In memory of my mother and father,
two rock-solid English countryfolk
who unknowingly exposed me
to traditions that last.

CONTENTS

1   An Introduction

7   The Great McLagan
12   The Two Faces of Young Mr George
19   All Aboard for Marble Hill House
23   Monty
36   Mixed Fortunes in Northumberland Gate Gardens
41   Arthur Halliwell's Uprooting
69   The Rathbone-Baker Prize for Artistic Excellence
75   Tact, Fact and Evasion
80   Mr Quill's Pet Poodle
87   Avril in the Summer Shadows
92   The Immortality of Miss James
98   His Own Worst Enemy
107   A Radical Set of Measures
112   Bless Me, Father
119   The Private View
125   The Makings of a Man
137   Near-Death Experience in Northwood Hills
139   The Long March
145   Man About Town
147   Lucy
148   Worlds Apart
149   Jo van Büren
151   A Friendly Enquiry
153   Typical of her Class
155   Unfamiliar Ground
158   Shadow Play
159   Weekend Break
161   The Duelling Ground
163   Storm in a Teacup
166   The Sadness of Nuala Singleton
168   Mr James Sutcliffe
169   The Nepalese Pavilion
170   Piccadilly Line
173   Second Class Citizen
174   A Point of No Return
176   Alderman Brown's Reception
177   Ursula MacFarlane, Spinster of this Parish
179   The Tall Stories of Gerhard Rohm
181   Darling of the Gods

INVERCLYDE LIBRARIES

Matador
9 Priory Business Park,
Wistow Road, Kibworth Beauchamp,
Leicestershire. LE8 0RX
Tel: 0116 279 2299
Email: books@troubador.co.uk
Web: www.troubador.co.uk/matador
Twitter: @matadorbooks

ISBN 978 1785898 914

British Library Cataloguing in Publication Data.
A catalogue record for this book is available from the British Library.

Printed and bound by CPI Group (UK) Ltd, Croydon, CR0 4YY

Matador is an imprint of Troubador Publishing Ltd

182 A Lesson Learned
183 The Wiles of William Crawley
186 Sweet Sixteen
187 The Understorey
189 Open to Debate
190 Sweet Hosannas
191 The Shadows Fade Away
193 Transitional Values
195 Seen from Above
196 An Odd Sort of Chap
199 Marcus Barraclough's Birthday
200 The Top Floor Balcony
202 Promenade
203 Contraflow
205 Writer's Block
207 Pinpoints of Consciousness
208 Eine Kleine Nachtmusik
209 The Bystander
212 A Turn-up for the Books
213 No Golds Today!
215 Digby Butterworth's Undoing
217 Decline and Fall
218 Max
220 RSVP
221 Still Early May
224 Plantation
225 On Holmwood Common
227 The Church at South Creake
228 Salve, Festa Dies
229 Like I Say
230 Young Fella M'Lad
231 October Revolution
232 The Skinflint
235 The Wrong End of the Stick
237 City Assignment
240 Hilda
241 The Number 65 to Kew Gardens
243 Running Commentary
245 A Welshman Born and Bred
247 Mysteries of the Tao

AN INTRODUCTION

In the majority of cases, these stories correspond with what 'a story' usually means when the word comes to mind; and, as such, they would survive well enough on their own, or so I like to think, without the commentary given below. Not infrequently, however, I tend to branch out from that simple definition into what I would describe as short 'literary entities' which, for the most part, retain a beginning, a middle and an end - whilst fighting shy of some of the more predictable features commonly associated with fiction. In this sort of work, the thematic development or storyline may be eventful, tenuous or merely the progression of thought on the part of a character or characters. And occasionally, it may be the narrator alone whose reflections follow a path from a beginning to a conclusion that was by no means always predetermined when the starting pistol fired.

Where the reflective element dominates, the so-called 'literary entities' mentioned above often take the form of what I can only describe as *Contemplations* in which, with or without an active human participant, the unexpected or the fundamental indeterminacy of things in general is looked at or made manifest in much the same way as objects are isolated and preserved, for example, in the fiction of a painting: perhaps a still life of flowers, a portrait of a peasant smoking a pipe, or a steam train chugging its way through a nineteenth century industrial landscape. Nevertheless, although familiar, these are reference points which, when looked at aslant and with detachment, can also take on the otherness of a reality that cannot be captured by laboratory instruments or deduced from mathematics or philosophy. In these 'Contemplations', I therefore wilfully confuse the categorical distinction between the everyday and the mystical; and I do so because that is the way I see things.

I do not like the term 'flash fiction', although the implied brevity may often cover what I do. At the same time, I do not necessarily disdain that description in relation to the work of other writers. On the other hand, in my own case, the words seem to have an underlying vulgarity at variance with the environment in which I instinctively operate - even if the content of a given piece concerns something that *is* vulgar, disparaging or merely comic.

Apart from my inability and disinclination to write longer works such as novels, there is the more positive motive of wanting to approximate to the nature and appearance of poetry or, as implied earlier, to works like paintings which have a limited size and are virtually accessible at a glance. And this, in a way, pins down what I have already suggested: namely, that what I aim at is often more contemplative than processional, thereby capturing what I think and feel in a form analogous to the plastic arts. As an example, consider Renoir's painting 'The Skiff' in which two young women, on a brilliant sunny day, are caught rowing across a lake against a background of woodlands and an imposing country mansion. But it is the painting's ability to *hold on* to the place and the event that interests me so much more than would be the case if I were standing on the shore gazing at the actual, down-to-earth, essentially imper-manent reality.

On the latter point, perhaps I can conclude with another example by citing 'The Return of the Native' by Thomas Hardy which I haven't read since my mid twenties - a very long time ago indeed. Sadly, I can no longer remember the story at all. What I do remember, however, is the opening sequence describing Egdon Heath: the atmosphere at nightfall, the almost religious gloom, the silence, the louring intimacy of land and sky and, in the distance, the minute ghostlike figure of the reddleman, the only living thing trudging almost out of sight along a country road. But although this is fundamentally a picture, it is also a *moving* picture with a beginning, a middle and an end. Yet despite being a picture that *moves*, my memory has enclosed it within a frame. And it is within a boundary like this that much of my work seems to emerge.

Not forgetting, of course, that the exceptions prove the rule!

* * *

Now, inspiration without divine intervention must be accounted for by less exalted origins. And at the physical level of genes, inherited characteristics, and the nature-nurture controversy, I can offer no insights when it comes to my own work. Both my parents were sane, unexceptional and, as the world sees things, very ordinary. My mother's mother gave birth to something like ten children - at least one of whom was conceived out of wedlock; and my mother's father, classed on his marriage certificate as a farm labourer, was described in acid terms by family lore as a clodhopper. On my father's side, things were more regular: although *his* father was a forceful character with a short temper, his mother was a gentle, forbearing woman who taught her son to embrace the virtues (in those days Christian ones) - which he very clearly did, despite being a reluctant doubter.

This introduction, in order to focus on what I've written, doesn't include a lengthy account of my background - a background, nonetheless, that provided me with a mother who was an entirely conventional countrywoman who, unlike her own mother, was maritally faithful. She was also a live wire with an amusingly forthright manner and an acute sense of humour much laced with sarcasm that required a cautious response. By way of contrast,

I had a highly aware father who stood on the sidelines, trod carefully, drove a delivery van and was universally admired as an English gentleman with a moral influence that only really took effect on me *after* his death. My parents presented just two other contrasting features. My mother spoke with a New Forest accent in a local dialect that included some highly colourful slang whilst my father spoke standard English with no regional accent at all.

* * *

It is a plain fact, I suggest, that genealogical tables alone are insufficient when it comes to accounting for how anyone thinks and feels. God, for me, lies forever at the forefront of a background - with all honour, rights and gratitude duly granted and mercy begged for. As a material being who is still alive, however, there is something else that bears down on me like a pleasant breeze - by which I mean the fields and hills of England.

Not far from my London home there is an unforgettable Surrey slope, agelessly tolerant of the wind and driving rain from the south, where the bluebells in springtime far outstrip the sky in their intensity of colour beneath the crumpled, green, half-open leaves of the beeches. As a boy, it was a place I knew well; as a rumbustious teenager, I never lost sight of it... And today, much later in life, it remains a visionary source of inspiration that acts as a template for all those many other places that are similar.

I still go there whenever an obliging friend can give me a lift. And over the course of a lifetime, it has never changed.

Michael Hill
1 July 2016

THE MAKINGS OF A MAN

In the nineteen forties, the Britannia Drive of suburban Redfield was solidly working class and law-abiding. A moderate proportion of those who lived there attended church, mostly chapel; and there was a strong community spirit - itself fortified by the wartime fear of invasion. It was into this compact environment, therefore, that an evacuee's shockingly obscene contribution exploded like a bombshell in the midst of a population where local gossip made banner headlines.

From 'The Makings of a Man', page 129.

THE GREAT McLAGAN

A little learning is a dangerous thing;
Drink deep, or taste not the Pierian spring:
There shallow draughts intoxicate the brain,
And drinking largely sobers us again.

Alexander Pope: An Essay on Criticism

Mr Alistair James Henry McLagan, seemingly all things to all men, and in his own view the fount of much of the world's wisdom, had (during his fairly long life) grown not only in knowledge and experience but also in his physical dimensions which, seen in relation to his under-average height, meant simply that he was fat. Among work colleagues and friends, there were inevitable jokes on this score which he didn't much mind. They were jokes that were always fairly cautiously expressed, thereby convincing the Great McLagan (this was his nickname in certain quarters) that he was well regarded... although it also enabled his critics to scorn his condescending ways under the pretence of well-meaning banter.

Before venturing to present Alistair McLagan with his trousers down (thereby revealing underwear from his local Marks & Spencer rather than from Bewes & Purvis of Jermyn Street), fair play demands acknowledgement of the fact that his career had not been without grounds for admiration. He had begun his adult life quite humbly as a jack of all trades in an insurance company where, by dint of hard work, he soon prospered - although not without a carefully contrived dose of self-promotion. After three years of improving prospects, he then moved on to a well known city bank on the strength of excellent references from his former employers who had been impressed, among other things, by Alistair's well rehearsed quotations from Cicero, some of them in the original Latin.

After a relatively short time in his new job, Alistair was appointed departmental manager in charge of investment strategy - in which rôle he proved extremely able. And it was in this prestigious and well salaried position that he remained throughout the rest of his career until his retirement at the age of sixty five when he was presented with a sizeable cheque and a bibulous farewell party during which sniggering juniors (entirely well-meaning, of course) dared to exchange whispers not only about his waistline but also about the incongruity between his sexual leanings (noticed by some of the better looking amongst his subordinates) and a philanthropic appointment to the board of Dr Barnardo's, scheduled to begin a week after his departure from the bank.

As the first year of retirement drew to its close, in virtue of spending two days a week at Dr Barnardo's instead of pruning roses in his back garden, the Great McLagan not only felt an enhanced sense of his own standing, but also an increasing conviction that his latter-day achievements required an airing. In general, this character trait was nothing new; his need to be admired was a longstanding one. However, being so recently deprived of deference from his former work colleagues, a greater onus descended on his friends - not all of whom were keen to genuflect to order. In the first place, it was humiliating; and in the eyes of at least one of his intimates by the name of Vincent Trevelyan, it wasn't justified by the reality behind the mask - a reality seen as falling short of the superior self-assessment that underpinned it.

* * *

After a successful start to his association with Dr Barnardo's, Alistair McLagan concluded his first year on the board by giving a party for a group of his friends. The venue was his modest maisonette in a somewhat characterless backwater half way between Worcester Park and New Malden. The gathering began during the late afternoon in the rear garden where, with drinks in their hands, the guests were treated to a tour of the roses and fuchsias which, to give Alistair his due, were as beautiful in appearance as they were small in number - to which it must be added that the garden itself was comparable in size to a pocket-handkerchief and was only just big enough to accommodate the seven or eight guests, a couple of benches and a deckchair. Nevertheless, the gossip was lively; good will was ample; and there was a lightness of heart in keeping with a fine summer's day and the several species of butterflies pursuing their crazy, symbiotic dalliance with the lavender.

In due course, rather red-faced from the heat after a couple of hours out of doors, the guests retired to the lounge for further, somewhat stronger drinks in preparation for an excellent smörgåsbord of hot and cold snacks served by a catering company employing two polite (and very presentable) Swedish waitresses. Before long, most of the visitors had subsided into the several ill-matching armchairs and an antiquated sofa whilst the Great McLagan remained on his feet and lectured them, rather pompously, on his comings and goings during his first year in office with so well-known a charity. And it was these comings and goings and the glowing colours in which they were described that developed into an entirely unforeseeable outbreak of unpleasantness.

At the moment in question, whilst the waitresses were distributing mediterranean-style, skewered king prawns with savoury sauce, sesame seeds and a sprig of coriander, the Great McLagan was boasting about a conference he'd attended in Switzerland concerned with child welfare. At the same time, relishing his own (second) batch of skewered prawns, Vincent Trevelyan was listening - but only in a superficial sort of way because he was far more interested in the prawns than he was in his friend's goings-on in Switzerland. After all, given the fifty years of his acquaintance with Alistair, he was no stranger to accounts of the latter's achievements!

So far, so good, one might say! But there then came a point in the narrative when the Great McLagan, standing with fellow delegates on the banks of the Zurich See, had witnessed a distant storm and, in its aftermath, an exceptionally spectacular rainbow. And it was this, or rather Alistair's account of it, that so suddenly and unexpectedly interrupted the smooth flow of the evening.

At first, it was wholly without guile that Vincent Trevelyan emerged from his preoccupation with food and declared rather too loudly that the Spanish for rainbow was 'arco iris'. It was a fact brought only recently to his attention; and it was not so much pride as the wish to share this seemingly odd snippet of information that led him to speak out. But the Great McLagan, vulnerable to competition, saw it as a challenge, denied the fact of the matter - and declared it absurd to suggest that the goddess Iris had anything to do with rainbows! The scene was therefore set for a tussle.

For three or four minutes, the pendulum swung to and fro whilst the other guests munched on. It soon became clear, however, that of the two opponents Vincent was the angrier - due in part to the rôle of alcohol but in larger measure to his certainty about the facts. Yet although he was the angrier, Vincent was also the more rational because it was to prove nothing at all that he had spoken out, whilst it was to demonstrate that he was always foremost with information that the Great McLagan had put his foot in it. Consequently the time had arrived, or so Vincent thought, to make use of his trump card.

Now Vincent's circle of friends was not all that much greater than

Alistair's, but it had the virtue of being more various. He therefore mentioned a long-standing Venezuelan acquaintance with whom he had recently been strolling in Regents Park during the course of a shower which, as in the Zurich example, had come complete with a rainbow - and it was from this friend that he'd learned that the Spanish for rainbow was 'arco iris'. To that stark declaration of fact and with a note of sarcasm in his voice, he then added 'Spanish is his native language, so he ought to know'... following which and thereby inflamed, the Great McLagan answered that Venezuela was an insignificant backwater out of touch with modern scholarship with no claim whatsoever to the last word.

Vincent then vengefully seized another skewer of prawns and staked his reputation on the evidence of the Victorian artist Atkinson Grimshaw, mentioning that his painting entitled 'Iris' in the Leeds Art Gallery showed a naked woman, rising from a woodland pool, whose head was encircled by the light of a rainbow. Having purchased the catalogue accompanying the artist's one-man show at London's Guildhall Art Gallery, he was also able to provide one or two more unanswerable details about the goddess Iris and her attributes.

Unfortunately for the Great McLagan, he had never heard of John Atkinson Grimshaw nor of his special renown as a painter of moonlight. And so, after a brief and angry silence, he turned away with a shrug - at which point, with the drinks still swilling copiously and snacks still being demolished, the argument faded away amidst the pleasant hubbub and indifference of guests who, in any case, had never managed to fathom what the disagreement was about.

Iris, goddess of Autumn, disobedient to her seasonal mission to wither the flowers, was changed into a rainbow as a punishment.

THE TWO FACES OF YOUNG MR GEORGE

In chapter ten of 'The Road to Wigan Pier', George Orwell shares with his readers what was, for him, the galling realisation that many a keen socialist aged twenty five had become, by the age of thirty five, a toffee-nosed conservative. As a comment on the age he lived in, on human nature in general and, unknowingly, on the sequence of events described below, he managed to hit the nail on the head with great accuracy. And whilst Orwell's own mind was undoubtedly focussed on the longer-term yearning for social change, the following story set in two village-like backwaters of London is a perfect, miniaturised facsimile of his underlying perception.

* * *

At a time when planet earth had travelled around the sun significantly less often than is now the case, I used to own a large terraced residence in Parsons Green which, even then, was an expensive and pleasantly leafy sort of area in West London - whereas today it is just as leafy but vastly more expensive... a transformation indicated by the fact that a house costing me relatively little forty five years ago is now valued at over three million pounds.

Much time has elapsed; all the same, it still seems odd that I remember neither the exact amount nor the source of the funds I acquired in order to purchase number 105 Bressingham Road which, for quite a few years, I let out on a room-by-room basis. This was at a time when planning rules were lax with regard to multi-occupation; and in retrospect, the rents were such that, by today's standards, the fifteen pounds a week I charged for a bedsit seem laughable - whereas, in fact, they were more or less average at the time. In all, there were six mixed single and double lettings; and there was never a shortage of young people who queued up to pay for the then novel experience of living away from the family.

I

Mr Leonard Beckinshaw was the sixty-year-old manager at a branch of the Westminster Bank on the outskirts of Doncaster. This placed him in a comfortable, middle-income position, well able to support a wife and an only child by the name of George Edward. His resources were insufficient, however, to provide his son with a much-coveted private education - though local influence, alongside his offspring's talents, secured the latter a place, at the age of twelve, in a local grammar school known as the Edgar Elliot High. And it was at the Edgar Elliot High that the Latin master found occasion to call him 'The Young Mr George' due to his consistently good performance combined with traces of his father's lofty manner. His fellow pupils naturally took note of this and latched on to it; and George himself rather liked it. Consequently, when his path finally crossed with mine, the nickname caught up with him again, having been revealed at 105 Bressingham Road by a visiting friend and former pupil at the Edgar Elliot High.

The reason why this son of a Doncaster bank manager ended up as one of my tenants was that his father's limited funds were still more than enough to cover the fifteen pounds a week rent - thus enabling the Young Mr George to accept a place at University College London where he read Financial Management and Maths during most of his time in Parsons Green. When interviewed, he had given a favourable, if rather cool impression, spoke well, was nicely dressed and provided a written undertaking from his father to send me a regular monthly cheque. Even forty five years ago, rent collection could be a nightmare - and for this reason, the Young Mr George's circumstances were attractive.

Whereas there were sometimes complaints from the neighbours about noise, plus intelligence from the cleaner about the diversion (through illicit cables) of the free electricity supply in the communal kitchen, no negative reports ever reached me about the behaviour of the youthful George Beckinshaw (not, at least, until after his departure). Indeed, he came over as a quiet, somewhat colourless character whose darkest feature was the unruliness of his black hair whose mop-like eccentricity was acquired as an expression of new-found freedom shortly after moving in. To this should be added his somewhat clandestine comings-and-goings and a persistent, perhaps nervous, inability to smile.

In due course, as time moved on, the cleaner brought me increasingly frequent news about a series of posters being pinned up in the shared kitchen - posters that suggested there was a left-wing extremist on board ship who was hell-bent on opposition to property owner-ship and who regarded all landlords as being on a par with Peter Rachman whose exploitation of his tenants had already made the headlines. Nevertheless, group solidarity obstructed any immediate solution as to who the perpetrator was. I also thought it unwise to get personally drawn into the controversy by organising an investi-gation. Instead, as an inexperienced landlord learning by leaps and bounds, I betrayed no awareness whatever of the poster campaign.

2

The name of the cleaner at 105 Bressingham Road during the time I ran it as a guesthouse was Mr Quill - now sadly in the company of his ancestors. He not only cleaned the premises but also collected the rents; and it therefore says a great deal for his handling of the tenants that he was always affectionately known to them as 'Reggie'.

Reginald Quill was in his mid fifties at the time of these events. He was completely reliable and regular; furthermore, he was the sole owner-occupier of a two-room, ground-floor flat situated conven-iently close to Bressingham Road. In appearance, he was absurdly short and plump, invariably wore a disreputable-looking belted mackintosh and rode about on an ancient red bicycle with his incongruously sparse but still golden hair blowing about in the wind. On top of these distinctions, Mr Quill was also a connoisseur of Victorian glass, particularly cranberry glass, which he picked up at jumble sales, in junk shops or in roadside skips. He then sold his acquisitions to fashionable dealers in London's Kensington Church Street where he was the darling of several blue-rinsed ladies with rather forced accents!

To save protracted uncertainty on the part of the reader, it has to be added to these basic data that Mr Quill was openly and unabashedly gay in every conceivable sense of the word. Nevertheless, his character was such that he raised many a laugh wherever he went but very few eyebrows - and he was consequently able to get away with blue murder. This enabled him, among other memorable achievements, to address a decidedly hefty young builder working near the guesthouse as 'my sugar plum'! Yet instead of arousing a more drastic response, his audacious familiarity produced roars of laughter from the entire team of workmen until the scaffolding virtually shook! In consequence, he secured occasional help with any heavy lifting jobs at 105 Bressingham Road; and, apart from the Young Mr George, he was popular as a confidant with virtually all of the tenants.

3

Time, measured by the earth's unstoppable motion but not defined by it, ticked relentlessly on. Residents at the guesthouse arrived and then gave notice regularly via Mr Quill. The exception was a pair of Welshmen in their twenties, Messrs Bradley and Pugh, who rather liked the location as well as the friendly ambience created by Reggie; and, as a consequence, they outstayed the other, more ephemeral lodgers by remaining in place for at least two years.

One morning, after what seemed like an eternity since the arrival of Young Mr George, a neighbour phoned me to complain about a party at the guesthouse on the previous evening. A description of great tumult was then related with emotion and accompanied by a great deal of effing and blinding, including the f-word itself. The caller, hugely embarrassed, apologised immediately.

The situation then calmed down; and after receiving my firm guarantees of closer oversight, I was told that one of my longer-term tenants - 'the one with that pile of black hair' - had been observed departing with his luggage about an hour before the phone call. And later the same day, the ever well-informed Mr Quill advised me that Young Mr George, having thrown a farewell party, had left for pastures new that morning.

As to his destination, I was obliged to await the next thrilling episode after a promise of further enquiries. Meanwhile, according to Reggie, one thing was very clear: namely, that the disappearance of all political posters had coincided with Mr George Edward Beckinshaw's early-morning exit! As to his rent, luckily, it wasn't he who was paying it - and a remittance, together with a formal note, was received shortly thereafter from Doncaster.

4

For several months after the political climate in the Bressingham Road kitchen had cooled down, nothing was heard of Young Mr George - nor was he uppermost either in my mind or in that of Mr Quill. Rents were collected or pursued; another party-giver was asked to leave; and Mr Quill himself just *slightly* overstepped the mark with a youngish male tenant who described his behaviour to me as 'a bit too fresh for his own good'. Other than this minimal upset, quickly righted by Reginald's genius for turning everything into a joke, calm conditions prevailed at the guest-house.

Another year passed uneventfully; and then one Friday evening, Mr Quill turned up at my flat with the week's rents which were interestingly supplemented by a news item. This came second-hand and in the strictest confidence, courtesy of Messrs Bradley and Pugh who had remained in touch with the Young Mr George who was apparently doing rather well.

After completing his studies, and oblivious to possible charges of nepotism, George had seemingly benefited from his father's influence and had acquired a junior post at the Westminster Bank's Hampstead branch where he worked hard, was soon noticed and then, not long afterwards, promoted. As I commented to Reggie at the time, commercial banks and family influences were a very long way away indeed from the thrust of George Edward Beckinshaw's poster campaign in the Bressingham Road kitchen!

More was to come; and three months later, I received a further report, similarly sourced, to the following startling effect. As a bank employee himself and the son of another, George had easy access to loans, had acquired a mortgage and had bought himself a nice little period cottage in Gospel Oak, not far from his place of work. This represented a fundamental transformation effected in record time. And it amounted to this: that the juvenile zealot who had recently pinned up a poster (among several) proclaiming 'Property is Theft' was now a proud property-owner himself.

5

It is well known that precipitate action among the young often ends up in disaster. At the same time, although there are those who never get it right, most people as they mature learn their lesson, move on and make good. Consequently, depending on their point of view, readers may be either pleased or irritated to learn that the Young Mr George, shortly after becoming a property owner, had found that the easy life cannot be guaranteed and that funds are not limitless. In short, stung by two months' mortgage arrears and the increasingly heavy costs of his nightlife, he soon found it impossible to make ends meet.

It is at this point in the narrative that I am both delighted yet disappointed to introduce readers to the dénouement - a dénouement that boils down to a final (and, I think, slightly shameful) deletion from the Young Mr George's sin list. This is particularly so, given the brief timescale; and those experienced in life's little surprises may already have guessed what's coming.

According to Messrs Bradley and Pugh, things became so desperate for George that, being within weeks of losing his home and possibly his employment, he decided to take radical measures not only by modifying his domestic arrangements but also by altering his *beliefs*. As a means of keeping the wolf from the door, he therefore placed an advertisement in the local newspaper and, in less than a fortnight, was playing landlord to a pair of young and very attractive female lifeguards from the 'Ladies Pond' on Hampstead Heath!

ALL ABOARD FOR MARBLE HILL HOUSE

Rosalie Wexford was on board the number 33 bus which had just stopped at the Alison Bradshaw Garden Centre in Barnes, West London. Occupying the outside half of a seat intended for two, with her shopping bags dumped alongside on the vacant half by the window, she was glued to the London Life pages of the Evening Standard, effectively shielded from the sharp looks of the new passengers clambering past in the overcrowded gangway. And to tell the truth, it was that vacant seat rather than the pale skin and drawn features beneath a clump of short yellow hair that drew attention to an otherwise unremarkable Rosalie Wexford.

Sally Parkinson was seated on the next bench along, her body scrunched right up against the window - this time with the shopping bags dumped on the *outside* seat. Although she was quite a lot older than Rosalie, she had grown no wiser: her hair, which was cropped and mannish, had been dyed aggressively orange - and there was a competing splodge of red lipstick to go with it. Neither were appearances improved by a crumpled black plastic mac, blue trousers and gold sandals.

For Sally, it was just a lucky coincidence that, as the bus started to move, the regular swaying of Alison Bradshaw's bamboos remained the chief focus of her attention - which meant that her eyes were conveniently shielded from those of a white-haired, male passenger whose puckered brow conveyed not only resentment at needlessly having to stand but also a rather scathing assessment of Sally's incipient moustache.

On the opposite side of the gender gap, the considerable bulk of Tom Fazakerley loomed large. He had an untidy, neglected appearance and was dressed in an old-fashioned, belted mackintosh with a long, red and white scarf wound several times around his neck.

He also had a leftover poppy from last year's Remembrance Day stuck in his buttonhole. His most remarkable feature, however, was an explosive halo of snow-white hair suggestive of an inflatable Father Christmas scared out of his wits by a schoolboy armed with a hatpin! Some might have said that his obesity justified the fact that he was occupying two seats at once. Nonetheless, this would have been too liberal an attitude - and one entirely at odds with the views of an overburdened Asian woman who was angrily looking him over. Sadly, she couldn't speak English and was fearful of the outcome of any pointing or gesticulation on her part. But she was finally reconciled to having to stand when the unfiltered air drifting across from Tom's direction came too close - not only to her, but also to a pair of schoolgirls who simultaneously squeezed their nostrils and giggled.

In the rear half of the bus, a third female passenger created a less startling impression. Her middling proportions were enclosed in a pink topcoat whose texture was admittedly reminiscent of a bath-mat; but a silver shoulder bag and a pair of well-ironed black trousers completed a pleasant enough picture. Furthermore, as St Luke puts it, Peggy Davenport shared one or two advantages with those shrewder 'children of this world' who 'are wiser in their generation than the children of light'. And there are good reasons for saying this: for although like certain other passengers she too was sitting on the outside of a half-empty bench, she retained a commonsense awareness of public pressure. This meant waiting until an unfriendly glance caught her eye - whereupon she rose from her seat with an obliging smile, and equally obligingly asked the elderly man glaring at her whether he'd like to sit down? But the ruse backfired when, being less obliging than she was, he proved just as unwilling to occupy the *inside* seat as the red-faced, flustered

Peggy who was left standing in the gangway... at something of a loss.

* * *

Ten minutes later, when the bus reached the halfway mark across Richmond Bridge, the time seemed right for another bout of tension; and the most conspicuous candidate was a Mr Brian Northcott who was leaning against the window - the outside seat alongside him having been vacated a moment earlier. For quite some time, Brian's jaws had been actively engaged in dealing with a mouthful of chewing gum - a fact which drew attention to an unnaturally large, square-shaped head with glinting eyes strongly reminiscent of Frankenstein's monster; and to confuse the picture further, the chintzy pattern on his blue umbrella clearly showed that it belonged to a woman - presumably his wife. At the same time, looking down from above, one of the frustrated standing passengers noticed it when Brian eased his right leg craftily sideways until the knee extended a good six inches across the now empty seat beside him; and, of course, even a casual onlooker would have taken just seconds to work out what his game was.

From his loftier vantage point, the eagle-eyed standee whose name was Patrick Ryan decided to strike while the iron was still hot. He was a willowy, anonymous-looking individual who, despite a bald patch and opaque eyes, nevertheless had about him the air of an unrelenting bluebottle impervious to being swatted. Accordingly, as he lowered himself into position alongside Brian's sprawling outline, he pretended not to notice when the latter's knee defiantly stiffened and refused to budge. This move forced Patrick to squat at an angle with his legs projecting into the gangway. All his movements, however, remained leisurely and relaxed, seemingly undisturbed by the intransigence of an obtruding knee. He pursued this approach resolutely; and shortly after having brandished a copy of the Standard, he even ventured a carefree chortle at one of the news editor's side-swipes. Accordingly, when he alighted at Marble Hill House, Patrick knew that the luck (or doggedness) of the Irish had prevailed and that Brian Northcott's hostile behaviour, having apparently escaped notice, ended up as ignominiously as a damp squib at a firework display!

* * *

That said, of course, one has to be reasonable. Today, tension is evident almost everywhere. For example, city-dwellers disturbed by a fast-moving world are well advised, when out and about, to tread carefully for fear of being knocked down by fellow human beings behaving like freshly fired cannon balls en route from A to B. The more leisurely pace of the past and many of the older courtesies are plainly disappearing. And particular to this story, there's that omnipresent dislike of sitting next to anybody else on a London bus - especially if you're the passenger crammed against the window on the *inside* half of the seat.

By contrast, however, there's a brighter side to the picture. You don't have to fly to the Cairngorms to find peace. The UK capital is littered with parks and open spaces where tempers can simmer down and dogs, together with their owners, can enjoy a degree of mutual regard rarely found in an underground carriage. And there's something else which, luckily, isn't the exclusive preserve of townies - namely, the widespread, easy-going manners still current among shop assistants and supermarket staff who are often very young people willing to smile more sweetly and act more obligingly than the po-faced likes of Sally Parkinson or the uncooperative, unreasonably gruff Brian Northcott as he journeyed on, unfulfilled, from the bus stop at Marble Hill House.

Children of this world: St Luke 16,8. KJB, slightly amended word order.

MONTY

The London Borough of Richmond Upon Thames straddles the watercourse with which its full name is compounded and includes within its borders many miles of exceedingly picturesque riverside walks linking Hammersmith Bridge on the city side with Petersham and beyond to the southwest; following this, the rough track continues uninterrupted and, after crossing the Kingston boundary, continues in the direction of Hampton Court.

Lining the banks in between these extremes, there are many well-known landmarks - not least among them being Kew's Royal Botanic Gardens which, from one well-known vantage point, overlook the historic façade of Syon House whose water-meadows on the river's farthest shore are prone to flooding at high tide. Further upstream, starting from Richmond proper, passenger boats travel regularly into Central London, then back again. And to cap it all, the pivotal rôle of the river is supplemented by the vast acreage of Richmond Park with its population of deer - all of which attractions and many others combine to ensure a steady supply of home-grown and foreign visitors.

On the brow of Richmond Hill, overlooking the view of the Thames near Glover's Island that inspired Turner's well-known painting in the Tate Gallery, stands the former Star and Garter Home for retired service personnel; and nearby are the flowery slopes of Hill Gardens which descend at a steep angle almost as far as the water's edge. It is no wonder, therefore, that Richmond has few rivals for scenic splendour in the whole of Greater London.

Just before the riverside path from Kew Bridge completes its two-mile meander at a point slightly short of Richmond's Old Town Hall and the nearby terraced esplanade, a rail bridge linking Hounslow and other suburban locations crosses the Thames, carrying passengers to and from Waterloo. This line tunnels briefly underneath the George Street and Kew Road shops on its way east to the metropolis via the next station along, North Sheen, which is itself distinguished by a grand overview of that most British of spectacles: namely, a group of allotments. These are the Manor Road Allotments which cover an enormous area bordered by the Sheen Court flats on the east side and Manor Road itself to the west.

The Manor Road Allotments, thus placed in their geographical setting, provide the background for a story which most of those associated with it have now forgotten - though even today, it still deserves a mention. Taken as a whole, it demonstrates those insignificant minor events that make up ninety per cent of human experience; but in the present case, it also conspires to tell a tale whose pathos is more than sufficient to rescue words like 'poignant' or 'touching' from their common misuse as exaggerations.

I

As allotments go, those at Manor Road were well managed, tidy (despite Mother Nature's generosity in the matter of weeds), and well endowed with a community spirit. The latter was centred on a small wooden shed selling garden supplies; and this, at weekends, provided social contact as well as seeds, bags of manure, bedding plants and a limited range of tools. On top of this, in a second shed nearby, the various functionaries gathered to discuss anything from the abundance of snails to unwarranted bonfires, neglected plots or broken fences. Among other matters of moment was the undesirability of feeding the foxes (often observed from the rail platform snoozing on a warm patch of earth); and there was once the vexed question of how to advise plot-holders that badgers were a protected species without divulging the whereabouts of a recently discovered set.

Whether in spring, summer or autumn dress, the Manor Road Allotments presented a picture of quiet contentment. The rigid ground plan was softened by abundant nature on the one hand and, on the other, by the inventive contrivances or inspired neglect of the plot-holders. Piles of surplus bits and pieces were rendered picturesque by the free reign given to the rampant, protruding spikes of fat hen; soil-filled containers or forgotten rubbish heaps supported the rough-and-tumble of red and yellow nasturtiums - all of them flourishing alongside bona fide crops such as the dangling clusters of runner beans or the crumpled umbrellas of the rhubarb. Wild bees, honey bees, bumble bees and butterflies provided ample pollination services; and robins, ever-faithful to their reputation, fearlessly dogged the heels of old and young as the first king edwards or maris pipers emerged triumphantly from the soil. All in all, the Manor Road Allotments were a haven of peace from March to October and, for a few of the most dedicated plot-holders, a source of companionship and relaxation throughout the entire year.

Apart from a ready supply of water, every plot-holder throughout the land has need of a shed in which to store tools or surplus crops such as potatoes overwintering until required at home. And it was these sheds, rather than the many, somewhat apologetic polythene greenhouses, that provided the Manor Road Allotments with their special brand of creativity and flair. One in particular, situated near the main gates, mimicked a colourfully painted suburban residence complete with a plaque bearing the text '1 Arcadia Drive'. Another reflected childhood memories of Treasure Island and consisted of a large shack where the Jolly Roger fluttered above a roofed veranda furnished with tattered armchairs and a coffee table. Furthermore, the timbered frontage facing the path bore the title Hispaniola in bright red paint - all of which earned the plot-holder the nickname of Long John which was a snide reference to his under-average height as well as a tribute to English literature.

Ramshackle but serviceable sheds abounded throughout the Manor Road site - some of them providing a regular meeting-point for time-honoured chums of one sort or another. These were places where innumerable cups of tea had been consumed over the years - together with many a ham sandwich prepared by absent wives who were thereby spared the freedom of speech often exercised away from censorious ears. Indeed, the term 'old boys club' was not out of place in some instances where ageing plot-holders, gazing wistfully over their shoulders, shared memories of youthful deeds unmentionable in a family context such as Sunday lunch with the in-laws!

2

This convivial, traditional picture of particular but representative British allotments is not quite as convincing when autumn begins to bite, when the leaves of the runner beans begin to turn yellow - and their pods (concealing the high purple of future generations) have gone to seed. Roses, forgetful of Picardy, shrivel and their petals fall. Nasturtiums fight on until the first frosts, and then collapse overnight into a tangled mess. It is then that the bonfires smelling like incense hang like a mist on the air. Then, too, the sharp caws of the crows sound especially ominous and the early mornings glisten with hoar frost. At last, despite its crimson splendour, the sun sets depressingly early and thoughts then turn wearily ahead to Guy Fawkes night, the winter solstice and the tinselled threat of Christmas.

It was in September, not so very long ago, that a stranger - indeed, a vagrant - first appeared and was spotted sauntering along the main concrete drive towards an allotment well cared-for by its owner, Mr

Stephen Poynter. Stephen was an ex-army officer in his late fifties who, although thinning on top, had never felt the need to surrender to a hat other than one indicative of his former rank when attending regimental get-togethers. Predictably, and in consequence of his background, he was affectionately known to many plot-holders as the General - by which title he was secretly flattered rather than offended.

On this occasion, Stephen was casually seated outside his shed which was among the more professional-looking structures on site - and one which also sported a patio of neatly laid paving slabs. He was in the company of another plot-holder by the name of Arnold Biggs, a friend and one-time grammar school teacher who was of similar age, equally thin on top - but who wore a tattered, somewhat incongruously smart style of cap originally purchased from Harrods. Arnold, whose nearby shed was of the undistinguished polythene sort, was of a quieter disposition than the General who betrayed, in his stern expression when caught off guard, a tendency to self-assertion unencumbered by an excess of words. Their discussion, until the stranger's grey silhouette came into view, was concerned with the recent outbreak of vandalism in which several sheds, beloved of their owners, had been wrecked.

At the time of these events, it was over a year since a pet known to all as the Manor Road Cat had been run over. And it was a plain fact that the strange presence ambling darkly along the path also appeared to be a cat. This was therefore a matter of particular interest to Stephen and Arnold who immediately exchanged glances, stood up and watched with rapt attention - Stephen with his arms folded across his chest whilst Arnold, out of awkwardness, kept his hands in his pockets.

There could be no doubt that the approaching animal, in addition to being a cat, was making progress with care. It was plainly on the alert, for although its tail was wagging from side to side, the word 'wag' implies too strong an element of positive, dog-like enthusiasm. On the contrary, this feline version seemed jerky and confrontational as if the tail's owner had been offended in the very recent past and was still fuming.

As the new arrival drew abreast of Stephen's shed which was set back a couple of metres from the path, it was met with the usual barrage of absurd human noises aimed at enticement - all of which it disdained, apart from a brief stop to deliver a defiant glare which the General mistook for friendly interest. In consequence, he stepped forward in order to further the acquaintance; but this was soon shown to be a mistake when the cat arched its back, lashed out with an angry paw - and produced an exceptionally protracted hiss. The result was an outbreak of military-style abuse swiftly followed by defensive laughter and a wide berth. The cat then moved on; but as it turned its back and ambled off, at least it answered one as yet unasked question: it was shown to be a tom and will therefore be referred to as such for the remaining duration of this story.

3

The distinctly hostile newcomer at the Manor Road Allotments must have been a fugitive from ill-treatment elsewhere: for he took up permanent residence and yet remained extremely aloof. Accordingly, he became known, rather dismissively, as the Prowler - with or without the definite article. Any intimate advances were met either with more hissing or a swift dive beneath the nearest convenient cover. Notwithstanding this, a few animal lovers provided an occasional saucerful of snacks which certainly disappeared overnight - although there was no early proof that the new boy on the block was responsible. This state of affairs continued for several months as conditions became steadily colder; but eventually, several plot-holders affirmed that the Prowler had been seen benefiting from these acts of human kindness. And as the weather worsened, three or four regulars, whenever they visited their plots, remembered to bring a bagful of leftovers or a tin of cat food. One of them even dispensed a supply of milk from an old medicine bottle.

This tentative, somewhat arm's-length state of play continued throughout the first winter and spring; neither was there much change during the following summer by which time Arnold had established himself as the most generous and regular of the charitable givers. However, as the weeks and months unfolded, a few close observers gradually began to feel that Prowler was slowing down, was apparently ageing - and consequently seemed less paranoid. Concurrently with these signs, when the second summer finally faded away, he was an already familiar sight on Arnold's allotment - although any indications of bonhomie dwindled sharply whenever the distance between the two parties fell short of around five metres. All the same, it was noticeable that whenever Arnold arrived on site, Prowler was usually there waiting for him.

In due course, the association between main benefactor and adopted stray became fixed. Prowler had his own tin plate, and tucked into the now daily snacks which were at their best on Monday mornings in the wake of the Sunday roast. All the same, as the temperatures plummeted and Arnold took to arriving more and more heavily clad, Prowler began to show clear signs of deterioration: he was often observed wandering about aimlessly; and he tended to stumble. But he also grew proportionally less timid - all of which indicated that he was no kitten when he first arrived at Manor Road.

Accordingly, as a second autumn began its offensive and conditions cooled, Prowler was found to be spending his nights on a sack inside Arnold's polythene shed - and *prowling* a great deal less.

From this point onwards, the old antipathy gradually dissolved. Food and drink were now deposited inside the greenhouse-come-shed rather than outdoors; and on top of this, Prowler began to peer at his benefactor from closer quarters and with a changed look on his face - one suggestive of growing familiarity and the beginnings of dependence. The days of flight from human contact seemed to be over - except on the one occasion when Arnold brought the General along to witness the transformation whereupon military dignity was met with another arched back and a rather less threatening hiss than on the first day of their acquaintance. Secretly, of course, Arnold felt a certain pride in his established special relationship whilst the General took comfort from having weathered the encounter without the humiliation of another scratch.

With only slight hesitation, it was at this stage as he weakened that Prowler first allowed himself to be touched - almost as if memories of better days and nicer owners were resurfacing under the influence of Arnold's benevolent attentions. Sadly, his grey fur was now a mass of clotted spikes. And one morning, just before taking delivery of the day's rations, curled up on a sack, he allowed himself to be stroked at length and without resistance. The walls of division at once came crashing down. The declining animal miaowed and began, albeit rather feebly, to tackle the chicken leftovers mixed with a helping of Whiskas; and it was at this point, too, that Arnold felt able to handle the brass identity disc without fear; and this lead to the discovery that Prowler's original name was Monty.

Monty continued relentlessly downhill in tandem with the shift from autumn into winter. He was by now virtually housebound - although he still ventured outside his polythene home for a short stroll where he continued to use a soft patch of earth as a toilet. Nevertheless, despite shelter and regular feeding, nothing could reverse his growing decrepitude which was worsened by the arrival of the first frosts and the louring monotony of the winter skies.

4

Good fortune intervened, but only briefly: a notice in the communal shed elicited the immediate services of a plot-holder who was also a practising vet. But sadly, one look at Monty was enough to tell him that he was dealing with an example of advanced old age exacerbated by the frosty weather; and he recommended that it might be in the animal's best interests to be put to sleep. Nevertheless, not wishing to upset anyone's feelings, he left the matter in the air and prescribed a mere placebo - more for Arnold's benefit than for that of the patient.

Arnold, although still in good general health, resembled the ailing Prowler in this one particular: namely, that he was extremely thin; and consequently, in tense moments, he was known to his wife rather abusively as a bag of bones. More to the point, and in a significantly different respect, he was also a considerate and sensitive middle-aged man who had plainly grown too fond of the once ferocious Monty to have him put down; and after consultations with the General who had apparently forgiven the recent arched back and hiss, it was agreed that the last days of a now well-loved pet should be as comfortable as possible. Neither of the men's wives would have countenanced a possibly diseased and certainly unsightly animal on its last legs in the house. Desperate measures were therefore needed; and it was the General rather than

Arnold who suggested the bright idea of a heater. The result was that he rescued an old wartime Valor lamp from his attic and passed it on to Arnold who, obtaining fuel from the nearby superstore, at once trimmed the wick and put a match to it.

That evening, as dusk fell, a faint glow lit up the polythene walls of Arnold's little greenhouse which, in ordinary circumstances, looked so miserably inferior alongside the General's sturdier wooden shed. Gradually, the transparent membrane steamed up, and the cluttered interior filled with a familiar odour first experienced tucked up alone in bed when Arnold was a boy; and this in turn was accompanied by a blanket of consoling warmth surrounding the battered orange-box where Monty, loosely curled up, dozed on the folded layers of sacking.

It was then that November established its remorseless presence on the Manor Road Allotments, making the provision of the lamp especially timely. The frosts had already begun in late October and by the second week of November the first snow had fallen. Monty's resilience continued to fail so that, now, he never left the warmth of what boiled down to a private nursing home where the heater burned day and night and the food supply was constant.

His deteriorating state was more than matched by his appearance. You can't bath a cat; and his fur, clotted with dirt, was a mass of spikes projecting at all angles like one of the characters in a Disney cartoon after an electric shock. At this stage, his light grey, almost colourless eyes remained wide open; and through them, the flicker of life within gazed outwards at a world whose allure was now negligible. The only thing that caused a stir was the now twice-daily arrival of Arnold - though food and drink by this time had to be deposited on the sacking in small tins alongside an invalid who could only struggle to his feet for a few instinctive seconds before collapsing back into a helpless pile. Such was his condition that he could barely eat. The sight was pitiful.

5

In circumstances such as these, the mercy mission at the Manor Road Allotments dragged on until the early snow, having melted away, returned with a vengeance in mid December accompanied by strong winds and drifting. The effect was like that of a world erased and the transformation was startling - almost as if a multitude of winters, remembered only by the most senior plot-holders, had reassembled to assert their former glory. Sheds and derelict bean posts that were once functional, productive and abuzz with activity, now looked as bleak and as useless as the charred relics of a bonfire around which, sparsely distributed, were the tentative tracks of a robin in pursuit of something to peck at.

By this time, Monty's quarters were roofed in snow too deeply frozen to melt under the influence of the lamp whose friendly radiance nevertheless breached the translucent polythene walls as soon as darkness fell. And despite the faint optimism implied by the hesitant flicker of the flame, deep and desperate was the nightly loneliness of that poor animal curled up in an orange box that he was now too disabled to quit. Moreover, every morning as if to deepen the pathos, his droppings (luckily still solid) were brushed off the rough bedding after Arnold had lifted him clear with his left hand from which he dangled like a fistful of weeds.

That year, the snow kept on falling for more than a week, putting a stop to all horticultural activity and maintenance at the Manor Road Allotments. The sky was not only a predictable grey but also, due to the thickness of the cloud, exceptionally grim. And on many such mornings, when Arnold turned up with snacks and a fresh supply of fuel, there were as few human footprints when he departed as when he arrived. And given these dreary circumstances on top of his family's indifference to Monty's plight, he was overcome by a sense of universal desolation whose influence afflicted him like a dead weight that he couldn't throw off.

6

One Friday morning, later than usual at about eleven o'clock and in the midst of continuing arctic conditions, Arnold opened the main gates of the allotments and noticed that the snow on the padlock had not been disturbed. A sudden break in the clouds unexpectedly cast an eerie white glare over the landscape. However, it was a brief moment of respite that ended almost as soon as it began, leaving an aftermath of even deeper gloom and the never-ending onslaught of a strong easterly wind.

Under conditions such as these, Arnold made haste. Dressed in a black overcoat, with his cap pulled down over his forehead and a long grey scarf wrapped several times around his neck, he began the familiar trudge to his allotment, doing his best to negotiate the frozen puddles on the concrete path beneath the snow. The sense of dereliction was intense as the wind whistled and the dead vegetation rattled like dry paper; and there were no tracks whatever in the snow - either of man or of beast. Arnold, accustomed to friendly chit-chat with the General or the usual succession of greetings from other plot-holders, had never felt so desperately alone.

The overnight weather had been such that it was necessary to kick away the fresh snow piled up against the stiffened polythene flaps of the greenhouse. No traces of Arnold's footprints from the previous night - nor any others formed since - had survived; and absolute quiet prevailed as he pulled back the flap and sniffed the warm and pleasantly familiar smell of burning fuel. It was on the cards, of course, that Monty had died; he was ready for that. But what he was *not* prepared for was the fact that Monty was nowhere to be seen - neither was he found alive or dead after every possible internal hiding place had been turned upside down.

Arnold then scoured the snow beyond the confines of the now empty greenhouse and among the surrounding plots for any tell-tale footprints - but there was no trace. He continued searching for over half an hour without result before giving up. He then renewed the fuel supply to the lamp, provided fresh food and drink, and left the polythene flaps slightly open in case the prodigal should return. Lastly and reluctantly, he set out for home with a heavy heart, knowing that he was closer to the spirit of Monty in the darkness and the winter cold than in the comparable chill of domestic indifference.

And such proved to be the case: for Monty's presence lingered on like a ghost at the Manor Road Allotments even though, despite the concerted efforts of many, no remains were ever found there. Nor was there any comfort to be gleaned at home; for speculation and regret were discouraged during the long winter evenings at number 16 Shackleton Drive where Arnold played a convincing second fiddle with quiet, but not unquestioning resignation.

MIXED FORTUNES
IN NORTHUMBERLAND GATE GARDENS

I

These swans look increasingly irritable. Self-absorbed, unwieldy on dry land, they are preening their feathers at the water's edge, indifferent to the two little girls who are bombarding them with stale crusts. They have an angry look in their eyes as if to say: bread is only a serious proposition after we have quit the shore and are safely afloat with our heads at the end of a graceful loop; dry foodstuffs must first be saturated in water before we are able swallow them. And please, do not expect much gratitude: we snatch by nature; and we *don't* say thankyou.

2

The sun has been dilatory so far today - but now, while briefly out and about, it spreads its soothing brightness over the broad prospect of land and lake like the warm extravagance of Provence in a French impressionist painting.

As I write, seemingly less positive, an ill-attended concert has started up on the ornamental bandstand. The tune steals over me, strangely familiar - though I cannot identify it. And the beat stirs memories as compulsive as the drums on a bank holiday afternoon at the Notting Hill Carnival.

With unforeseen suddenness, my eye is drawn closer to home. A jack russell which, with loud admonishments, has just been conditionally untethered, is not constrained by the fraught misgivings and moral exhortations of his human companion: he has spotted a squirrel amidst considerable urgency and commotion, and has given chase. As a further provocation, the sight of those mocking, glassy eyes staring down from the safe haven of a gnarled and sanctimonious oak tree has prompted a fresh outburst of barking which has now attracted the interest of a gang of toughs whose ancient affinity with the hunt has seemingly roused their enthusiasm.

Sadly, the sun is now taking an unwelcome leave of absence behind a cloud. And a chilly breeze is surreptitiously filling the vacuum. *Oh, to be in England now that April's there* is no longer a quote I can reasonably offer as evidence of seasonal dependability. And so, given that the sky has withdrawn its former benefits, grey melancholy lurks with downcast gaze under the darkening limes. Distant voices sound hollow - like the boom of empty vessels in the weightless air; and silence seems suddenly louder than all competing noise - as if unreality has gained the upper hand.

Even so, impetuous townies cluttering the lawns like discarded litter remain forever zealous in their loyalty to a make-believe summer after stripping down in premature readiness for hopes that are determined but unfulfilled.

3

I have just observed a toddler, aged about four, chasing and trying to kick a feral pigeon which, unlike the swans, is a tireless enthusiast when it comes to stale bread. And the parents have taken no steps to stop it. Indeed, I surmise that, as believers in freedom of expression, they see no grounds for taking any steps at all - unless, as now, they are suddenly affected themselves by having to struggle up from their comfortable tartan rug in order to prevent the child from straying.

Observation has at last given place to involvement. A young man, by no means an obvious ruffian, has just sat down on the bench beside me and seems to be in a downcast, introspective frame of mind. I would have liked to suggest a shave, a shower and a good night's sleep if he is to clear his head sufficiently to surmount his troubles. But there again… even the band seems more despondent now: it has modified the beat as if weighed down with recollections of a shared regret. And in consequence of that, I too am feeling the onset of melancholy and I am moving on.

4

As I wander slowly off across the broad acres of green, those dare-devil groups of sunbathers persist in the notion that summer is here and are prepared to risk discomfort under pressure from the cutting edge of the wind. Yet, in the ups and downs of incessant change lies their hope of fulfilment: the laughter of woodpeckers in a city park is promisingly auspicious; a cloudy interval seems of little consequence to passers-by talking at ease in their native language on a cheap weekend break from Stockholm. And see how the grey geese are flying below the level of the treetops while the page on which I scribble grows steadily brighter.

And now, unexpectedly, the sun has re-emerged with a vengeance and I have withdrawn to the shade. When shining unimpeded, it is surprisingly pleasant; but when hidden behind a cloud, the cold is uncomfortable. At the end of the day, this is England; and ironically, amidst her inconstancy, it is England at her most predictable.

Meanwhile, a strutting, well-heeled gentleman with a smart, pin-striped suit and a pot belly is enjoying an afternoon stroll. He is soothed by a tunnel of dappled, citrus-green light beneath these burgeoning London planes and is benefiting from the intimate acquaintance of an old-fashioned, polished walking-stick with an elaborate silver finial.

Here too, at the stroke of three this afternoon, it seems as if all Perugia, in full voice and at full throttle, is passing by and is taking great pains to stress each and every penultimate syllable with a maelstrom of mediterranean intonations and emphases. And as I cast my eyes once again among the sunbathers, I am struck by one further reflection. In Northumberland Gate Gardens, now as in the past, I have noticed that love is still very much alive among the many sufferers from that condition who either stroll or sprawl in the grip of sometimes shameless self-absorption. But whether the sun will shine as benignly upon them this time next year as it has seemingly done for the last fifteen minutes remains opaque and fundamentally uncertain.

5

I have just visited the Castle Gallery which is an important feature of these world-famous gardens. I was *not* looking for uplift - and in that regard, I wasn't disappointed. I *was* disappointed, however, by the fact that I wasn't even *interested* in the spectacular lifetime accomplishments of one Nick Barlowe comprising new and historic photomontage, works woven, painted and built - including densely compacted text elements. Plus thoughts on anti-philosophy, and long-winded diatribes against didactic, class-ridden interpretations.

Concerning important critical acclaim, I noticed no multi-layered, non-judgemental propositions - and found nothing indirectly expressed that was at the same time of much interest. And, indeed, I nearly wet myself when I read that avant-garde music is élitist, given that it rejects the classical tradition supposedly so greatly loved by toffs. And in any case, are we not deafened on a daily basis by bottom-upwards rumblings from politically correct advocates of the lowest common denominator by whom we are bored as stiff as the stiffest of proverbial pokers?

After barely ten minutes of superior boredom, I have therefore left the gallery with no idea whatsoever as to the 'portentous issues' on which Barlowe has focussed. I am in the open air again; and as I look ahead of me, I sense a fresh clarity of vision - rather as I imagine a horse must feel when relieved of its blinkers.

6

Happily, I have now put the blues behind me; and leaving the Castle Gallery to its own devices, I am making haste slowly towards the broad and liquid expanse of nearby Castle Water. As I amble across the crowded, stone-clad bridge linking the northern and southern shores, there is a trembling at the surface as if the Angel of Bethesda were at hand beneath the waves where a cormorant is depleting the fish stock. Here too, strollers of every ilk are gazing downwards abstractedly - as if compelled by the lake's primordial connection with their own distant evolutionary origins.

It seems that my ramblings are drawing to a close. The sun, now at last on the permanent staff, is in a warm and cheerful vein. And the lake, whose surface is a network of orderly ripples, reflects an inverted, complex world well beyond the scope of Barlowe's genius.

Here too, the crowds are casually enjoying the ordinariness of an afternoon outing. And they are watching, as am I, the bobbing flotillas of paddle-boats whose colour is like a bucketful of open sky boiled down to an evocative, blue concentrate underpinning this panorama of unexceptional, peaceful human activity.

Oh, to be in England... Robert Browning: Home-Thoughts, from Abroad; 1845.

Angel of Bethesda: St John 5, 1 - 4.

ARTHUR HALLIWELL'S UPROOTING

It was all the familiar trivia that he'd left
behind that meant so much more to him than the
downs or the seaside picnics. That was the truth
of it; and the particularities he cited were no
more than half-forgotten aspirations that summed
up his sense of a far greater loss.

M. H

I.

Depending on age and circumstance, no one who has reached adulthood will fail from time to time to look back at some past event that persistently crops up for reasons that may or may not be obvious; and although occasionally the less fortunate may be reminded that the present is a great improvement on former, unhappier days, there is a larger cross-section for whom retrospection and nostalgia are interchangeable. And for these, the lucky ones, rose-coloured spectacles may not always be needed in order to recreate moments of genuine pleasure: sudden flashbacks, for example, recalling an incident before the first shadows have darkened a child's mind.

There are others, of course, who live only for the present, for whom the past is not only another country but also a bore. The characters in this story, however, are not of that ilk. And to illustrate the influence of events that refuse to fade away, it's worth mentioning a particular, but seemingly unremarkable incident that left Will Halliwell in possession of words and images that remained with him for a lifetime - notwithstanding the fact that the occurrence itself lasted only a few short minutes as he lay in his pram while his mother wheeled him across a South London common of no great distinction.

Long after the names on their headstones were obscured by lichen, he still remembered their faces: the faces of two elderly women, in appearance as timeless as icons, black-hatted and benevolent as they gazed down at him beneath the hood of the pram, muttering their old-fashioned, well-meaning phrases. There is no clear reason why that brief assortment of compliments became lodged in the mind of a child so young. Nevertheless, it was then that the infant Will was spoken to in terms he could only have understood in retrospect.

Circumstances like this are by no means unusual. And whether they are dramatic or indistinguishable from a thousand other similar events, it sometimes happens that apparently trivial memories travel like a beam of light into times and places distant from their starting-point. This at least was Will's experience when, many years after his father's death, on no special day and for no particular reason, he remembered the faces of the two elderly women gazing down at him from a rectangle of sky formed by the hood of his pram.

* * *

It was in a flash and entirely without warning that he heard himself uttering one of the phrases that still struck him after so many years. Unsurprisingly, as he mused on, he asked himself what possible connection there could be between those two old women, his father's misfortunes and the brilliance of a fresh spring morning. The juxtapositions were spontaneous; but they came without answers; and so, equally spontaneously, he allowed his mind to stray as the sudden warmth of the sun struggled to make up for what had been a grey and profoundly forgettable winter.

Almost like a vessel becalmed at sea with its sails drooping from the masts, he stayed put exactly where he was on Hampstead Heath, reluctant to abandon the comfort of the bench he was sitting on. He glanced at the dense foliage where, indifferent to passing traffic, blackbirds were singing their ancient, unchanging song; and above his head among the taller trees to his left, he spotted a flimsy platform of twigs where a woodpigeon was incubating a clutch of eggs which childhood experience reminded him were as smooth and as pale as ivory.

It was early days. As the northern hemisphere tilted more and more towards the sun, he knew what familiar changes to expect as the year advanced. But throughout April, although rain would continue to fall and although in May there would be the same annual glut of flowers, there would be one irregularity that disfigured the age-old order of things: namely, the fact that he was no longer likely to hear the sing-song, see-saw sound of cuckoos perched by the reed beds. And he reflected that if anything demonstrated the short-termism of the past, the fragility of the present and the uncertainty of the future, it was the sudden silence of the cuckoos.

There was just over a week left before Easter - which reminded Will, now sixty four years of age, that it was at this season fifteen years previously that Arthur Halliwell, his father, had died in circumstances which had been overshadowed not only by the natural tragedy of death but also by another factor operative for many years before that terminal event. Unsurprisingly, therefore, and not for the first time, Will glanced over his shoulders and embarked on yet another assessment of his former life and its many entanglements.

When cancer finally caught up with him, Arthur Halliwell had been thirteen years into his second marriage which followed the loss of Emily, his first wife and Will's mother. Emily's death had occurred three years before the moment when Will, having been asked to approve the new liaison, had freely done so. And important to an understanding of the subsequent course of events is the fact that both marriages had been happy ones, although very different in character. For Arthur, on the other hand, after remarrying, something had gone wrong along the way which (as it turned out) was only indirectly associated with his new wife, Ann, who was a wise and understanding woman gifted with a patient, caring temperament.

Unfortunately, removing the fly in the ointment was beyond the scope of mere marital relationships - even good ones. Eventually, Ann deduced what the problem was, but never discussed it with Will. And it was not until much later that Arthur, in need of sympathy, told his son about it - whereupon Will made a point of never discussing it with Ann to avoid seeming to point the finger. In any case, at so late a stage in their lives, the only solution would have involved an impossible upheaval. All the same, for Will, many years after Ann as well as Arthur had died, the problem retained a disturbing subtext that repeatedly raised questions; and to his way of thinking, it was a matter of regret still largely unresolved.

When the trouble first presented itself, although it ended in a stalemate, it had a background that can be explained easily enough by pointing out that when Arthur sought his son's support, the latter was in the throes of an adult but still hectic, youth-oriented private life. In consequence, he failed to grasp the seriousness of what his father was telling him and responded with an absurdly naïve platitude which must surely have sounded dismissive. Although all the signs were there, and although Will could easily have understood them if he had only placed himself in his father's position, he failed to pay sufficient attention; indeed, he failed to pay the right *sort* of attention. And the matter was never raised again.

With luck, new attitudes can sometimes follow in the footsteps of experience. And time, the great healer and the great destroyer, had latterly altered his perspective, giving rise to fresh insight as he approached pensionable age. Sitting on a bench on a warm spring day at a distance of seventy miles from the epicentre of his recollections, and after a lapse of so many years, Will thought back over that brief conversation with his father and over what little he knew about him beyond his own personal experiences as a child in the family home before his mother's death at a very early age. Consequently, he surrendered to the drift of his own thoughts and once again focussed on the backlog of events which demanded, or so it seemed, a radical reassessment.

One thing that demonstrated Arthur Halliwell's blood relationship with Will - apart from the plain fact of it - was their shared respect for their own and the nation's history. This was something Arthur had never consciously foisted on his son. Indeed, from the start, one of his chief concerns had been never to impose his personal opinions after having himself endured an overbearing Victorian father. But despite a consistent laissez-faire policy, both parties had ended up with a similar picture of reality - one which was hostile to the mid-to-late twentieth century passion for cocking a snook at patriotism, at traditional practices and, above all, at values long taken for granted. In consequence, both father and son looked aghast at what they saw as the left-leaning smash-and-grab raid on their cultural heritage embodied in the many changes that so greatly disconcerted them.

During the course of his life so far, in a more fluid age than his father's, Will Halliwell's outlook had matured and settled, enabling him to look back with deeper understanding at his younger days and in particular at his failure to recognise the tundra-like bleakness which had once led Arthur to solicit his help. Consequently, at sixty four, in the spring sunshine, in a moment of quiet retrospection on a park bench, he was able to assemble with greater ease the conflicting influences of historic rootedness and unforeseen developments that had cast a shadow over Arthur's final years - notwithstanding comfortable circumstances, Ann's steadying influence and her patient cosseting.

2

This is a story that takes a few steps backwards, but no more, into the circumstances and events whose gradual build-up impaired what the world might at first regard as the good fortune of a bereaved husband. It is not a life history; neither is it an exhaustive biography of one or other of the two main characters of whom no one would ever have heard but for the recollections of one of the principals, namely Will, who was the only person who survived to tell a tale that reveals why his father's final years, although cushioned by his second wife's affection, were so fundamentally undermined.

Will had gleaned regrettably little information about Arthur's early life beyond the entry on his birth certificate showing that he was born on the second of January 1902 in Maidenhead. He also knew that he was the only son of Walter Halliwell, an itinerant gardener, bee-keeper and carpenter. From snippets of conversation, from odd asides and from the indirect evidence of several family albums, Will made other fragmentary discoveries about his roots - including the bare fact of Arthur's boyhood attendance at a junior school in Dunscombe, a village near Bath, where over a period of several years, Walter earned his living as a nurseryman.

Later on, still following in the wake of wherever work was to be found, the family ended up in a tied cottage in a South London suburb which at that time, in the nineteen twenties, was still leafy. The cottage proved seminal. It was attached to four or five acres of land owned by the Summerhill Dairy which supplied the local community; and it was here that Walter was placed in charge of the kitchen garden whose produce was sold mainly to those customers whose milk was delivered to their doors. He was also tasked with the bee-keeping that provided the dairy's other seasonal side-line, honey. Unfortunately, as it turned out, this was also Walter's final place of employment after a more or less obscure career that nevertheless reflected well on Victorian England's horticultural and other, mainly rural, traditions.

After he grew up, Arthur, still living at home, had also taken up employment at the dairy as a driver - to begin with, the driver of a clumsy, overworked horse with a wiry black mane, leather blinkers and a nose bag that absorbed any unauthorised impulses and ensured docility. In other words, barely out of his teens, Arthur became a milkman in charge of a milk float; and although the horse soon disappeared and was replaced by a motorised delivery truck, it was a milkman that he remained for the rest of his working life both before and after he married Will's mother, Emily, who was a spirited, no-nonsense former housemaid born and bred in Dorset.

Walter was already a widower on the verge of retirement when the marriage took place - after which the newly-weds lived alongside him in the cottage where all three of them shared the more than ample accommodation until, in the natural course of events, Walter died. This left Arthur and Emily as the sole occupants of what was actually a large house (rather than a cottage) built in 1868 where, in the early years of their marriage, they resorted uncomplainingly to an outside water closet very much indebted to the inventiveness of Thomas Crapper.

Time moved on; and it was in the bedroom formerly occupied by Walter and his wife in what was by then a long-established family residence that Will was conceived and born. As another only son like his father, he grew up there, was dragged off to infants' school from there, survived the Second World War there; and when it was over, he continued to live there with his parents throughout his formative years at the Henry Lichfield Grammar School for Boys and for many more years after he completed his studies and started work.

Being a grammar school boy was a source of considerable pride in those days when no one else from the families of either parent had managed anything like it. It provided an education which, at the age of nineteen, enabled Will to move on to the Updike College of Art & Architecture from which privileged position he was able to look down his nose at some of his less fortunate cousins - one of whom, for example, ended up as part of a small team of taxi drivers based outside the railway station at Three Bridges.

It was not long after successfully completing his four-year course at the age of twenty three that Will finally left home and moved into rented accommodation on the strength of his first job with Bainbridge Jones & Frampton Architects where he remained until, by the time he was thirty when his mother died, he had become a junior partner. This, of course, was another step up the social ladder of which Arthur felt quietly but genuinely proud. It made Will feel proud, too, when he took out his first mortgage on a small but fashionably situated mews cottage in Kensington.

Will's mother died more or less suddenly. Sadly and dramatically, it was from the same bedroom in which her son was born that she was rushed to hospital. And with similar urgency, it was during a holiday in Mumbai (still Bombay in those days) that a telegram reached Will, leading within hours to a spare seat on board a flight home. He landed at Heathrow in time to reach Emily whilst she was still able to utter a few meaningful sentences. But it was in the same

South London Hospital for Women, only a week later, that he came face to face with Arthur, in tears at the head of the stairs outside his mother's ward.

There are occasions when actions genuinely speak louder than a few mumbled words. Thus prompted, Will immediately made his way unaccompanied through the swing doors and crept behind the curtains drawn discreetly around the bed. And he was struck not only by his mother's closed eyes and motionless features but also by the stunningly obvious fact that this was the last glimpse he would ever have of a woman who had been a live wire at family gatherings and the scourge of the local butcher when his produce was judged below par. Barely middle-aged at sixty six, she had died only minutes before his arrival.

* * *

Andrew MacFarlane, managing director of the Summerhill Dairy, was swift to ease Arthur's situation by giving him more than enough time off to deal with the unavoidable aftermath of a death. And it was from the company's main gates, in the presence of the entire workforce, that the funeral procession departed for a picturesque country cemetery in Sussex on the slopes of the South Downs near Newhaven.

There was history in the choice of that out-of-the-way spot which, on a sunny spring day, witnessed a simple ceremony high above the flood plain of the Ouse. The site of the grave overlooked an impressive panorama that had long-standing associations with the home of Emily's sister, Rose, and with the many summer holidays the Halliwells had spent there. For some of those present, there was a mysteriously charged atmosphere: half-forgotten, half-remembered fragments of the past seemed to hover invisibly overhead in the descending sunlight which, although indifferent to the circumstances, nevertheless enhanced and transformed the landscape. The chirps of sparrows in the hedgerow seemed timeless; the nostalgic smell of the sea blown inland from the docks added to Will's competing recollections; and there was an elusive permanence and appropriateness in the air which, if anything, had a soothing influence on the minds of the chief mourners.

In the weeks and months after the funeral, Arthur lived alone with his thoughts in a very large and suddenly very empty house. He was regularly visited by Will who sometimes stayed overnight; and he was fed on a daily basis, free of charge, in the Summerhill Dairy's staff canteen. Fortunately, despite the inevitable loneliness, it was these two factors that helped him make the best of the much needed continuity and support that reached him from a familiar environment, sympathetic employers and a wide range of warm-hearted customers. Indeed, his customers were more like old friends who still anticipated the clink of the bottles when the same milkman rang their front door bells and greeted them with a smile that was just a little more drawn than they were used to.

3

Against this background and helped along by a lifetime of routine comings and goings, Arthur continued with his rounds. He was still greatly liked, even admired, by his customers who had always been aware of his many virtues. This was especially the case when seen by those with ageing eyes against the background of a changing world whose standards were uncertain. He epitomised reliable and predictable behaviour beyond the strict demands of a humble occupation; and he was always punctual. Significantly, too, over a longer timescale, people had noticed that he had an intelligence and sensibility not obviously associated with his position in life; and this was enhanced by the way in which he spoke with a quiet confidence that suggested he was a man worth listening to. There was another feather in his cap, too, which was known only to a selection of his older customers: namely, that throughout the conflict with Germany and particularly during the blitz, he had been an air raid warden, based at Summerhill's but with the added responsibility of monitoring the blackout in the surrounding rabbit warren of traditional cottages which, as it turned out later, were under greater threat from urban development than they were from Hitler's bombs.

The fact that everyone knew about his bereavement increased and broadened the friendly welcome he was always given. He was much talked about among the several clusters of neighbours who knew each other; and the dairy not only continued to supply him with regular meals but also, acknowledging nearly forty years of service, it issued a guarantee that he could remain as long as he wished in the house he'd lived in for his entire working life. The result was that during the three years following Emily's death, and despite his permanent sense of loss, the raw edge of his misfortune was mollified by the continuity of his circumstances along with the widespread personal encouragement he received.

Something else, however, was brewing in the background of his daily life - something of which, in the first instance, Arthur himself could not have foreseen the consequences. As time wore on, an entirely new factor came into play which altered his situation and presented him with the prospect of a brighter future than either he or anyone else could have imagined. It was not only Will who was taken completely by surprise!

Great oaks from little acorns grow - and sometimes they do so more rapidly than the author of this fourteenth century proverb might have thought. To begin with, for Arthur as well as for acorns, it was a slow process. But in due course, the widespread welcome received from his customers gained extra significance in the leafy, pleasantly middle-class surroundings of Copythorne Crescent, and especially at the front door of number 33 whose rear garden overlooked an equally pleasant, tucked-away little park. The owner of the property, Ann Blanchard, having devoted her adult life to caring for a recently deceased maiden aunt, was conveniently unmarried. And the cast of mind which had made such a selfless commitment possible also enabled her to see with particular clarity the virtues that everyone who knew him saw in Arthur. Affection developed gradually: and after time had made its contribution, it became clear that the regular chats on the doorstep were something that both parties looked forward to. In consequence, the next stage was reached sooner rather than later, ending up in the kitchen each week with a cup of tea and a slice of homemade cake. And the subsequent step was even shorter, reaching the point at which these convivial get-togethers in a tidy, well-stocked modern kitchen became something that both parties increasingly depended on.

The course of events as well as natural sensibilities were such that Will had no means of knowing precisely how things moved towards their conclusion. Nevertheless, it was obvious that a proposal had been made and accepted. Consequently, mulling the matter over without a shred of evidence to back him up, Will wondered, as he looked back, whether it was *Ann* who first made the suggestion and Arthur, reticent by nature, who agreed to it after a brief pause for consideration. Whatever the truth, the pace of events gathered speed and reached a happy ending - although not before Arthur had phoned Will (who was still in bed), astounding him by asking whether he would mind if he got married again!

Caught unawares, Will burst out laughing, offered his unqualified support, and then, sitting up in bed, listened to a prepared plan of action which relieved him of a growing worry because, given that his father owned no property, what was to become of him in his old age had long been a concern. This was now taken care of: Arthur, already nearly seventy years old, was to resign from the dairy - following which, after getting married, it was agreed he would move into Ann's ready-made home which was far more comfortable and secure than the tied cottage whilst being less than a fifteen minute walk away from it. Significant continuity alongside substantial betterment was therefore guaranteed.

It was a master-stroke. Will, of course, attended the registry office wedding at which only one other person (Ann's next-door neighbour, Pat) was present. Further guests appeared later on: it was a perfect summer's day; and this enabled everyone to celebrate together in the back garden of 33 Copythorne Crescent where, among the well kept flower beds, there was much laughter, small talk, and a choice of ham or egg-and-cress sandwiches followed by homemade trifle. Pat handed out tea or coffee through the kitchen window, whilst Will introduced himself and two other male guests (at Ann's prior bidding) to a modest range of bottles in a cupboard next to the cooker.

Among the many minor incidents that marked a jolly and convivial afternoon, there was only one that passed virtually unnoticed by everybody except Will whom it secretly amused (and slightly embarrassed). He was asked to introduce the high point of the occasion by opening the champagne; and as he did so, firing the cork half way down the garden, he observed his father, with a sheepish grin on his face as he kissed his new wife, with modest brevity, on the cheek. It was just a passing instant caught in the crossfire of congratulations and hand-clapping. But it was clearly the bridegroom rather than the bride who did the blushing!

4

A detailed account of the thirteen years Arthur spent with Ann between their marriage and his death would seem much like a thousand other marriages and consequently of little interest to those not associated with it. As regards their personal relations, it was a successful match unimpaired by friction. Furthermore, Arthur never lost sight of the benefits of his new home and of the daily companionship that went with it. Living amongst the general public instead of in a tied cottage on private land was at first a satisfying novelty - as was eating quietly at home instead of having to make conversation in the noisy and sometimes ribald atmosphere of a works canteen.

From the start, married life went ahead smoothly and none of its many advantages was affected in any way by a downside; but accompanying Ann on frequent shopping trips to destinations further off than the small cluster of local retailers involved Arthur in direct contact with a world previously experienced more or less exclusively through newspaper reports, the BBC and doorstep gossip. As a result, he became aware of change, often for the worse, and of the tremors affecting an environment formerly perceived as stable.

In one particular matter, somewhat surprisingly, Arthur reacted with uncharacteristic haste. This came about after a prominent national newspaper, whose values he'd always treated as his own, sought to increase its circulation by printing audacious photographs of pin-ups on the inside pages. In a moment of indignation, Arthur strode to the newsagent and changed his existing order in terms that embarrassed the proprietor - after which he remained a loyal reader of The Times throughout the rest of his life.

Not long after cancelling what was once his regular source of news, Arthur also noticed (as did Ann) that when the owners of the house opposite sold up and moved out, the new, much younger residents did little more than nod their heads in response to the cheerful 'hellos' and 'good mornings' of their neighbours. It seemed as if the well-remembered bonhomie, widespread during and after the war, was beginning to go out of fashion.

With increasing frequency, more inauspicious signs bubbled up from nowhere during the first few years of Arthur and Ann's life together. To begin with, the small local shopping parade began to alter: Cullens, previously the friendly grocer, sold out to a supplier of spare parts for lorries. The butcher where Emily had so often complained about toughness changed hands and, during an election campaign, displayed radical left-wing posters alongside the lamb chops and tripe in the window! The owner of the launderette, too, was deemed to have taken leave of her senses when she transformed the conventional appearance of her shopfront with a large mono-chrome photograph of a sparsely clad white male seated in the lotus position and accompanied by an invitation to attend yoga classes. There was no end to it; and when the John and Mavis Maltravers Garden Shop with its many glass houses and nursery beds on Palace Hill was demolished in preparation for a council estate, Ann declared it was the last straw during what turned out to be the most pivotal luncheon ever consumed at 33 Copythorne Crescent.

In the middle of the washing up, as a consequence of a worsening situation about which both parties felt similarly, Ann's plan of action (already long in the making) was reiterated with a new emphasis to which Arthur submitted without reserve despite a pinprick of hesitation so slight that he barely noticed it himself. And the continued darkening of their private world, such as the closure a week later of Turnbull's Pet Shop, proved a red line that had to be crossed. Turnbull's, after all, was the mainstay of Timmy, Ann's middle-aged black spaniel, equally beloved of Arthur before and after he and Ann were married. And so, seeing that the world was changing to the detriment of man and beast, Ann and Arthur Halliwell reached a decision to respond urgently - and to do so before they were too old to take the required action.

The consequence of a decision, once made, is often an end to uncertainty and the beginning, however short-lived, of a period of stability. A leisurely correspondence was therefore entered into with Ann's cousin who was the wife of a retired judge. The couple lived in Lewes. And after a brief toing-and-froing of letters, Ann and Arthur were invited down to spend a pleasant weekend in the imposing flint-faced house owned by the former judge and his wife. The building was perched on a knoll at the upper, western end of the town not far from Lewes Castle. And it was there during two days of generous hospitality that they received encouraging advice from a man, once prominent in his profession, who for Arthur in particular spoke with the voice of experience. Arthur was no cringer; but he was also a traditionalist who was naturally conscious that a judge, retired or otherwise, was somewhat distinct from a former milkman. Nevertheless, the two men established a warm, companionable relationship; and this enabled Arthur to relax into an easy-going conversational manner which, throughout a very pleasant weekend, betrayed an undercurrent of respect that went down well with Judge Alan Warburton.

It proved a fruitful two days away from home; and en route to the station, before returning to London, the visitors were introduced by their hosts to a reputable high-street estate agent whose two senior partners were out of the office at the time, valuing new properties. Left in charge was a junior assistant who, in addition to being extremely affable, was noticeably assiduous in recording all the necessary personal information and contact details required from the new clients. His manner, like his black pin-striped suit, was rather exaggerated; and he was somewhat too unctuous. On the other hand, wise woman that she was, Ann decided that due allowance must be made: after all, still very inexperienced and at the outset of his career, his oozing benevolence identified him as nothing more pernicious than a young person trying to do his best - and making sure that he was seen doing it in the presence of a local gentleman of acknowledged standing!

5

Will's contemplation of his intimate past continued. He had no commitments that day and was disinclined to budge from the wooden bench on which he'd been lounging for over an hour. The location was a high-point on Hampstead Heath not far from Jack Straw's Castle - a former public house latterly renamed and converted into a centre for physical well-being. Beneath him was a steep slope of rough grassland darkened by scattered clumps of gorse; and where the gradient eased off was a village, the Vale of Health, comprising picturesque period dwellings surrounded by dense woods that concealed all evidence of the city beyond. It was a place of particular charm: a sheltered, tucked-away little enclave forming part of the broader Heath whose history was preserved not only in the paintings of John Constable but also in the veteran oaks that continued to sway and creak in the wind as they had done for centuries along the ridge that links Hampstead and Highgate.

From his position above the rooftops, Will had the advantage of height, enabling him to scan almost the whole of East London stretching away uninterruptedly towards the Essex borders. But despite the welcome (if uncertain) arrival of spring and the soothing warmth of the sun, the city sprawl in front of him was depressingly colourless, its details dissolving into the grey uncertainty of distance. It lay there, monotonous and muddled, in striking contrast to the fresh green environment where he sat. Indeed, to a temperament like his, the outlook seemed as oblivious as a corpse to the pleasure he felt when a robin, with instinctive boldness, appeared beside him on the arm of the bench.

For Will, whose adult sensibilities were still coloured by those of his childhood, moody reflections such as these remained characteristic of his thinking whenever he was alone. They went hand in hand with a tendency to leap from awareness of the present to recollections of events long over and done with. Consequently, disregarding the sandwiches in his knapsack, he imagined himself once again caught up in the past, alighting from a bus in the Sussex village of Barsden Mappley on that very significant day, nearly thirty years before, when he first visited the bungalow into which his father and Ann had moved only a fortnight earlier. Then as now, he was mindful of having had to hold back in deference to a tradition that required everything to be in order, well polished and tidy before even close family members were given a chance to glimpse the outcome of a courageous decision.

Although he had never set foot there before, Will at once noticed that it was a place rigidly divided into two distinct parts. To the right of where he stood at the bus stop was the village green receding at a gentle uphill gradient towards a broad, blunt summit where, half hidden by a screen of elms, he observed the tower of a church flanked to right and left by the red-tiled roofs of typical guidebook-style cottages.

By contrast, on the opposite side of the busy main road between Lewes and Lower Dicker, he was confronted by a reality that so often defaces those English villages that are greatly admired by trippers and yet wrecked by developers who add numberless modern, pink-bricked dwellings built on the cheap because only the well off can otherwise afford to live there. Nevertheless, having phoned his father from the station, Will was partly reconciled as he sauntered towards him when he appeared from a side road. He took note of the grass verge dividing the kerb opposite from the pavement where, through the happy fault of negligence, no mower had yet obliterated the profusion of dandelions which, in their random abundance, outshone by far what is so often seen elsewhere: namely, those municipal patches of daffodils planted artlessly in the hope of imitating nature.

And so, in the warmth and brightness of the midday sun, and further influenced by the triple cooing of the doves, Will had reserved his judgement by the time he and Arthur reached the opening into Glyndebourne Way - the sheltered cul-de-sac with its neat front gardens which (he hoped) would become his home from home and a permanent point of access to the grandeur of the Sussex downs.

Rather like the first few hours after the launch of a new business venture, that day at the start of another epoch in the lives of both generations proved a cheerful one. No shadows had yet been cast;

everybody was in high spirits; and the atmosphere was strangely familiar in a home whose settled, lived-in appearance had been reached in a remarkably short time. The couple, by reason of age, had downsized intentionally from their former, four-bedroomed house to a modern, two-bedroomed bungalow involving less maintenance and lower fuel bills. This meant that no new furniture had been needed - and the walls were already hung with photographs and watercolours familiar not only from Copythorne Crescent but also from Will's boyhood recollections of his own home with Arthur and Emily.

After a fifteen-minute guided tour of the noticeably spick-and-span bungalow (and accompanied by a glass of sherry each), Ann served lunch in the garden on the only piece of newly purchased furniture: namely, a fold-up table made of regrettably synthetic material which, given the occasion, in no way diminished the enjoyment of homemade chicken and asparagus soup, bread rolls and a glass of white wine. This was followed by Ann's unique version of rhubarb crumble which would have persuaded any aspiring chef to reconsider his or her more predictable choice of crêpes suzette.

The general picture was therefore unblemished: taken altogether and looked at from an independent point of view, it was almost as if this modest, intimate occasion was being orchestrated by some invisible well-wisher: it was a perfect summer's day much enhanced by the twittering of birds; and the regular buzz of bees making their acquaintance with an already partially stocked garden was especially soothing. For a while, there was a reassuring impression of permanence and a slowing-down, or so it seemed, in the forward motion of time.

Will had been invited for a 'long weekend' which, to him, seemed very little longer than a short one; and consequently, he voiced none of the desire he felt, even on the first day, for a glimpse of the downs. Instead, the afternoon was spent in a shady corner of the garden on deckchairs imported from Copythorne Crescent; and the evening was centred on cold duck followed by lemon soufflé with cream. The day then concluded with television and an early night in preparation for a trip promised for the following afternoon.

The next morning, after a bacon and egg breakfast, Will killed time before the scheduled outing by taking a look at the small cluster of village shops which, like almost everything else on the modern side of Barsden Mappley, were characterless in form and built of the same monotonous pink bricks that proliferated everywhere. His visit was short-lived. Apart from a butcher, a small supermarket, a dry-cleaner, a pet shop and an Indian restaurant which was up for sale, there was so little worth seeing that the only option was to move on. In the older, historic village, however, the picture was certainly brighter; but the church, after a recent theft of carpets and candlesticks, was closed and the cottages looked under-occupied except for one of them where washing was flapping cheerfully on a line in the front garden. Otherwise, only the inscriptions on the graves in the delightfully overgrown churchyard were of much interest.

After a sandwich lunch, everyone (including the dog) set out for the coast at Seaford with Arthur at the wheel of Ann's antique Ford. It was so old that the mechanic who serviced it during the Copythorne Crescent years repeatedly joked about it, saying that it must have discovered the elixir of life. But luckily, on that auspicious day, with benevolent forces still active, there were no hiccoughs and the drive was as smooth as it was short.

An archetypally English afternoon was to follow from the moment the car parked on the Esplanade which was dominated to the east by the towering chalk ramparts of Seaford Head. Straight in front of the visitors was the pebble beach murmuring softly under the influence of the incoming tide; and in the distance, emerging from the mist on the far side of the bay, stood Newhaven harbour which was protected from the rigours of the sea by the stone semicircle of West Pier and its lighthouse.

All around the car, rising from the paving stones and from the wider landscape, the sun's accumulated heat imposed a pleasant hush on all environmental noise so that even the seagulls' pencil-sharp cries were blunted. It presented a picture of a world in which nothing whatever was amiss - even a pessimist might have been persuaded to let well alone by not looking too closely.

The first item on the agenda, of course, was that all three visitors went for a stroll together - the sort of stroll undertaken because it was a custom so embedded that no one even thought of questioning it. Nevertheless, it was kept short at Arthur's suggestion so that the ageing Ford was never out of sight - although everyone paused for a few minutes to watch the ferry from Dieppe glide slowly past the pier into its anchorage at the mouth of the Ouse. The prospect of refreshments was then raised; and so, like a carbon copy of a thousand similar outings, everyone returned to the car and sat down uncomfortably inside it with the doors thrown open whilst Ann dispensed tea from a thermos flask and handed round slices of homemade fruit cake.

* * *

The passage of time can either confirm an impression or prompt reconsideration. And so, many years later on and looking back at that cloudless afternoon, Will's inward eye bore down on it with fresh openness from his vantage point on the summit of Hampstead Heath. Personal and social events had altered him; but he remembered the suspicion he'd felt at the time: namely, that despite the conviviality of a seaside picnic, it was in the course of that unremarkable event that the tranquillity of the afternoon was darkened by an almost imperceptible shadow. From his own parallel recollections, he could still feel it nagging at the back of his mind; and he was now convinced that an awkward lull in the conversation meant that Arthur, in his own differing way, was experiencing similar memories of the past they shared - a past which was staring back at them from the other side of the bay.

Will's capacity for recollection required no special effort. After all, only a few miles of water separated him from the quaint back streets of Newhaven where so many summer and Christmas holidays had been spent with Emily's sister, Rose, when the world was a very different place. He cast his mind back to the rock pools and the nearby sandy beach where he first learned to swim; it was also a fair guess that his father, while watching the ferry sail into port, had been thinking about Rose's husband, a wireless operator serving on the same channel crossing before and after the war - someone Arthur had greatly admired as a well informed, well travelled man who spoke French and had connections in Paris. Indeed, it was because of all these associations that Emily had been buried in the neat little graveyard on a hillside just to the north of the town.

Still reclining on a park bench and gazing out across London's East End, Will continued mulling over that afternoon on the Esplanade at Seaford. He could still remember quite clearly what his thoughts were at the time. And it struck him that, although on such a day of celebration, neither father nor son would have dreamt of dampening Ann's pleasure or each other's, neither could have been unaware that on a prominence just visible a mile inland from where the ferry lay at anchor, the mother of one and the first wife of the other had been buried only a few years earlier almost within sight of the pebbled shore where those who survived her were peering nostalgically across the water and drinking tea.

6

That which seems familiar, that which presents itself as everyday experience, that which governs the universe, is taken for granted by the world and is known simply as 'time'; but it remains an incomprehensible enigma despite all equations and descriptions of its workings. Nevertheless, it carries everything along with it; its range is immense, and yet it condescendingly and minutely concerns itself with dust particles, gale-force winds and the routine scheduling of trains. Neither human beings nor planets can evade its mysterious authority. And so, under its pervasive influence, Arthur, Ann and Will grew older, albeit slowly; and the perturbations in their progress, their everyday ups and downs, seemed for a while so minor that they passed unnoticed. Arthur and Ann believed that Will was doing well at work; Will took it for granted that Ann and Arthur were happy together; and none of them suspected that anything was amiss until a point was reached when the air that chafed the downs blew colder and made itself felt.

From the safe distance of the present, Will asked himself how a matter of such fundamental concern could have passed unnoticed for so long; and the effort gradually brought to mind the many occasions when, on his way back to London, Arthur had driven him to the station at Lewes following a weekend much like any other at Barsden Mappley. He recalled the unconvincing smile on his father's face whenever the pair shook hands and said goodbye on the pavement. And he also remembered what he had only half-noticed on those occasions in his hurry to reach the platform: namely, the left-behind, helpless-looking figure of an elderly man standing beside the car and watching him as he finally turned and waved before disappearing through the station entrance. It had been something that happened almost every time - something so recurrent that he took it as a normal feature of inter-generational family farewells instead of a symptom of something so much more far-reaching.

Notwithstanding the mild influence of the Vale of Health glimpsed from above, there was another factor that affected Will and gnawed at his conscience as he contemplated those family relationships recorded long ago on death certificates or held in abeyance between the covers of photograph albums. It is not only God, of course, but also the human mind that is sometimes inscrutable; and perhaps it was the sheer openness and freedom of the heath that enabled Will's thoughts, without conscious effort, to focus on the seamier side of his past.

And so, unknown to anyone other than himself, but no less regrettable on that account, his private recollections of the Christmas breaks spent at Barsden Mappley resurfaced uncomfortably and unprompted as he remembered how bored he'd been when the weather and festive obligations had combined to keep him from the quiet lanes and empty paddocks that had their attractions even in winter. Awaiting him in London were the usual seasonal get-togethers; and not least among them was the annual New Year party attended by friends from his college days - an occasion characterised by much alcohol and, unsurprisingly, by the ribaldry and laughter that went with it. Compared with such eagerly anticipated events, Christmas at Barsden Mappley was dreary; and Will was always eager to be on his way back to Victoria. He hoped that Arthur and

Ann had no inkling of what was in his mind. But now, imagining the dullness and drudgery of the clearing up after his departure, he could feel the pain of it *in principle* - never mind whether or not his contrived show of enjoyment had been convincing.

7

Clear insight into the problem that affected Arthur and Ann Halliwell finally came about as suddenly as a burst of gunfire despite the trail of clues that Will had failed to notice. It was during one of his many regular visits to Barsden Mappley when the elusive secret, so long left undisclosed, came abruptly into the open. The time was mid-morning on a typical winter's day. Will and his father were out walking Timmy the spaniel on the village green. Both of them, as well as the dog, were well wrapped up in suitably seasonal clothing. The sky was rainless but profoundly grey; and although there was no frost, the wind was biting. Nothing could have been more desolate: the elms surrounding the church were shorn of leaves; and country living had seldom looked less attractive. Unfortunately, this was a sentiment to which Will made an oblique but ill-judged allusion.

Arthur responded instantly and emotionally. It seemed that Will had hit the nail on the head, providing a long-awaited, now irrepressible opportunity for his father's pent up unhappiness to emerge into the open. Or so it appeared, given there was no preamble to a declaration that left the younger man stunned and embarrassed when confronted by desperation so great that his only reaction was to withdraw behind the first ill thought out cliché that came to mind.

Arthur was quick to pay tribute to Ann and their life together. But this was no more than a bare fact - a fact that could only partially relieve the desolation he now admitted to feeling about life in

Barsden Mappley. There was nothing there, he said; there was little to do; the downs were all the same; and they had few local friends apart from what he described as 'the two old biddies round the corner'.

'In London', he went on, 'I could always visit the Natural History Museum or the Science Museum' - a reply that sounded a very hollow note alongside the incongruity of that proposition in relation to his past practice. Clearly, Arthur was having trouble pinpointing precisely what he meant - or perhaps, in the muddle of emotion, he was unable to assemble the much larger number of seemingly trivial regrets which were the real reasons why Barsden Mappley had assumed the rôle of an endurance test.

However confused or otherwise his outburst really was, it was followed by a pause; but it was his next remark, emerging from the brief silence, that unsteadied Will and knocked him off balance when his father mumbled... almost whispered 'I sometimes wish that I'd never been born'. A second, very awkward pause was the sequel; and it did nothing to offset the shock of so abrupt and uncharacteristic an outburst from someone who, until that moment, had been a perfect example of mildness and self-control.

Embarrassed by the turn of events and uniquely unprepared, Will defensively countered the level of emotion thus unleashed with a particularly ineffectual answer. 'But you never went to the museums in any case', he replied, hoping against the odds that a plain fact, clear and unembroidered, would prove helpful.

In response to a true statement that so completely missed the point, and despite his overwrought condition, Arthur pulled himself together and made a comeback that showed considerable insight not only into his own nature but also into human nature generally.

It was an answer on a par with a theological distinction made by an experienced, worldly-wise cleric countering dissent from a naïve parishioner. And it was this answer that Will still remembered word for word as he reclined on his wooden park bench on Hampstead Heath's highest and most exposed vantage-point.

He could even hear his father's voice blurting it out.

'I realise that', said Arthur in reply to Will's point of order, 'but I knew the museums were just a bus ride away. And I knew I could always go there if I wanted to'!

THE RATHBONE-BAKER PRIZE
FOR ARTISTIC EXCELLENCE

At root, Amanda was a genuine art lover open to the possibility, however remote, that among the large or small-scale bric-a-brac, ironmongery and objets trouvés, there might be a few worthwhile paintings, drawings or sculptures. Notwithstanding this, but for the loan of a friend's membership card, she would not have been present at that year's Rathbone-Baker Exhibition because, on the strength of her past experience, it was sure to be a waste of money - like many other of the Quantum Gallery's allegedly ground-breaking events. That, at least, was the way she saw things.

She justified this superficially ambivalent course of action in the belief that paying for entry would impose an obligation to take the show seriously - whereas free admission as the prelude to a casual walkabout would provide opportunities for lighthearted scorn, a disparaging phrase in her notebook or the simple pleasure to be found in superior condemnation. Indeed, Amanda relished the prospect of a deliberate, almost flippant diatribe, having long ago formed the view that there were occasions for disapproval which, all things being equal, could also be transformed into a recreational pursuit. In this frame of mind, therefore, she waltzed into the exhibition, looked about her with interest and prepared to confirm her prejudices.

As is common at many art exhibitions, women were in the majority; but at the age of forty three, Amanda was younger than the average female visitor that day. She was also somewhat distinctively dressed in that the exotic self-consciousness evident in many of the other women's costumes was absent from her own neatly urbane ensemble. This comprised a newish-looking, heavily pleated black-and-white check skirt reaching just below the knees - to which was added a pale blue blouse with matching cardigan supplemented, as a finishing touch, by a modest necklace. To cap it all, her hair, consonant with her years, was light grey, unostentatiously groomed - and short enough to reveal a pair of silver ear rings. Her unmarried status was subtly underlined by the absence of any jewellery on her fingers; and there was none, apart from the necklace, elsewhere. On the other hand, her image thus described, if suggestive of a grey eminence, was redeemed and set alight by her fresh pink complexion and the sparkle in her steely blue eyes - all of which, given her occupation as a university lecturer, hinted at the self-possession and poise needed to assert her seniority.

* * *

As Amanda began her exploratory walkabout, the fact that the first artist she encountered shared her gender did nothing whatever to disguise the pretentious vacuity she expected to find - and found. That the work actually comprised oil paint on canvas was a good start that swiftly foundered before it really got going; and having glanced around the walls at about a dozen geometrical designs that reminded her of paint charts or tests for colour blindness, she began to peruse the equally technicolour prose in the printed guide that accompanied the exhibition. Here she encountered much talk about volume and space which, given the flatness of the paintings, were qualities conspicuous by their absence. Also in short supply was any back-up for the artist's declared need for the handmade character of her work to be evident - given that every example shown looked more like a print than a painting. Triumphant in her predictions and following in the proverbial footsteps of Jack Robinson, Amanda made her way to the next salon with a throw-away, I-told-you-so smile on her face.

The second artist chosen by the selection committee was male - a fact merely coincidental, Amanda decided, with the fact that his work comprised an over-literal pictorial *examination* of the industrial landscapes present in a Midland town. Having glanced at the brochure, she was struck at once by this umpteenth example of the obsession, widespread among curators, with the word 'examination'. She also felt that, whatever else might be said, the pictures were outstandingly dull, lacking in focus and, as she mumbled quietly under her breath, not a patch on *Lowry's* industrial landscapes. Out of a sense of duty both to the painter and to her own presumptions, Amanda then glanced for a second time at the brochure where she discovered that the artist eschewed mere observation in favour of a participatory approach with an emphasis on space and personal input. But her trouble proved fruitless: she was, if anything, more negative about this second seeker after fame than about the previous one - feeling, as she moved on, that he had successfully killed off what might well have been an informative and, given sufficient talent, a memorable addition to a show that, so far, was fulfilling every prediction. Roused - but as yet by no means fed up - Amanda set out for pastures new which would almost certainly boil down to more of the same.

In the following gallery, somewhat flattened by an immediate impression of emptiness, Amanda decided at the outset to consult the exhibition brochure by which she was further flattened (on the one hand) and amused (on the other) to find an unprecedented level of meaninglessness bearing no observable relation to the mixed media structures all around her. The text declared that depicting a World War II tank as if it were both a dada poster and a cubist fantasy brings it to life and transforms how the work as a whole is to be interpreted; and this process, or so the text asserted, sheds an entirely novel light on the experience. *Almost* genuinely bored by this time, but still smiling, Amanda fled to the next port of call without actually looking at any of the individual artworks.

It would be repetitious, a strain on the reader's patience and super-fluous to requirement to describe the work featured in the next two galleries in the course of Amanda's walkabout - or to outline her response. The final salon, however, was (up to a point) a different kettle of fish insofar as it contained submissions from a subsequently highly acclaimed individual whose reputation is familiar to most people interested in the arts; for which reason it would be unnec-essarily controversial as well as immaterial to the present story to mention the actual name of this now well-known painter. He was, nonetheless, the only contributor in that final section whose work Amanda felt was worth considering - although she couldn't help thinking that the originality of many of the pieces sometimes failed to match their enormous size.

Having spent more time as well as having paid more attention during this, the last lap of her visit, Amanda felt it was time to alter course: by now she was tired; and the pleasure of verifying her own convictions had worn thin. As a result, an exorbitantly priced cup of tea seemed tempting - given there was nothing left to prolong her interest. But the moment she made up her mind to depart, she also experienced the need, a combination of weariness and contempt, to discard the exhibition brochure which, to her way of thinking, was little more than the current year's parade of superlatives handed down from a repetitious past. She felt that the grandiose language in which it laid claim to meaning was mere befuddlement; and for her, implicit in every word, the presumption of superior insight was vexatious.

Given this attitude of mind, though perhaps with an element of impishness colouring the disdain, she cast about for the obvious means of disposal - but was then reminded that she had never seen a waste bin in the gallery other than in the toilets. Nevertheless, luck was on her side; and as she turned towards the exit, she spotted a pile of newspapers neatly tied with string alongside a door marked 'staff only'. This stroke of luck provided a ready-made alternative; and so, with a casually surreptitious gesture, she dumped the unwanted brochure on top of the newspapers. She then made straight for the exit; and as she did so, feeling the satisfaction of a deed well done, the exhibition and everything to do with it began to fade from her consciousness - in much the same way as the filament in a light bulb, after a flick of the switch, surrenders to oblivion.

* * *

Before she was quite gone, however, a sudden unexpected event checked her immediate withdrawal. It was as brief as it was arresting; and, once she finally emerged from the exhibition area, it formed a picture in her mind which has persisted and caused amusement at intervals ever since. It was something she observed at the very last moment, out of the corner of her eye, just as she was passing through the double swing doors where the youthful male attendant, previously meditating at his guard post inside them, leapt off his stool and sped across the intervening space towards the heap of newspapers from which he retrieved the crumpled exhibition guide with an impatient, snappy gesture. And it was only then that Amanda noticed a small white rectangle fixed to the wall above the pile - at which point the penny dropped: the newspapers, so neatly and beautifully tied as she now vaguely remembered, actually comprised one of the *exhibits* - one which she had so satisfyingly and, she judged, so significantly failed to identify!

It was a fitting conclusion to the afternoon's events - and one that caused her to chuckle. Reconciled to the day's experiences by this curious turn of events and heedless of the cost, Amanda retired to the members' room, flopped out on a leather sofa, and enjoyed her exorbitantly priced cup of tea - added to which was a very nice slice of chocolate gâteau for which, with similar nonchalance, she willingly paid through the nose!

TACT, FACT AND EVASION

Martin O'Sullivan fibbed and cajoled his way through life in a manner that treated truth and untruth as equal partners in the struggle to secure an easier passage through the build-up of days that comprised his relatively comfortable existence. He did not lie - at least, not always - in order to gain benefits such as those a corrupt politician or a fraudster might pursue. Instead, he lied simply as a means of clearing the path before him, hoping to circumnavigate the pitfalls and inconveniences inherent in playing the game straightforwardly.

Among the many situations that benefited from a black or white lie were those that involved a change of mind when obligations willingly entered into (often with a morally laudable purpose) became a burden from which he sought release. This happened quite often in Martin's case; and it created the demand for a quick and easy way out - an approach less shaming than admitting his batteries had run down... or perhaps, more honestly, that he'd lost interest. Protraction was naturally the most obvious and least onerous device; but in the end, something had to be *said*, and this implied a considered choice between half truths, white lies or frankly black ones. Consequently, in many such circumstances, a tall story overcame the need for a tricky amalgamation of fact, tact and subtle evasion; it also minimised discussion with the injured party by depriving him or her of any recognisable ground that might be questioned.

Martin's characteristic modus operandi extended beyond mere words and personal relationships. The many years of subterfuge that had so far shaped his adult life had not averted the need for a somewhat inelegant crew cut designed to camouflage his slowly advancing baldness. But unfortunately, it was a measure that failed to deceive those of his work associates who, although peripheral to his inner circle of friends, had successfully coined *Bristles* as a popular, widely adopted nickname - thus incidentally earmarking their general, albeit subliminal, reservations.

This atmosphere of doubt was also operative at a darker, less innocuous level. When it came to oiling the works of life's everyday ups and downs, although in Martin's case practice had long since made perfect, the ease with which awkward events were provided with sharply defined, instant explanations left some of his well-wishing family, friends and work associates in a state of limbo due to their own experience of the fact that the world was seldom as simple as Martin liked to make out.

Mrs O'Sullivan, of course, who exemplified the female genius for looking years younger than husbands of similar age, cannot be left out of the picture - and this is for reasons far more significant than the supporting rôle played by cosmetics. With an instinctive grasp of reality, she had devised her own programme in relation to a spouse who, although devious, had kept her suitably entertained, well provided for and, with two exceptions in the past that she didn't know about, untroubled by rivalry from the dreaded 'bit on the side'. She further majored in having a strong character of her own and a very clear idea about what she did and didn't want in a variety of ongoing circumstances. Consequently, as long as things went her way, she was happy to allow herself to be 'deceived' in smaller matters without necessarily believing in the deceptions as literal truths. Martin, meanwhile, convinced that he'd pulled this or that fast one, was satisfied that he'd probably got away with it.

* * *

There was, by contrast, the special case of Martin's two long-standing friends, Paul and Patrick. One of them (Paul) was also a distant relative; and both of these acquaintances were at one in being ill at ease with the O'Sullivan brand of well practiced, over-confident smooth-talk by which they were seldom convinced.

Before elaborating further, the respective family circumstances of this loosely aligned duo need to be mentioned because there was one crucial difference between them which may have had a bearing on their divergent responses to similar views of Martin's character. This difference, easily stated, was as simple as it was elemental in that Patrick was the spouse of a plump and agreeable wife - whereas Paul was the recently bereaved husband of a painfully thin, chaste and irritable malcontent who had borne him no children. The consequences, real or incidental, were these: that Patrick was generally more willing to let matters ride - whereas Paul, much more easily offended, was prone to react.

Having pointed out their contrasting circumstances, nothing more in the way of judgement or detail is material to the present purpose; yet for both parties, Martin's apparent flippancy in relation to serious affairs seemed closer to fantasy than to fact. This was crucial, for in the eyes of these particular individuals - who, by the way, had *shared* their negative conclusions long ago - it was the principle that fundamentally mattered. There was also a further complication in that they both felt a rooted uneasiness lest it be thought they were naïve enough to be taken in... all of which sat uncomfortably alongside a desire to keep the peace and preserve a long-established friendship with the increasingly damaged reality that was Martin Aloysius O'Sullivan.

The ambivalence engendered on the one hand by their underlying reservations and on the other by the binding influence of the past complicated the attitudes of these two individuals who, apart from identical insights into Martin O'Sullivan's character, were very different people indeed. Perhaps for this reason, they had never discussed contingencies, plans of action or possible outcomes - neither had they exchanged views on whether or not things were tending in a consistent direction. In fact, they seldom met and had never betrayed any inkling of impending issues despite the fact that their meetings with Martin and each other had become less frequent. However, it was this latter, barely noticed trend that transformed what may seem like a collection of anecdotes into an emerging narrative.

If anything, Martin's fiercest critic, Paul, was the sharper of the two, having finally realised that the future might well bring change. Notwithstanding this, he was instinctively wary of making a precipitate move at the wrong moment and in mistaken circumstances. He therefore bode his time in the privacy of his own consciousness, concealed his clairvoyance and hoarded his knowledge in preparation for the possibility of that ultimate rainy day when he would no longer care about being seen as old hat.

This latter perception, true or false, lurked at the heart of a sense of decay - a feeling that his friendship with Martin had become a game they were both playing for the sake of appearances... and about which *both* were in denial. Indeed, during long evenings in his now desolate living room, he often imagined the instant when he was finally ditched. After all, he told himself in a moment of scorn, he'd been aware all along that Martin O'Sullivan, so lacking in self-knowledge, was a social climber whose network of acquaintances, as it grew, was consistently associated with upmarket villas and expensive cruises in the Caribbean. Furthermore, if and when the crisis arose, he revelled in the foreknowledge that Martin would pass the buck with great skill - or deny the situation altogether. In other words, even as victim, be felt himself superior to the situation in which he found himself!

In the long run, Paul decided, time and tide would be the chief determinants of change. The conclusion that seemed most likely, of course, was that the past and its vanishing storehouse of memories would simply dissolve like the end of a hectic and futile day. For several years, the 'ancien régime' had been a source of diminishing returns in the partial vacuum of a vulnerable mind. If and when the moment of closure finally presented itself, he had already planned his realignments. He was uncertain whether Patrick would be part of them; but he was confident that he was ready for the necessary wrench.

And he was sure that he'd survive it!

MR QUILL'S PET POODLE

To the amusement of everyone who knew him, Mr Reginald Quill had a pet poodle, a flimsy little bitch by the name of 'Tootie' - the double *oo* being pronounced as in 'sooty'. The reason why this was widely regarded as a joke had a more complex basis than the sound-quality of the name itself which was instantly trivialised, of course, by the inherited, peculiarly English tradition governing what is absurd and what isn't. To add grist to the mill, and despite having no connection with immediate reality, there was the further effect of the crossover between 'Tootie' and 'tutti-frutti' which, although the mere description of an Italian ice cream, has always provoked parochial British smiles. This ran in tandem with the now politically incorrect derision associated with Chinese or Japanese words. All in all, therefore, it was against this general background that a friendly grin crept across people's faces whenever they heard Mr Quill calling out the name of a pet that forever lagged (until it could lag no long-er) behind its master's heels due to the frailty that accompanies age.

There were other supplementary reasons, much nearer the mark than sound, that amused close and casual acquaintances equally. In the case of Reginald and his dog, there was an assortment of revealing answers to the rhetorical question 'what's in a name?'. And at the root of them all was the simple fact that people were entertained not only by Tootie but also by Mr Quill himself whose own name had a somewhat humorous ring to it. Further to this, the comedy implicit in both names was exquisitely reflected in the fact that Mr Quill played to the gallery and had long cultivated the art of making his listeners laugh. He was, as it happens, a born comedian who, like many well-known stars of stage and screen, was driven by his own personal demons to make a butt of fun out of *himself*. And people loved it because it transformed any desire they might feel to mock Mr Quill into apparent admiration for his skill as a showman.

In a world inclined to protest against virtually anything, I must be careful how I put what follows. It is a simple truth, however, that Mr Quill's delight in the histrionic went hand in hand with the further simple truth that he was gay. And not to put too fine a point on it, he was very gay indeed! In practice, such was his talent as a comic (albeit one who lived by cleaning windows and scrubbing floors) that he managed to entertain captive audiences with tales of private goings-on which he presented as if they were fiction rather than fact. And he did it so cleverly that people were reduced to tears. And consequently, they were always ready for more.

His fans, of course, were not to be found in a packed auditorium: instead, they included a suburban flower-seller on the corner of Lillie Road and the Asian owner of a bicycle repair business in the equally run-down Dawes Road. By contrast, there was also the blue-rinsed proprietress of an antique shop in the infinitely posher Kensington Church Street who regularly purchased items like the nineteenth century toby jug memorably rescued by Mr Quill from a skip near the North End Road Market.

Some of his devotees, given common prejudice, were particularly unlikely. For example, take a surly bigot like Sam, formerly a boxer of admittedly catholic taste in matters of sex. Who could have imagined seeing someone like him melt into peals of laughter when Reggie (hopefully trawling the Queens Head pub) called him 'babe' in front of his beer-swilling pals? And then there was Rob, a handsome road-sweeper, who virtually wetted himself on hearing Mr Quill's favourable assessment of his anatomy!

* * *

So far, all that can be concluded about master and hound, taken as a duo, is that they shared aspects of their somewhat bedraggled appearance, that they set each other off - at least to a degree. This apparent convergence was not without firm foundation, however. In Mr Quill's case, there was the pot belly that betrayed an age approaching that of Tootie if measured by any of the traditional tables of equivalence. Furthermore, at only five and a half feet tall, Mr Quill's under-average height was reflected in the diminutive proportions of his pet. On the other hand, whether due to sheer luck or the vagaries of his hormones, Mr Quill (aged sixty six) still had a great deal more energy, relatively speaking, than his dog - something of great benefit to his sideline as a comedian. And as if to emphasise this distinction, Tootie had fared far less well in terms of general health, and was only kept alive by Reginald's devotion alongside that of his neighbour, the obliging Sally Entwistle, who dropped in regularly when Mr Quill was out on his rounds to ensure that the dog was properly fed, watered and fussed over.

At this point, the mention of Sally Entwistle justifies a brief digression which adds little to the narrative but much to the picture. It relates to an incident during one of her visits to Reggie's home whilst he was out helping with the washing-up in a local café favoured by taxi drivers. Very unfortunately, as she searched for a rag with which to mop up the mess around Tootie's feeding bowl, she chanced upon a half-open drawer. Spotting some black-and-white photographs, she was unable to resist having a look - at which point she was confronted with vivid confirmation of what she already knew in the form of some wildly explicit shots of young gentlemen up to no good. Sally was a devout Catholic and never for a moment questioned the beliefs of a lifetime. All the same, she knew Reggie well and very much liked him. She therefore mulled over what she had seen at some length; and after a few days, she concluded that people had only limited control over what they were or were not. And so, on the basis of 'to understand all is to forgive all', she left the question of judgement to a higher authority - and resumed her previous warmth of sentiment.

Returning to master and hound, no one could have failed to notice Tootie's gradual deterioration, despite being so well cared for; and Sally had long ago discovered that, in response to the gentlest of prods, the poor animal simply collapsed on to the carpet with a whimper and had to be helped back on to its feet by hand.

To this there is little to add other than a few more, hitherto unmentioned points of convergence between a dog and a dog-owner who, as a joint act, became known to their neighbours in Wallerton Avenue as 'The Happy Couple' - something partly attributable to sightings of Tootie in the basket attached to the front of Mr Quill's rusty bicycle. Other observers, perhaps those with differing attitudes and a taste for schadenfreude, concentrated on the link between the sparse remnants of Mr Quill's honey-coloured curls and the fact that Tootie was virtually naked, with little remaining in the way of hair other than thinly distributed fluff which left large, distasteful-looking patches of pink skin exposed to view. The only genuine hair still to be seen was the white tuft at the end of a tail which, by reason of being the sole surviving characteristic specific to a poodle, evoked a mixture of laughter and wonderment from those with enough curiosity to pay attention.

* * *

Stories featuring Mr Quill, his way of life, his ups and downs and his narrow squeaks have been told elsewhere. And there could well be other tales to come if and when memory serves - although this is little more than wishful thinking unless there remains a survivor other than myself for whom he hoovered floors, polished furniture and from whom he collected a weekly envelope whose contents were unlikely ever to have been submitted to Her Majesty's Revenue & Customs.

Meanwhile, time has moved on; and it is now nearly twenty five years since Reginald Quill passed away, leaving behind very few people who knew his *full* name which was Reginald Arthur Quill, son of Ethel Winifred Quill with whom he is now buried. Sadly, it must also be mentioned that anyone who can rediscover the whereabouts of his grave will notice that none of those to whom he left bequests has troubled to add his name to his mother's original tombstone which, in turn, makes no mention of any male partner. Concerning Reginald Quill, it is a sobering fact that the world that once applauded his wit seems to have forgotten him - with the added sting that even the exact whereabouts of his grave, like the name of his father, is now uncertain.

By contrast, despite so grim a picture, I choose to hope that I am not the only person who still remembers Reggie. How could I forget him? And how could I ever erase from my mind the lively character at the heart of so many electrifying stories? He has left behind a rich and varied account of absurd and often risky goings-on in the back streets of London; or again, there were tales of surprisingly smutty banter in a Parsons Green pub during the Saturday night sing-songs. In relation to the present storyline, however, these were mere incidentals among the many staging-posts in the course of a lifelong journey which Tootie rather than Reggie brought to a sudden, if interim, conclusion. And it was Reggie alone who was taken by surprise or, as some might say, 'caught with his trousers down' when the inevitable happened!

In Tootie's case, the fact of mortality had long been on the menu. Indeed, for most observers, her departure for a higher and better version of the Battersea Dogs' Home looked more and more imminent. The energy and joviality of her owner nevertheless acted like a camouflage and seemed to imply the possibility of permanence in an imaginary 'world without end' situated not all that far from the hurly-burly of Fulham Broadway.

And so it was that although the physical appearances of master and hound overlapped, the wider expectations diverged fundamentally; and this was brought into sharp focus on a dull grey, mid-February afternoon in nineteen eighty four - at a moment of abstraction when Reggie was concluding a profitable deal in the Kensington Church Street antique shop where he was sipping a glass of sherry in tandem with the same gushing proprietress who, with boundless cordiality as always, secretly looked down on her visitor!

It was Sally Entwistle who discovered the body when she arrived on that rainy afternoon, in Mr Quill's absence, with a tin of dog food that, sadly, was never going to be needed. Tootie, limp and more naked-looking than ever, lay as if she had just toppled over near the foot of the stairs not far from the open door of the toilet. But Sally, who had her wits about her, realised in an instant what had happened and sprang immediately into action by returning the tin of dog food to her bag in case Reggie arrived home unexpectedly soon. For the same reason, she then filled the kettle in readiness, after which she began shaking out and rearranging the grey flannel blanket in the cardboard box that had long served as Tootie's night-time retreat after serving the same purpose for most of the day as well!

Tootie was still warm and loose limbed; and this enabled Sally to lay the body out, neatly curled up on the blanket and looking neither

THE FIRST HINTS OF PURPLE

obviously alive nor particularly dead. Furthermore, she determined never to reveal that this long-standing companion of an eccentric old man had died in a manner other than comfortably tucked up in bed. She then switched on the radio at low volume, twiddled the knob until she found some soothing music - after which she sat down and waited until, as soon as she heard the key in the lock, she got up and made her way quickly and in full charge of her wits to the front door.

The expression on Sally's face and the fact that she gently took hold of his arm was enough to tell Reggie what had happened. Looking him straight in the eye, she filled in a few details and embroidered a few others to which she added well chosen words of comfort spoken quietly and with feeling. She then accompanied him into his remarkably old-fashioned and untidy front room where she switched on the electric heater standing in the fireplace and pressed the button on the standard lamp whose pink shade brightened and bestowed what limited benevolence it could. Lastly, almost in slow motion, she withdrew into the kitchen to make the tea, leaving Reggie in the armchair alongside his pet's remains where he wept in uncharacteristic silence and without embarrassment.

Later that evening, Sally returned along with her husband who offered his condolences. She also brought with her a bottle of gin and a bottle of orange cordial. Reggie's favourite drink was 'gin and orange'. And never since he lost his mother had the prospect been more welcome.

What's in a name? William Shakespeare: Romeo and Juliet, 2,2.

AVRIL IN THE SUMMER SHADOWS

When trumpet blasts
rouse bodies that were men,
these marvellous hills
will lure me home again.

M. H

Avril trudged irresolutely along the narrow woodland path that sloped gently downhill from Richmond Park's Bog Gate towards the busy Sheen Road ahead of her. The meagre gradient matched the mood of indecisiveness which, from the start, had imposed low spirits on her walk home; and ironically, the reason for this was the simple thought of actually *arriving* there, of finding herself back within the four walls from which she had so recently sought respite. Unfortunately, and to her great discomfort, she was unable to resolve the ambivalence.

On her right, bent over loosely into broad curves, one or two wild raspberry canes rocked hither and thither in the wind a few feet above the ground. Attenuated by lack of light beneath the oaks, they were the clear losers in their battle with the sturdier brambles. All the same, just a few days earlier, Avril had picked and eaten the only five or six bright red berries she could see; and it now looked unlikely that this tiny annual crop would be supplemented before yet another year had added to the marks of time on her features - features which increasingly lacked the power of feral nature to rejuvenate at the coming of each successive spring.

Avril was a woman in her mid seventies and was what our forebears once disparagingly called an old maid. Her health was good; the navy blue trousers she was wearing in conjunction with a lighter blue blouse were tidy and looked freshly laundered. Perhaps to liven things up, a diminutive gold cross hung around her neck whilst a single imitation pearl embellished the lobe of each ear. Despite these positive signs, however, there was a vacancy in her colourless eyes and a corresponding emptiness in her mind that July's summery abundance all around her failed to eradicate. All the same, summer was not without its influence: like silver coins scattered on the ground, the roundels of sunlight among the leaf shadows affected her sufficiently to hold despondency in check. And frustration centred on the uneventfulness of her life was marginally diminished by the stillness and heat among the empty spaces where a white butterfly seemed to appear and disappear as it fluttered through patches of brightness and gloom. It was almost as if a mischievous child were turning a light switch on and off in a darkened chamber. And there was Avril, an incidental and faintly bemused witness, looking like a lost soul beneath a nimbus of wispy grey hair.

As she continued on her way, she tried hard to confront her demons; and an opportunity soon arose in the form of a black-and-white spaniel that stopped to sniff her hand with eager curiosity and, as she bent down to pat its head, with apparent pleasure. She was stirred by a sudden emotion which the dog, gazing up at her through complacent, watery eyes, seemed to appreciate. But this brief, unpremeditated moment of connection with something alive ceased abruptly when the dog's owner grabbed it by the collar and dragged it away, muttering some unsmiling, unconvincing moral exhortation about the 'lady's nice clean clothes'. It was a snappily expressed assertion of exclusive ownership that acted with the keenness of a blade - and it killed stone dead the few friendly words of greeting then forming on Avril's lips.

It was an experience that can, and so often does, wreak havoc when some lonely or troubled individual of any age group is met with discourtesy or disregard at just the wrong moment - perhaps after receiving bad news from an ageing relative or on the anniversary of a friend's death in a car crash. And so it was for Avril on a day when she was particularly overwhelmed by feelings of purposelessness and langour.

* * *

Depressed by the prospect of finding herself back again so soon in her all-too-familiar second-floor flat, Avril flopped down on a way-side bench. The effect, or so it seemed, was to obstruct the forward motion of time, thereby moderating the disorderly mood-swings affecting her. This in turn enabled her to subside into the stillness of the wood and to take heart from the monotonous, dreamy purring of a woodpigeon high up and out of sight in the branches of an oak.

Reminiscence is not uncommon in circumstances like these, especially when life's shadows are lengthening; and Avril's stream of consciousness followed that same familiar course by regressing into a range of visual memories focussed on the spirit of place. Images and cross-references of this sort were ever-present at the back of her mind; and they were not entirely the product of rose-coloured spectacles. As a means of grappling with depression, she reminded herself of the certainty that formerly inspirational but long unvisited landscapes were still there to be drawn upon, at least for her, as the strongholds of permanence! She also wagged her finger at herself, pointing out that at least one of them remained well within reach… and this consideration produced forceful, positive emotions because, for Avril, there was a presence abroad in dramatic landscapes which had so often proved a remedy for the doldrums before age and lazy habits had taken their toll.

At the head of the list, therefore, she resurrected the picture of that delightfully modest little river, the Mole, flowing curvaceously around the foot of Box Hill on its way through Surrey to the Thames. And she remembered one particular day, while she was still a young woman unmindful of age, when the splash of a leaping fish broke the noonday silence, there, where the comforting shelter of the downs was at its best.

That was an otherwise ordinary moment which memory had fortuitously fixed whilst leaving more significant events out of account. Furthermore, long before then, as a child evacuee, she had first encountered the Mole during the Second World War and had revisited it many times as an adult - although not for at least ten years, now that she was getting old. And so it struck her, with bleak suddenness, that this interval must have marked the turning of the tide. She knew, of course, as a plain matter of fact, that the steep banks along the water's edge, enriched with burdock and nettles, were still less than two hours away by bus; and as a West London resident, it would be so easy to go back again. Consequently, in her imagination, her mind enlarged the memory of that rural idyll; and as she pondered, the picture-image in her head was transformed into a daydream that revived vivid recollections of her last-but-one visit when she was driven there for a day out by her one remaining relative; but even *he*, she reflected, was now nothing more solid than the inscription on a headstone with neither cross nor quotation to distinguish it.

Life, it seemed, as well as God, moved in a mysterious way. Remembering that unremarkable trip dredged like sunken treasure from the past, Avril's inward eye now focussed on an insignificant leaf, prematurely discoloured, which she had noticed falling into the water - a sight whose symbolic force had often struck her since. Standing by the bank with her cousin, she watched it receding, carried away by the current and rocking absurdly from side to side until it was finally swept out of view at the first bend - a bend shimmering with light as the stream altered course, broke up chaotically, and consequently caught the sun from so many angles that it seemed almost to dissolve into molten silver.

Although as frail and insubstantial as the daydream itself, that leaf, its turbulent passage and its abrupt disappearance saddened Avril who abandoned her seat in an effort, as best she could, to pull herself together. All the same, the recollection was not wholly negative; and the glitter of the stream in her mind's eye acted as an antidote. Its brilliance proved persistent in defiance of the years; and the flicker of sunlight at the bend, in seemingly perpetual motion, came back to her surprisingly vividly. It proved a turning point in more senses than one. And as she resumed her walk home, it strengthened her resolve to take action by renewing her acquaintance with a river that was still a friend-in-waiting - and disarmingly easy to get to.

God moves in a mysterious way / his wonders to perform.
William Cowper, Olney Hymns, 1779.

THE IMMORTALITY OF MISS JAMES

I

We are looking back at the mid nineteen fifties on a bright and cloud-less Sunday morning. The location is Bedford Hill, South London, at the church of St John the Divine where Solemn High Mass to mark the Harvest Festival is just beginning.

The principal celebrant that day was the vicar, the Reverend Nicholas Oldland, a plump and jolly Anglican cleric who, in addition to being a dedicated bon viveur, was also a keen collector of eighteenth and nineteenth century English porcelain teapots. He was assisted by his curate, the Reverend Hugh Purvis. Hugh, still in his twenties, was a recently ordained East Ender from Bethnal Green whose rather flamboyant hairstyle was known in those days as a 'duck's arse' due to the way in which it was swept back either side to a point at the nape of the neck. Furthermore, he kept it in place with a generous helping of Brylcreem which caught the candlelight and led, among certain teenage parishioners, to uncharitable quips about a halo!

* * *

At a time when High Church Anglicanism was still seen as conten-tious, the congregation was steady but on the small side. It comprised about forty five regulars among whom were odd characters such as Harold, the ageing verger, who headed the procession at the beginning and end of Sunday masses brandishing his staff of office and clad in a sombre black gown. He was exceedingly short; and on other less formal occasions, just as evening began to cast shadows in the side-aisles, he was observed by last-minute visitors in a somewhat humbler rôle as he crept hither and thither like a ghost, extinguishing candles and locking doors. There was also the livelier Bill Shrimpton, a grey-haired sidesman and unofficial parish handy-man who, on one unforgettable occasion during mass, assisted a protesting Kensitite's removal from the church with a kick in the pants!

Slightly more aloof at St John's and less susceptible to comment were the Tinsons, a husband and wife team who kept the parish accounts and handled public relations whenever necessary. They were also associated with a very nice little bungalow in a superior part of nearby Wandsworth; and this widely known evidence of their good fortune tended to raise their standing in the eyes of those whose judgement was not governed exclusively by gospel values.

* * *

Given that circumstances are similar today, there is nothing surprising about the fact that many of the most regular worshippers in the nineteen fifties were women; and at St John's, two of these still deserve more than a passing mention. By no means least was Miss Godfrey-Fawcett who was confined to an invalid chair - and who consequently had to be wheeled to mass every Sunday by one or other of the two teenage altar boys, Michael and Tim. Miss Godfrey-Fawcett was widely regarded as a person of superior class because she occupied a large house with mullioned windows facing the broad green acres of Tooting Bec Common. Furthermore, she was rumoured to have money; and consequently, there were frequent whispers in dark corners - including insinuations from Tim's mother, Beattie, who put it about that the vicar's warm regard for his wealthy parishioner reflected hopes of financial benefit when that good lady finally regained the use of her legs in the world to come!

Whilst everyday human failings are present even in the most morally committed circles, we must not imagine that the only saints in the modern world are confined to stained glass windows. Tucked away in obscure backwaters, slogging it out in awkward circumstances, there are still many innocent souls whose true merits are known only to the one person qualified to offer a well-deserved reward. Bent almost double and a regular worshipper at St John's for more than thirty years, Miss James was just such a person. Her murmured conversation was always deferential; her mumbled prayers were usually audible but never decipherable and, if she could have stood upright, she would not have exceeded five and a half feet. Furthermore, as if to press home her unassuming character, Miss James was always dressed in black, her skirt reaching to within an inch of her ankles; and she also possessed a broad-brimmed black hat which often obscured the benevolent eyes that gazed from behind a pair of spectacles whose lenses were so perfectly circular that they evoked recollections of a Simon Tofield cartoon.

2

The Reverend Oldland had, in addition to his priestly calling, a genius for the arts of display and decoration. Indeed, had it not been for his mission to save souls, he could have made his name as a top window-dresser at Harrods or Fortnum & Masons. Accordingly, the Harvest Festival at St John's was always a sight for sore eyes - especially for the likes of Miss James coming from a dingy two-room flat into what, by contrast, must have seemed like a foretaste of Heaven!

The altar that day was supplemented on each side by a small table supporting a polished brass vase of yellow chrysanthemums that glowed among the abundant dark green foliage fresh from the vicar's back garden. Each table was flanked by an enormous, free-standing candlestick bearing its restless flame at least seven feet above the floor; and the altar itself was resplendent with smaller vases full of tea roses and ears of barley. In addition to this, the brilliant white altar frontal together with the matching chasuble and dalmatic worn by the clerics, were generously embroidered with clusters of wheat and grapes; and the whole glorious ensemble was lit by enough candles to keep the suppliers in business for a month!

After the entry procession had reached the chancel with Harold in the lead; and after the processional cross carried by the crucifer had done likewise without striking the brass lamp overhead (as happened the Sunday before), the five members of the choir took their places in the stalls and continued with the first hymn. The teenage acolytes, Tim and Michael, having exchanged meaningful glances, made the best of their disappointment after the mishap with the cross failed to recur; and Bill Shrimpton, acting as master of ceremonies stood to one side of the thurifer while the Reverend Oldland censed the altar unsparingly from one end to the other. The mass then proceeded without a hitch through a sequence of popular hymns and plainchant, scriptural readings and the Reverend Oldland's well delivered sermon about providing for the poor and needy - although he was rather too forthcoming with the catchphrase 'waste not, want not' with which everyone was all too familiar.

* * *

After the sermon came the offertory which, at a St John's Harvest Festival, was the point at which members of the congregation made their way to the sanctuary with gifts destined for a local hospital. These were laid either side of the altar, on the steps, leaving the central sections clear for the clergy to come and go. On this occasion as on every other, the gifts were somewhat predictable and tended to reflect the worldly estate of the donors. A tin of Cadbury's Chocolate Digestives occupied a middle rung on the social ladder; a can of tomato soup suggested a somewhat lower position whilst a neat basket of fruit and vegetables from the Tinsons' allotment represented a much higher level of suitability for a Harvest Festival - placing the benefactors well ahead in the estimation of close observers.

Miss James made her humble contribution at the tail end of this ceremony; last but not least among the charitable givers and bent double out of necessity, she tottered up to the chancel steps which she was helped to climb by an obliging chorister. Carrying a bulging paper bag, she then continued unassisted to the second set of steps at the foot of the altar where she had difficulty, due to her ailment, in depositing what turned out to be a bag of apples. Unfortunately, whilst wondering how to accomplish this task, the bag burst. The apples then fell on to the first step and rolled off it; and having acquired momentum from their fall, they continued rolling back towards the congregation across whose faces the smiles spread rapidly.

Miss James's apples then seemed to gain a life of their own, rolling down towards the nave - but at very diverse angles. And they did so at a seemingly leisurely pace, acquiring a weird and spellbinding dignity - rather like bowls gliding along the length of a perfect green on a summer afternoon.

Whilst Bill Shrimpton quickly rescued the apples and consigned them to the safety of the Tinsons' wicker basket, Miss James was consoled with good humour and escorted back to her seat by a member of the congregation. Meanwhile, the pent-up hilarity had infected the priests who managed to conceal their smiles by bending over the altar as they prepared the eucharistic vessels. They failed, however, to elude the eagle eyes of Michael and Tim as they took refuge in the obscurity of the lady chapel where they dissolved into an unstoppable outburst of boyish giggling.

The mass then proceeded and concluded without further mishap. Well-wishers gathered around Miss James at the end, made light of the incident and induced a reciprocal smile. At the same time, the Reverend Oldland and the Reverend Purvis shook hands with departing members of the congregation with whom they also exchanged many winks and nods. They then left Harold and Bill Shrimpton to lock up - after which they made off to the vicarage where the Reverend Oldland's mother served luncheon consisting of a leg of lamb with all the trimmings... followed by strawberry trifle and a bottle of dessert wine.

3

Almost sixty years have come and gone since that Harvest Festival at St John's. The church, after radical internal alteration, is now a nondescript set of offices within the original redbrick exoskeleton which has gathered much dust. Only the cross and weather vane on the roof still bear witness to the glory days.

Inevitably, the Reverend Purvis is now in his grave - as is the Reverend Oldland whose funeral expenses were not mitigated by Miss Godfrey-Fawcett who passed away years earlier without mentioning him in her will. All the adult members of the former congregation have likewise passed away; and only a few ageing survivors can still recall the splendours of a past which will never be forgotten in another place where the dead still live.

First and foremost, Miss James has been relieved of her ailing back and is now absolutely clear that *her* apples (but not Eve's) really were and still remain a genuine laughing matter. Furthermore, this carefree attitude has found powerful allies: for whenever Miss James repeats the story to triumphant newcomers, there is much light-hearted banter among the angels. And I think we are on fairly safe ground if we suppose that a smile has even stolen across the face of the highest authority of all!

HIS OWN WORST ENEMY

Daniel, still sitting up in bed, had just extinguished the light standing on the small wooden table beside him after browsing some rather difficult poetry: Geoffrey Hill's 'Mercian Hymns', to be specific. He had read them before, but because they could not be understood in any literal sense, their unyieldingly mystical content combined with their timelessness made them highly re-readable. Meaning clearly lurked in and between the lines; but, for Daniel, the level of ambiguity gave free rein to his imagination - for which reason he had now returned to them after a lapse of more than a year. However, after his usual late-night limit of twenty minutes' reading time, he became drowsy - with the result that he decided to concede defeat. After all, to Daniel, the poems did not appear sequentially linked; and this made it quite legitimate, or so he thought, to stop and start whenever it suited.

He had long ago paid off the mortgage on his flat which occupied the top floor of a redbrick, architecturally undistinguished block - one of six similar buildings which, together, comprised Pettigrew Mansions - a well maintained thirties development just off Upper Ravenscourt Avenue. To use a verb beloved of the estate agents who sold it to him, the flat 'benefited' from a view of Richmond Park. In reality, and to be more precise, it was little more than a view of the treetops of Conduit Wood situated just inside the north-western boundary of the park which was otherwise obscured by a foreground of generously proportioned, detached dwellings costing upwards of two million pounds each.

As his eyes grew accustomed to the dark, he gazed out through the window panes at the melancholy slate-grey of a sky which was un-interrupted except for the leafless crown of an oak to the left whose trunk rose majestically from among flower beds and lawns similar to those surrounding the other blocks on the estate. And also, given the impact of the night, there was an almost imperceptible barrier in the form of a faint amber radiance from the street lamps which were hidden out of sight beneath the window-sill. He noticed this curious effect, felt that it somehow chimed with the mood of the poetry; and he concluded that the invisible moisture in the atmosphere must be absorbing the light - which would account for what he was seeing. He also glanced at the block opposite, a mirror image of his own, and especially at the white window frames whose colour was transformed by the same unnatural orange influence of the sodium lights.

In contrast to these familiar circumstances only a few metres away, Daniel also spotted the headlamp of an aircraft making its barely perceptible, diagonal, perhaps rather eerie descent from right to left across the dim rectangle of the window. No part of the plane itself was visible due both to distance and the darkness. In consequence, such was his state of feeling, that he was reminded of the Star of Bethlehem; after all, nothing other than a pinprick of moving light was apparent - which left more than a little scope for imagination. And so, gradually, the Mercian Hymns and the gloom of the night sky coalesced and exercised an indefinable yet unsettling influence.

Caught up in the ebb and flow of his thoughts, Daniel was unaware of any identifiable sound other than the noise of tyres on wet tarmac from the cars passing at ground level along Upper Ravenscourt Avenue - a road which, during daylight hours in particular, was a busy one. It was a repetitive, husky sound - rather like the needle scratching away at an old-fashioned record that continues to rotate after the song is over. And it was this that added impetus to his growing uneasiness: for in some curious way, that inarticulate noise felt like an echo of the vast spaces - and their terrifying emptiness - out there in the darkness far beyond the comfort zone of his flat.

It was a wilderness, or so he pictured it, where even the Star of Bethlehem would have had trouble finding its way.

As a rule, despite his advanced years and the fact that he lived by himself, Daniel seldom experienced loneliness in a form that might be described as uncomfortable. At seventy five, not all that many of his friends were left. But the number was sufficient; and even with the few who lived too far away for frequent face-to-face encounters, there was still regular contact by letter or telephone. On top of this, in the majority of cases, there was a community of shared interests, whether in relation to the arts, politics or cultural attitudes in general. And with regard to culture, a London resident like Daniel had ample, cost-free opportunities to keep him happy at virtually any time of the day. So with enough friends (and no foes) to call on, whatever tendency he had towards anxiety or depression was usually held effortlessly in check.

Also of benefit to Daniel, there was another downside sometimes associated with the elderly to which he had never fallen victim: namely, he did not look back on his past with the slightest sense of loss or regret. He had never experienced anything that corresponded with the idea of a 'gilded youth'; and his career had occasionally been onerous. Consequently, he had anticipated his retirement for decades and was not disappointed when it came. Board meetings at the drugs company that employed him for thirty two years had often been stressful or tedious experiences; and it was a relief that there were no more conflicts with the hyperactive elbows of ambitious colleagues. As a result, retirement for Daniel was a liberation that left him free to pursue his interests as never before. And he was still enjoying it. All the same, he could not hide from the fact that he was getting older. He could see that his hair was thinning; and despite being healthy (a condition maintained by a few very ordinary drugs), he felt a growing vulnerability when things went awry.

* * *

Such was the overall state of play for Daniel on this *particular* mid-January night. And particular nights are likely to differ from others, especially if they are as sullen as this one when the hours of darkness are long, when a cold wind is blowing and the first signs of a frost begin to whiten the lawn. At the time in question, there was also a peculiar silence in the flat itself to which the distant hum of the freezer somehow drew attention: and in these circumstances, Daniel felt threatened (albeit irrationally) by some amorphous, non-human source of instability. So his resilience began to weaken; and in consequence, the fact that he was alone if not exactly *lonely*, began to tell.

Fortunately, after snuggling down under the duvet and pulling it up over his shoulders, the slow drift into sleep provided welcome respite. But this only lasted until he was disturbed in the early hours and awoke to the same gloom as before - a gloom rendered even more sinister this time by the snarling and squealing of foxes settling some grievance among the bushes that divided the flats from the road. And so the inner darkness deepened to a degree that made his plans for the coming day more like a challenge than a pleasant prospect, given the effort he knew he would need to force himself into action. Plainly, the same melancholy grey cloud confronted him as it had done before he fell asleep; and the coming dawn, thereby delayed, was evident only as a thin blood-red ribbon that separated the uneven skyline of leafless boughs and straggling chimney pots from the featureless emptiness above it. Even the lawns which soon after nightfall were covered with frost crystals were now dumbed down by the subsequent rain that dissolved all trace of their former sparkle - rather like a once attractive fabric whose inadequately fixed dye has begun to fade.

This was the worst moment of all for Daniel to whom dawn was usually a spirit-raiser - and it looked as if his normal resilience was about to be overwhelmed. Nevertheless, when his alarm broke the silence at six o'clock, he responded at once, put on his dressing gown and made his way via the bathroom into the kitchen where he rallied, albeit only slightly, under the influence of two cups of tea, preparations for breakfast and the sight of that equivocal red glimmer along the horizon below which the occasional glare from the bedrooms of other early risers warned him of a world on the move which he might well have trouble contending with.

Daniel completed his routine morning tasks not only out of habit and need but also on the strength of the self-knowledge which persuaded him that to do so acted as a steadying influence on his weaknesses. He knew that to have lingered in bed would have encouraged a sense of helplessness exacerbated by the failure of the light. In keeping with such resolution, he therefore switched on the BBC news and listened to the reports which, animated by a world beyond his own narrow concerns, usually engaged his interest if and when it was flagging. On this most fraught of mornings, however, with accounts of terrorist attacks close to home and contentious economic squabbles, it all had the opposite effect by presenting a universe far removed from the one in which he remembered growing up as Daniel Matthew Sillitoe in the security of the late nineteen forties.

By eight o'clock, shortly after sunrise, the outlook from the kitchen was still extremely dismal and the chance of glimpsing the source of what little light there was seemed negligible. The glowing red band along the horizon had widened somewhat, but looked more like a distant conflagration than a sign of better things to come. Apparently, colder air was also drifting in again over the city from the east - something evident from the fact that the earlier drizzle was now turning into sleet. And the occasional fully-fledged snow-flake, caught in the light from the kitchen window, was fluttering towards the ground accompanied by the now continuous whirr of wet tyres on the surface of Upper Ravenscourt Avenue.

* * *

After rinsing, drying and tidying away the clutter of breakfast, and having improved his appearance in the bathroom, Daniel found that he was still at odds with himself. The complete negativity of the outside world continued to take its toll, depriving him of all emotional interest in the various, previously formulated plans for the day. At the Tate Britain, for example, there was an exhibition of Ravilious watercolours; the National Gallery had a major Rubens exhibition; and at a small gallery just off Piccadilly there was an exhibition of sixteenth century Russian icons.

Inertia and reluctance therefore continued to prevail. On a morning as unpropitious as the present one, all the possibilities which would normally have galvanised his interest produced insufficient energy to lure Daniel beyond the bounds of home and into the livelier city environment which, he knew from experience, almost always set him up for the day. Instead, he found himself in a protracted state of conflict - scarcely able to bestir himself on the one hand and, on the other hand, seriously intimidated by the knowledge that he was his own worst enemy. Consequently, he began to do battle with his demons, averting his mind as best he could from armchairs and books, turning instead to the prospect of just being himself in the busy thoroughfares of London's West End with its many options and interesting venues. Firstly, he took a swig of whisky to arrest his growing anxiety en route to taking charge of himself. He then put on his overcoat, a bright tartan scarf and a hat, after which he made for the bus stop across the road - but not before a long-drawn-out check on all the taps and electrical devices in the flat which he could never quite convince himself were safely turned off.

The outcome was more or less as anticipated, but still as surprising as it was welcome. Daniel almost immediately felt the resumption of stress-free self-assurance - rather like the gradual restoration of feeling to an arm once the weight of a sleeper's body has been removed from it. In the remote corners of his mind, of course, he knew from the start that this change would happen despite the lack of any discernible improvement in the weather. And now that at last he'd broken free and was out and about, he found the winter grey and the cutting edge of the wind were egging him on rather than holding him back. At heart (and he was aware of it) he was a funda- mentally *outdoor* person - one for whom rain and ice, field, forest and lake were almost as important as human companionship. And so for Daniel, the day, despite a miserable dawn, had begun in earnest.

Glancing up and down as he stood at the end of the queue with the peak of his flat-cap pulled low for protection, he felt more and more at ease - sufficiently so, in fact, to take an interest in a group of elderly women waiting for the red, single-decker bus to the station. They were all generously wrapped up in woollen scarves and uniformly tawdry coats surmounted by old-fashioned, rather absurd hats. Daniel wondered if they had just finished an early-morning stint, mopping the floors at the two, locally well-known hotels at the top of the hill. Whether or not that was the case, they obviously knew each other and were enjoying a traditional British moan about the snow which was still falling in combination with barely frozen sleet. Daniel, on the other hand, allowed his thoughts to move on. He had already noticed three or four windswept, insidious-looking crows swaying among the leafless twigs of the horse chestnut on the other side of the road next to a public house. Somehow, their tenacity stood for freedom and the sort of loneliness that can also be life-enhancing - and this at once reminded him of the flock, seemingly of blackbirds, silhouetted against a winter sky in the painting 'Caravans' by Eric Ravilious. It was a lovingly remembered cross-reference that chimed surprisingly well with the Crown and Anchor pub opposite where, as in the painting, a tree served as a refuge for similar-looking birds doing battle with whatever the wind threw at them. In fact, the similarity was even greater: in the scene before him, the tree was to the left of the pub - and in the painting, to the left of the caravans.

It was only then that Daniel felt fully in charge of himself; and out of the choices previously vying for attention but eluding a decision, he finally concluded that Tate Britain and the Ravilious watercolours were the most compelling option for the day ahead. Until that point, he had remained in a quandary. But at last, observing the scene across the road, he felt an enormous burst of eagerness for what he had made up his mind to do. Indeed, such was his regard for Ravilious, now bolstered by his sudden release from conflict, that he made up his mind to treat himself to the hardback, more expensive version of the exhibition catalogue which he knew would be displayed with commercial prominence in the gallery bookshop!

* * *

And so for Daniel, on that particular day, both the decision and the act of making it were rooted in an entirely fortuitous set of circumstances. Indeed, the experience seemed like a clear demonstration that life, despite itself, carries on regardless at its own insistence and against all the odds. But Daniel, well aware of what it meant to be seventy five, was also aware that there was more than one side to his somewhat brittle nature. Consequently, he renewed yet again a former resolution: namely, that if he wanted to remain his own master indefinitely, he would need to remember that faith in himself and the will power to back it up were the essential preconditions of independence. But it would be a hard slog - and as the bus drew away from the stop, he was already attempting to brush that worrying thought to one side.

A RADICAL SET OF MEASURES

Jeremy Dinsdale - forever to remain a lone wolf as will be shown in due course - lived in splendid isolation or in purgatory, depending on how the reader chooses to interpret the picture here presented of a private life played out in a uniquely spotless apartment on which no eyes but Jeremy's own had so far rested. This latter fact underscores an enigma; but for the time being, whilst his story unfolds, we need only bear in mind that the key to everything about Jeremy Dinsdale lies in the tellingly simple word *private* with its many layers of undisclosed but not unimaginable implications.

The young man in question and the premises in which he performed his daily tasks were together the scene of a repetitive lifestyle in a world painstakingly constructed and set apart to suit his special needs. This world began and ended at the entrance of his flat which was sealed off from outside influences by means of a towel rolled up lengthwise like a snake and forced to block the gap between the base of the door and the varnished parquet beneath it. In pursuit of the safe haven thereby signalled, this device was aimed above all else at excluding any unsavoury smells arising from the other flats above and below Jeremy's own at number 3 Abergavenny House, Earls Court, London. Unfortunately, there was just one snag: namely, that given the multicultural environment of the Royal Borough of Kensington & Chelsea, the merest whiff of Murgh Musallam could defeat all the defences ranged against it.

As the product of a compulsive imagination, his flat had become a virtual hermitage where cleanliness supplanted godliness as Jeremy's main preoccupation. To start with, he had spent a great deal of money on replacing the original kitchen and bathroom which, to his way of thinking, were sullied not only by wear and tear but also by the contagion of previous lives. In addition, he had painted all the walls of the two-room flat in a rather characterless emulsion whose pale insipidity was countered by calling it 'magnolia' on the manufacturer's colour chart. This undertaking was completed just before the delivery of a new lounge suite which, being light grey, was intended to conceal whatever traces of dirt Jeremy's efforts were unable to remove.

So far *not*-so-good! There was, however, one truly effective measure taken as part of the general makeover: namely, that the wall-to-wall carpets that came with the flat had been taken up and thrown away at the very beginning in order to avoid harbouring dust. This exposed a good-quality, honey-coloured parquet floor which had been sanded immediately and then sealed with heavy-duty varnish. It was an initially negative action which nevertheless added a sparkle to an otherwise drab picture.

Within this somewhat Spartan environment, the furniture other than the lounge suite was merely practical; and the only explicit embellishment to be seen was a black-and-white wedding photograph of Jeremy's parents hanging in the hallway. There is very little else to be said about the flat's internal conditions: they represented, of course, in their own way, a radical set of measures aimed at creating personal space. And the central objective was plain: namely, to provide a defence, flimsy though it might be, against the challenges of the outside world.

Despite its non-mystical character, his adopted régime, taken in its entirety, was in a roundabout sort of way Jeremy's closest approach to religion - the other mainstream faiths being in conflict not only with his rather vague views about origins but also with his felt need to steer clear of all verities beyond his own imperfectly understood compulsions. Buddhism, which might have appealed to his quietistic side, was complicated by the smell of incense (which he disliked), by flowers that dispensed pollen and by the clutter of images, wall-hangings and shrines. Furthermore, for a mindset like Jeremy's, home-grown Christianity was particularly unattractive: he felt its dogmas were too pointed and demanding; in addition, he found the thought of Christ's blood and the chalices that contained it a repulsive proposition.

Last but not least, the doctrines of Islam had scarcely crossed his mind despite the fact that, in theory, there was a link between the Prophet's radical puritanism and Jeremy's delicate abstemiousness. His broad perception, however, and the thought of various cultural constraints represented an absolute barrier; and these considerations, taken together, pointed to a line of thinking in which he had never willfully indulged. At the same time, his reservations were confused with the many other, quite unrelated fragments of received tradition at the back of his mind. And the net result was the virtual hermit's cave in which, of his own choosing, Jeremy Dinsdale had established his presence.

* * *

It's worth pointing out, in the light of the foregoing, that Jeremy had no male visitors whatever and even more surprisingly that he had no female ones either; nor did this state of affairs indicate any particular sexual leaning on the part of a man to whom all bodily functions were repugnant. Indeed, the only regular human contacts he had were his brother who acted as confessor-come-therapist when he visited him from time to time in his Basingstoke semi - and his widowed mother who, when the need arose, dressed her son's wounds in a dowdy two-up-two-down in Stockwell. Defining precisely what these wounds were, of course, remains an impossible task, hidden as they are not only in a pool of silence but also, perhaps, in the ancestral gene pool. But their existence was clear enough to anyone observing the crestfallen look that his face unfailingly presented - not to mention the mechanics that struggled wearily into play whenever he forced a smile.

It needs to be emphasised that Jeremy was a fairly young man, no more than thirty five years old, whose features were sufficiently drawn to make him look somewhat older; whose skin was as pale as parchment; and whose closely cropped, faintly auburn hair was, by reason of its shortness, just one among several aspects of his personal hygiene which, but for constant vigilance, demonstrated that his demons were always ready to pounce.

Given all of this, one might have expected him to pay more attention than he did to his appearance - and yet he did not. No doubt his clothes were well laundered, but they were not particularly well pressed. In all weathers, he wore blue jeans that were on the loose side, black shoes, a white shirt and (when needed) a dark grey plastic mackintosh. In summer, the mackintosh gave place to a flimsy, straw-coloured blouson; and if it rained, a plain and rather incongruous baseball cap was added to the ensemble. This dreary-looking scheme of things set against the contrasting orderliness of his flat never varied. Neither was there any mitigation attributable to a splash of aftershave.

Understanding such a complex hinterland of threat and containment makes it easier to grasp the function of Jeremy's immaculate, hermetically sealed apartment where, highlighting a particular advantage of the digital age, he was able to earn his living on a computer - thus enabling him to spend vast periods of time behind closed doors in a flat from which he ventured out only occasionally in order to buy food or to liaise with the secretarial agency that employed him. Other than this, he lived in silence: no sounds of radio or television were ever heard; the only intermittent signs of activity were the wheeze of the hoover or the rumble of the washing machine; and no cooking odours were ever detected, thereby fuelling the suspicion that he lived on a frugal, vegetarian diet which contributed to the willowy, deprived appearance that he shared with the other patrons of his local health food shop. But there was just one symptom of his presence that he could not conceal: and this was the intense smell of carbolic soap, detergents, polish and disinfectants that signified Jeremy's constant campaign against dirt whenever he opened his door on the communal landing.

Very sadly, this final, definitive articulation of his obsessions brings us no closer to a silver lining as we observe the colourless backdrop to Jeremy's life. This was a life, of course, which despite so-called magnolia walls, bottles of Dettol and indifference to sex, necessarily included those bodily functions common to all of us. Unfortunately, these were functions that left Jeremy intensely uncomfortable - a plain fact evident to anyone who noticed that, even on winter nights with the snow falling and the north wind blowing, the bathroom windows at number 3 Abergavenny House were sometimes thrown so widely open as to test the endurance of the hinges.

Splendid isolation: headline in The Times 22.01.1896. See the Oxford Dictionary of Quotations.

Murgh Musallam: a curried whole chicken dish with virtually the full gamut of Indian spices. See 'Mrs Balbir Singh's Indian Cookery', published by Mills & Boon 1975.

BLESS ME, FATHER

Lent was late that year; and it reminded Eric that time was running out for *him* as well. Not to put too fine a point on it, Ash Wednesday, the first day of the forthcoming penitential season, was only four days away - and it happened to coincide with his seventy eighth birthday.

Seated until then beneath the leafless trees all around him, it was only the sight of two nuns strolling past that had suddenly interrupted Eric's daydreams which were focussed on the twenty years since he retired from teaching. It gratified him that he had little or no sense of nostalgia: he had never looked back longingly on his former career; and in the interim since it ended, with his strong interest in London's wildlife and open spaces, he had never been bored. Indeed, it was a point of special pride whenever he recounted how he had once spotted a fox in St James's Square.

As he lounged comfortably on that bench in Holland Park, he continued to think about Lent. He was reminded of the Latin words formerly used by priests during the imposition of the ashes: '…pulvis es, et in pulverem reverteris'. That was when he was a boy, of course; but things had changed. He reflected on the present-day English translation: 'remember that you are dust, and to dust you shall return'. So naturally, at the age of seventy eight, this stark reminder had a sobering influence. However, instead of compensating with a warm drink in the nearby café, Eric took heart from the brightness of the March sun, the daffodils in full bloom beneath a veteran oak and the pair of magpies energetically nest-building about forty feet above him.

Despite these encouragements, there was nevertheless an encroaching shadow that bore down on him and affected his composure. This was the product of his considerable self-knowledge which warned him about his private shortcomings alongside the seasonally appropriate need for remedial action. The backlog of failure was long, though not particularly heinous; and as a practising if imperfect catholic, he decided it was time to put the record straight. In short, remembering it was a late Saturday afternoon and Sunday the day after, he decided to take advantage of the fact that the confessionals would be operating in the nearby church. He therefore abandoned the bench he was sitting on and set off with a modest spring in his step.

* * *

Eric made his exit from the wooded area of Holland Park via the picturesque Kyoto Garden which was centred on a realistic-looking waterfall playfully negotiating a steep, rocky descent. At its foot, he crossed the zig-zag bridge spanning a pool where he noticed that virtually all the coins hopefully cast into the water for good luck were copper. Passing a Japanese stone lantern, he then encountered two rather drab peahens as he made his way along a path to the so-called 'formal gardens' with their alternating beds of yellow and pink primulas. Overhanging these, he also noticed the drooping boughs of a prunus whose white blossoms on leafless twigs were reminiscent of a snow flurry. Lastly, having briefly deviated to take in the pink and white camellias behind the Belvedere restaurant, he skimmed past the ice house and the surviving frontage of Holland House, emerging from the park into the Duchess of Bedford's Walk.

Here, the first thing to command his attention was Campden Hill Gate. This was an apartment block on his left whose vast length and towering height embodied a redbrick and stone-faced façade in marked contrast to the character of Holland Park - although by no means was it a comedown with its immaculately clipped privet hedge and its soothing welter of pink camellias in nicely maintained front gardens. Furthermore, as a finishing touch along the length of the hedge and mounted on brick plinths, there were ornamental urns alternately planted with purple pansies and scarlet primulas.

Typically for him, although he was anxiously pondering what he was going to say to the priest, Eric absorbed all of these pleasant-enough details before crossing the junction ahead and then veering downhill along Holland Street where the dwarf magnolias lining the lefthand pavement were struggling into flower. It then suddenly dawned on him that at no point between Holland Park and the church would there be a single property worth less than a million pounds. In reality, his own private circumstances were by no means dismal; nevertheless, in such opulent surroundings, his lean figure, his drawn features and the balding scalp beneath a beret somehow went hand in hand with an underlying sense of dissatisfaction.

Continuing on his way to the lower end of Holland Street at the point where it crossed Hornton Street, Eric's largely positive contemplation of the urban landscape was briefly interrupted by the sight of a stationary police van into which a drunk, with disarming willingness, was being loaded with comparable courtesy and consideration by three officers. But in the absence of sufficient spectacle to detain him, Eric forged on, turning left into Gordon Place whose white-fronted villas, subject to a win on the lottery, struck him as being ideally suited to his requirements. Next, as he neared the end of his journey, he turned right into Pitt Street and right again into Dukes Lane where, having passed the elegant period façade of Queen Anne Cottages, he reached his intended destination in Kensington Church Street.

* * *

As soon as Eric opened the door and encountered the familiar smells of polish, candle wax and the previous Sunday's incense, he felt (as he always did when entering certain churches) a strong awareness of homecoming - of enclosure in a sacred space free from the uncertainties of time and tide. And, for him, this was a particularly atmospheric church which, in common with many others in central London, was open on weekdays as well as on Sundays. Not only that, but you could virtually guarantee there would always be one or two people kneeling quietly at prayer in the gloom; votive lights burned unfailingly at almost every shrine - and this was especially so before the image of the Virgin of Mount Carmel to whom the church was dedicated.

Our Lady of Mount Carmel is, as a matter of plain fact, a parish church in the care of Carmelite friars whose monastery is part of the same complex of buildings. Consequently, there is never a shortage of priests - with this result: that having arrived and taken stock, Eric had the satisfaction of finding two of the confessionals already in operation. The names of the priests functioning at any given time are always displayed above the respective confessional doors - and in this instance, Eric had never heard of either of them. He therefore decided to chance his luck with a certain Father Athanasius - partly because he was rather taken by the name and partly because the queue outside *his* confessional was shorter than the alternative option provided by Father O'Connor.

In due course, with his mind made up, Eric edged his way on to a pew in a position clearly acknowledging the several people before him - this being in marked contrast to his daily experience of twenty first century metropolitan bus queues. But the point needs further clarification because queues for confessions seldom comprise straight lines; instead, people sit randomly and simply *remember* the order of precedence. Eric then paused, coughed nervously, and having settled himself comfortably, he made the usual sign of the cross and composed, as best he could, the form of words to be used for the more embarrassing of his sins - most of which were equally embarrassingly recurrent!

* * *

When at last his turn came, Eric knelt down in the dimly lit confessional and, as he listened to the priest's prefatory blessing uttered on the far side of the grille, he could make out, more or less clearly, the features of a very old man in the brown habit of his order over which was draped the priestly stole of office. Eric then mentioned the approximate date of his last confession and began, somewhat uncertainly, to make a clean breast of his failings.

At this point, readers need to understand that in outlining the perfectly true story that follows, I am entitled (if not obliged) to shelter behind the seal of the confessional. Prurient details, all of which the venerable father would have heard many times before, are not the object of this tale. Of much greater interest, on the other hand, is the character of the priest himself as revealed incidentally in the course of a ten-minute conversation... and of similar interest is the beneficial effect he had on his likewise ageing listener.

I have no idea - nor can Eric remember - what caused Father Athanasius to mention that he had spent most of his priestly life as a missionary in Africa in conditions which had been very rough and ready - and where the local politics had often been threatening. It was clear, nonetheless, that he had taken it all in his stride and had seen it as part of the life of sacrifice that he'd espoused as a youth of eighteen on the Island of South Uist off the west coast of Scotland. He had clearly never looked back with any regrets; and, as far as anyone could guess from his words and demeanour, he had never doubted his faith. We may conjecture that he had perhaps at times felt nostalgia for the cooler climate of his boyhood years; but it was entirely without emotion that he gave ill health as the only reason for ending his days in the relative comfort of an English monastery.

It must have been his wealth of experience, including some of the horrors he must have witnessed, that caused Father Athanasius to pass lightly over the particularities which Eric had most dreaded having to mention. Contrary to expectation, he was at once put at ease by the old man's understanding which was plainly founded on absolute personal innocence unsullied by his encounters with the exact opposite. His advice on these matters was consequently brief, to the point, and centred on prayer.

What really surprised Eric, at least initially, was what happened after he'd got the worst of his shortcomings off his chest - and here I have his consent to break the seal of the confessional. Having mentioned his recurrent habit of swearing, and considering the easy ride he'd been given in relation to much more delicate matters, he was bemused by the fact that Father Athanasius should bother to concern himself with mere bad language. From the start, he had been at pains to point out that he never swore as a means of abusing others. Instead of obscene nouns intended to wound, he was more inclined towards coarse adjectives which he used merely as 'colouring agents' to enliven his conversation. Neither was he attempting to minimise discussion when he emphasised the point.

Eric was therefore taken aback - but later on rather amused - when Father Athanasius seemed to think that, instead of being morally deficient, he (Eric) might perhaps be unfamiliar with the scope of commonplace English idiom.

'There is no real problem here' the old priest advised him. 'There are plenty of other words you can use - for example, what about *good heavens...* or *great scott...* or *stone a crow?*'

* * *

Eric naturally expressed agreement with these wise recommend-ations - though he wondered whether his response, which he had difficulty in formulating, might have sounded rather inadequate. But later on, whilst kneeling in the pews with his anxieties dissipated, he not only felt that a weight had been lifted from his shoulders by a familiar routine; he also felt the even greater benefit of another man's goodness - notwithstanding the fact that, as he began reciting his penance, an observer might have thought that the smile on his face was somewhat inappropriate!

Pulvis es: the full Latin form 'memento, homo, quia pulvis es, et in pulverem reverteris' translates into English as 'remember, man, that you are dust, and unto dust you will return'.

Stone a crow: short for 'stone the crows' - an exclamation, probably mid nineteenth century.

THE PRIVATE VIEW

The terraced house situated at 134 Arbuthnot Gardens looked taller than it actually was because, in the first place, it was a particularly narrow building. At the same time, the effect was reinforced by an extra storey above the bay-windowed ground and first floor levels; and this lent a slightly lanky, but far from inelegant appearance to the white stucco frontage visible to passing strollers. Indeed, this favourable impression remained the case even when the casual eye, largely focussed elsewhere, missed much of the detail. For example, pedestrians hurrying to the shops in the Fulham Road usually failed to grasp that the bay windows on the lower floors were replaced on the top storey by an entirely flat front which, topped with an open balustrade and pierced by simple rectangular fenestration, extended along the whole length of the terrace.

Inevitably, there were a few people such as the lonely or those at a loose end who with luck, on this or that day, might spot a secluded garden with a life all its own beyond the windows at the back of a darkened lounge. Some of them would be amused by the self-important stance of a black-and-tan airedale gazing down at the street from an open door; and others might feel a pang of envy or the brunt of exclusion at the sight of a shocking-pink cyclamen glowing like a lamp on a drawing room window-sill.

There were other features, however, more immediate by reason of their closeness to the pavement and thus more likely to arouse the admiration of the general public. At number 134, for example, there was an american cotinus tree that blazed into technicolour splendour each year when autumn's short-lived alchemy worked wonders on the sap. And in spring, a dwarf magnolia stellata took charge and dignified the half-hearted progress of the front garden with its white-pointed, bulletlike buds whose fully open petals, as the season advanced, acquired a sprawling, rather suggestive flaccidity.

The house had further compensations, too, on top of being situated in the most exclusive part of London's South Kensington. It was, for example, within an inch of The Conran Shop, a venue renowned for its elegantly modern furniture, fashionable designer goods and the highly luxurious versions of almost everything needed to smarten up the homes of business executives, younger up-and-coming whizz-kids or even, in the view of local diehards, the East End attics of champagne socialists!

There were prices to match all this, of course. And there was no shortage of bulging pockets to pay for expensive acquisitions after a Pieds de Porc Rémoulade lunch in the foyer of a shop which also boasted the distinction of having once housed the Michelin Tyre Company's offices. The evidence of this was still strong; and between an introductory Saffron Crab Tart and the Pieds de Porc Rémoulade, diners could examine at their leisure the display of wall tiles illustrating a variety of early racing cars.

* * *

Only a little further away than The Conran Shop was the Victoria & Albert Museum next door to the Brompton Oratory whence, after the pomp of Sunday worship, the owner of number 134 Arbuthnot Gardens, Mrs Lucille Baldwin, had only to walk a few extra steps eastwards along the Brompton Road in order to immerse herself in the white-marbled, brightly lit glare of the cosmetics department at Harrods (an establishment needing no introduction). Here she dawdled, imagined, indulged recollections of the primrose paths of days gone by - and sometimes made purchases. But after this, whether or not she added to her store of skin creams, she always made her way into the adjacent, world-famous food halls where the cheese counter was her favourite source of a lunch-time snack after having treated the Oratory twenty minutes earlier to a candle in honour of the Virgin of Guadalupe. After that, she only took a taxi home when there was a downpour or when the winter was at its lowest ebb; otherwise, she enjoyed the walk in anticipation of a nice French Mont d'Or la Tradition cheese, a crispbread and a glass of wine. And if, in due season, the wisteria was blooming in all its purple magnificence around the blue panels of her front door, it was a welcome bonus.

The railings enclosing the frontage at 134 Arbuthnot Gardens bore a plaque with the name 'Knebworth' in weathered gold script which Lucille's husband, by now fifteen years in his grave, had comm-issioned in memory of his mother whom he took on a day-trip to Knebworth's superb gardens shortly before she died. Lucille had left the plaque as it was out of respect; and the same unaltered condition of things was also the case inside the building - not only out of respect, but because that was the way Lucille liked it. The house had been bought, decorated and furnished gradually over the years from her husband Gerald's income as a banker; and his savings, by the time he died, together with insurance policies and the like, had left her comfortably off. And now, fifteen years down the line, she was a more or less contented widow with a small sprinkling of friends (some of whom joined her each week to play bridge) and an abiding interest in the arts which she indulged regularly. Apart from that, afternoon walks by the Serpentine or a leisurely trot around the Japanese Garden in Holland Park were her repeated but never-failing enjoyments.

* * *

Despite tolerable health and frequent exercise, Mrs Lucille Baldwin looked not a day younger than her seventy eight years. She was pale beneath the powder, more than adequately wrinkled, and exceedingly thin; in fact, one might reasonably have described her as the archetypal skinny lizzy were it not for the fact that such language would undermine the residual dignity that survived, notwithstanding the added disadvantage of her slightly below-average height. Alongside all this, she was aware (and perhaps *tragically* aware) that she needed to look to her laurels; and unfortunately, this inspired some markedly futile trips to the Harrods cosmetics department... which in turn, and from time to time, tipped the balance against her better judgement when set alongside additions to her wardrobe from Selfridges or a once-in-a-blue-moon stroke of luck in the Notting Hill Nearly-New Shop.

It would be fair to say that many of Lucille's obsessions and strategies were in response to the assaults of nature - something she could hardly be blamed for. Neither could she be blamed overmuch for a conspicuous instance of her growing susceptibilities which became obvious to a sprinkling of those present at an exhibition entitled 'Turner's Later Paintings' at the Tate Britain Gallery. It was a private view day; and Lucille always looked forward to attending the private views of major exhibitions to which she had automatic access by reason of being a fully paid-up 'friend' of all the main London galleries. By seeming to set her apart, not only did this privilege subdue any doubts about her own dwindling significance brought on by age; it also countered the nuisance of overcrowding which, on other days, contributed to obscuring her view when some thoughtless individual blocked her line of sight. Counter to these positive considerations, however, there was one all-too-predictable pitfall. Stemming from privileged access, there arose a consequent need so often evident at the galleries: namely, the need to dress in a manner deemed appropriate to the occasion, thus affirming, rather obtrusively, the wearer's artistic leanings tacked on to the worthier celebration of great art and its ability to raise sometimes downcast spirits above the humdrum of daily life.

In pursuit of this familiar practice, Lucille had spent half the morning preparing for her walkabout at the private view; though in fairness to her, it must also be said that her love of Turner's work, whether virtually abstract or plainly figurative, was at least equal to her desire to look her best. Unfortunately, however, on this occasion, she failed to adapt the means to her age. Instead, she mimicked the half-memory of some bright young thing surviving at the back of her mind from the days when she was a bright young thing herself! It would be mean-spirited to paint too detrimental a picture of the flowing extravaganza of flimsy blue cotton ending in points below her knees as she sailed into view among the many other art enthusiasts. Contrived affinity with the colour of Turner's mediterranean skies did nothing to diminish the disparity between the outfit and its wearer; and despite the blandness of a simple silk scarf around her neck, there were far too many rings on her fingers - not to mention the topping of unnaturally white hair held in place by a tortoiseshell slide. And so, to her discomfort, out of the corner of her eye, she gradually became aware of the occasional censorious glance or vague smile that her appearance was producing.

After the first five minutes of euphoria contemplating her all-time favourite picture of 'Norham Castle, Sunrise' and having moved on to 'Landscape with River and Distant Mountains', Lucille attempted to soften her growing malaise by focussing on the tumultuous seascapes incorporating marine monsters or gloomy wrecks at the height of a storm. But although she ended up forcing herself to imagine she was out at sea with the painter, straining to catch a glimpse of the shore at Margate through the wind and the spray, the plain fact that she was regarded by some as a 'mess' finally struck home. And so, after a few more brief encounters with revered works such as the idealised realism of 'The Blue Rigi', she made her way towards the exit door en route to the cloakroom.

Having collected her handbag and a surprisingly unremarkable black overgarment, Lucille's discomfort deepened; and although her journey from South Kensington to the gallery had been via the underground system, she made an instant decision to return home by taxi in order to escape as swiftly and invisibly as possible from the sense of disappointment that, at the same time, she was already attempting to suppress as the cab drew away from the gallery and turned west into John Islip Street. But her dilemma could not be set aside easily; for although she sought to dumb down her feelings as best she could, she nevertheless knew how faulty her judgement had been. In a shadowy way, she realised that had she thought more deeply, or consulted one of her friends and acted more imaginatively, she would not have provoked such a negative reaction to the incongruity of her attire compared with her age. The lesson began to sink in.

Slowly, having entered into a virtual trance and emerged from it again as the taxi chugged along, Lucille began to understand that with just a little more consideration, she would have garnered the respect (if not the rapt attention) of which she felt such a pressing need. And almost at once, that thought began to dissipate her inner gloom whilst also encouraging a growing perception which climaxed as she passed the Oratory. This immediately proved decisive and initiated a learning curve that brightened into a new determination. And so, as she climbed the well-worn steps at Knebworth, she had already more or less decided that the penny which had so painfully dropped would be reinvested in a better planned, wiser and more appropriate future - beginning with the next private view.

THE MAKINGS OF A MAN

This is a tale that is not the straightforward result of a theme long thought about and carefully planned in advance; and for that reason its timing is likewise fortuitous. In essence, it brings into focus an abrupt, unpremeditated series of childhood recollections. At the same time, it is a story which, in its own small way, reflects a peculiar affinity with the cosmic microwave background - by which I mean that it shares the same weird ability of the past to catch up with the present to which it returns as if from a foreign country.

Hitherto neglected by memory, the particular recollections in question here have lain dormant whilst on a course set in motion during the Second World War and only now completing their journey back through time in the reawakened memory of an old man. That elderly man, when these events first took place, was a naïve, inexperienced boy summarily evacuated to a West Country town still unaffected by Hitler's bombs; and for him who in the early forties was seven or eight years old and is now at the penultimate stage of his life, those remote years radiate their freshly restored influence. Today, happily, he is still in good health; and he is also the only person alive whose antennae can pick up those well-travelled signals and pass them on.

* * *

The effect of this virtual time warp is not only the revival of personal memories; it also marks the passing of a world that no longer exists. The terraced ranks of Bristol's working-class dwellings, not unlike those associated with the paintings of L. S. Lowry, may not have been flattened by enemy bombs - but nevertheless, they have survived only to be fundamentally transformed since their heyday. Nearly all the lives once lived in them have long since ended, as the local graveyards attest; and in those municipal burial grounds, the bodies (among others) of Leonard Williams, his first wife Rosie who died at an early age and his second wife Laura, all cluster beneath the turf where they are now as silent and forgotten as the mutterings of the nonconformist ministers who laid them to rest with a promise of everlasting life.

Today, the uniform West Country accents in Britannia Drive where this family lived have all but faded away. Polyglot communities now predominate; and the redbrick air raid shelters that once occupied the entire length of the road between the terraces have been demolished. Furthermore, the unforgettable odour of the fish and chip shop on the corner, and the inimitable taste of the chips themselves (at threepence a bag) continue to reassemble in the now adult mind of the former child evacuee. Sadly, that shop closed in 1950. All the same, it has left enduring echoes, given that other fish and chip shops, in the city centre and on the street corners of new estates, have been opened up by the world and his wife whose accents come from much further afield. Strangely redolent of the old tradition, however, the chips still smell and taste the same; nor is it any easier today than in the past to match their unique qualities at home.

Likewise disappeared from Britannia Drive and from its pavements are the chalked squares scrawled by children playing hopscotch. Most of these too, in common with their parents, are either dead or not far off it - together with all trace of their secret transactions in the dark interiors of empty air raid shelters. Nowadays, of course, such goings-on have faded like a dream from the memories of the few survivors of that dwindling generation. Furthermore, the handful of old men and women who still live on in the homes they grew up in are mostly housebound; and when they gaze like lost souls out of their front room windows, it isn't youngsters playing hopscotch that they see but brightly clad teenagers tearing past on skateboards or gathered in tight-knit huddles around the glinting screens of smartphones.

Such is the backdrop of an almost forgotten story which, although dead and buried for so long, has been rescued from the drifting sands in the nick of time.

* * *

The workings of the advancing years remain constantly active, conspiring to make this a good moment to point out that the former child and the ageing adult of today are one and the same person now known to the world as James Salter who, in his younger incarnation, was evacuated with his mother to the Redfield district of Bristol at the height of the London blitz. In those days, but no longer, everyone called him Jamie.

The dominant force in Jamie's wartime redoubt was known to him, somewhat inaccurately, as his Uncle Leonard. Unsurprisingly, given his age at the time, he never really grasped the fact that Leonard, rather than being a blood relation, was actually a cherished survivor of his father's school days and that those childhood bonds - notwithstanding strong political differences - had endured until the time of the present tale when both parties were in their forties.

Years later, after the war and during his teens, Jamie, in a series of short-lived bursts of retrospection, gradually reassembled his memories and realised that this boyhood association of his father's, precisely one generation before his own, had been the reason why the two long-standing chums, and himself with them, had embarked on a day trip to the village school in Willsbridge just beyond the reach of Bristol's cramped suburbs. It also explained that day's references to masters' and mistresses' names and provided a background for the rather tedious recital of boyhood pranks. Yet strange as it may seem, he never forgot this seemingly unremarkable outing to a spot still rural in those far-off days; and this was because it represented a break from what was, for him, the claustrophobic character of inner-city Bristol's narrow, monotonous streets.

Given these attitudes, it's worth mentioning that although Jamie was born and bred in Greater London, his circumstances there were entirely unlike those facing him in Bristol. His father was a member of the maintenance team employed by Appledon Park not far from Croydon town centre. It was an extensive piece of land which provided a refreshingly countrified outlook when viewed from the bungalow across the road where Jamie lived with his parents. Indeed, until he was evacuated, he had never experienced life in an ordinary, built-up urban environment - least of all in a uniform row of terraced houses where he felt fundamentally ill at ease.

* * *

In his later years as an adult, James's capacity for hindsight strengthened. Once again, he was able to conjure up memories of his childhood companions in Britannia Drive. Yet although he had no concept of class in those early days - and despite his family's humble position - he perceived from the start that the local boys were rougher than he was used to. He naturally made friends, as children inevitably do. But without explicit awareness of social division, he nevertheless felt a certain *apartheid* without sufficient experience or knowledge to understand why he felt it or what it meant.

It was at this time of association with the local youth that Jamie's dark side made its first unequivocal appearance. Dirty words were nothing new to him - nor were rude investigations in back alleys. And of course, no one needs reminding that schools, even infants' schools where boys predominate, were always hotbeds of the sort of language associated with life's seamier side. It was therefore no fault of Britannia Drive's 'rough' boys that Jamie had at least this feature in common with them. And it was entirely his own fault that he set out to impress them by writing an obscene verse in the privacy of one of the air raid shelters - after which, sharing a fit of giggles with a single local collaborator, he popped the offending (and extremely feeble) rhyme through the nearest letter-box.

* * *

In the nineteen forties, the Britannia Drive of suburban Redfield was solidly working class and law-abiding. A moderate proportion of those who lived there attended church, mostly chapel; and there was a strong community spirit - itself fortified by the wartime fear of invasion. It was into this compact environment, therefore, that an evacuee's shockingly obscene contribution exploded like a bomb-shell in the midst of a population where local gossip made banner headlines.

The repercussions were drastic and immediate. That weekend, it happened that Jamie's father, the somewhat retiring Mr Gordon Salter, had left London for Bristol to join his wife and son under the hospitable roof of his friend, Leonard; also visiting was Leonard's own blood relative, a nephew by the name of Oscar whose presence didn't help. It should be mentioned, too (and Jamie somehow knew this), that Leonard was looked up to by his neighbours because, apart from his conspicuous uprightness and his attendance at chapel, he was also admired for his contribution to the war effort as a worker at the local aircraft factory. Indeed, his job proved the final feather in his cap by providing a vantage-point for gleaning and dispensing news not otherwise available in those anxious days.

The sequel was very unpleasant. A routine Saturday morning knock on the front door followed by subdued voices and the rustle of a sheet of paper ended in a damning silence broken finally by a gentle click of the latch. There was then a short delay, the ominous thump of footsteps, and finally a summons to gather in what in those days was known as the 'front room'. The entire household was present: Jamie's parents were acquainted with the circumstances and, amidst expressions of consternation, their quizzical response was masked by their downcast, conspicuously red faces. At the same time, Leonard's wife Rosie, from a shared sense of shame, withdrew to the darkness furthest from the window whilst Oscar, aged eighteen, eagerly stationed himself at the forefront.

Strangely, it is at this point that James's communion with the past seems to weaken. None of the words or phrases used by his Uncle Leonard have survived the journey through time. What does survive, however, is a picture of the man himself, in shirt sleeves, who towered above a small boy dwarfed even more by an embarrassed assembly of family and friends. There, as James now remembers it, stood Leonard, a bright star of the community: his jaw, always peculiarly square, became rigidly fixed; his colourless eyes glinted with anger; and the striking pallor of his face is something that Jamie, even as a mature and thoughtful adult, is unlikely to forget.

* * *

Every cloud has a silver lining; and so, in due course, Jamie's humiliation, if not forgotten, was set aside as the war rumbled on and the evacuation continued. Meanwhile, at the opposite end of the story, not only recollections of concrete past events but also early indications of the sort of person he was to become re-emerge at intervals in James's present-day consciousness.

So far, no picture of the interior of the little terraced house in

Britannia Drive has been given; nor is it material to the present purpose to dwell on the latterday Victorian gloom and the somewhat artless contents such as an iridescent fairground vase or the painted china alsatian on the cluttered mantelpiece above an empty grate. We can set these reminiscences aside except, possibly, in the light of the occasion at the age of nineteen when James (in air force uniform) and his father attended the funeral of Leonard's first wife. Without a word, they gazed down at her now unrecognisable face as she lay in her coffin in that very same front room which James remembered so well amidst the protective silence that marked the passing of the late Mrs Rosie Williams whose full name, Rosalie, inscribed on the coffin lid, had never been used since she signed the register, so long ago, at her marriage to Leonard Williams in the nearby Bethesda Baptist Chapel.

* * *

Jamie's mother, Florence Salter (forever known as Florrie) was a far more vivid and forthright character than her husband and, despite her son's tender age during those wartime years, she often made surprisingly sharp observations or pointed out wounding ironies, putting things in her own characteristically lively way; and eventually, these expressions had a formative influence on the adult James's use of words. Such was her native and regional fluency that she had no hesitation in pouring scorn on the back garden at number 10 Britannia Drive on the grounds that it was 'no bigger than a pocket handkerchief'. One might reasonably have expected that Jamie's freezing experiences in the outside (and only) toilet would have given him cause to share her cynicism. On the other hand, this particular pocket handkerchief, by its informal and open-air nature, was the only feature of Britannia Drive that he really liked; indeed, he can be said to have loved it.

Florrie's so-called pocket-handkerchief-sized garden was only about thirty feet square - and it really was a square rather than a rectangle. But for Jamie, its rural character was not only reminiscent of home: it was also a miniature paradise in its own right. First of all, the garden along with the whole of Britannia Drive, was on a hillside; and at the bottom end furthest from the house, there was a flint-faced wall which overlooked a panoramic view of the city. This not only provided an escape from containment; it also aroused a certain exaltation. In bright sunlight, the receding acres of rooftops, the factory chimneys belching plumes of white smoke, the effects of distance and the ample sky with its billowing clouds seem, today, to have laid the foundations for James's enduring love of painters like Constable, Turner and, by contrast, L. S. Lowry's industrial landscapes.

Visible through a hole in the toilet door when in use, Jamie could glimpse the garden that he'd learned to admire. The colours of the flowers delighted him - though naturally in those days, he had no idea what to call them. Nevertheless, their picture in his mind's eye remains so clear that they live on still in evocative, homely names like marigold, antirrhinum and michaelmas daisy - flowers whose yellow, pink and sky-blue heads, shaken by the wind, continue to reappear in a thousand subsequently much-loved gardens.

In that wartime microcosm, other aspects of the natural world left their mark and remain influential. There are few splendours in a summer garden that impinge more forcefully on the retina than the wings of a red admiral opening and closing as it basks in the sun - all the more impressive, perhaps, in the smoky suburbs of a place like Bristol in the forties. Or consider a fritillary probing the purple heads of a buddleia outlined against the backdrop of that city's industrial landscape.

All these experiences and many others like them proved pivotal, working on Jamie like a tonic during those years of imminent danger. Formative fragments of the past, they have travelled through time and back towards the present where they continue to revisit him today. Effective healers, they loom larger than life - and *considerably* larger than a pocket handkerchief.

UNFAMILIAR GROUND

I knew of course, that it was myself rather than anyone else who was thinking these things; but it was still Father David who was giving voice to the words. I looked around me; I carried on with my walk. And I let the sound-patterns reach me from whatever source they might be coming.

'For a brief while', (surely it was Father David speaking to me now), 'notice there is a lull as if the wind has been constrained by a vow of silence. I hear the cracked voices of an ageing couple... seated on a bench... in thrall to recollection. And I draw your attention to the blades of the mower lopping the dandelions' yellow flower-heads that will burst forth again presently like an Easter Proclamation'.

From 'Unfamiliar Ground', page 156/157.

NEAR-DEATH EXPERIENCE
IN NORTHWOOD HILLS

Something tells me we are at the height of spring. Some vague prompting or transient impression… something unaccountably tenuous tells me that today is a spring day. And yet… I sense an equally unaccountable flaw in the evidence.

As I emerge from the underground by way of a draughty staircase, two teenagers having been at pains to look as if they have taken no trouble with their appearance squat open-legged on the steps, stuffing their mouths with chips. The girl is gazing star-struck into the eyes of her lover whose hair has been heavily greased and combed into spikes so as to preserve the fiction that he has just stumbled bright-eyed and bushy-tailed from the shower.

Outside the station, I am confronted by a nondescript shopping parade along each side of a main road where the supply of basic amenities is thin on the ground. I observe one dry-cleaner, two Indian restaurants with no customers; and I feel a strange sense of aimlessness associated with the few people I encounter passing a run-down garage next to a closed-for-lunch pet shop. It is rumoured to be Wednesday - and yet I have a weird suspicion that the world has come to a standstill and that days no longer have names.

* * *

Light drizzle has been falling on Northwood Hills all morning. Ahead, strangely remote, I catch tantalising glimpses of spring in avenues receding at different angles from the roundabout like the spokes of a spider's web where red-tiled roofs are outnumbered three to one by the bounteous greens of treetops rising like a rainforest from eco-friendly back gardens.

The drizzle has now thickened and forms a veil. Even as it falls, white light from no particular source fades to the wishy-washy colour of powdered ash; and water rattles morbidly through the network of choking drains. And yet, although I have taken the name of Northwood Hills in vain, I begin to wonder where I really am. Perhaps the world in some curious sense has stopped turning after all. The sight of bluebells rotting in a tub seems to be warning me that I am profoundly nowhere; and I grow more certain by the minute that this is neither the time nor the country where I used to live.

Is it therefore conceivable that I am a ghost? Perhaps *that* accounts for the feeling that no one notices me... perhaps they cannot see me! Alternatively, am I some insubstantial visitant gazing at a parallel universe? Things are becoming clearer: I am nowhere at all... and I am deeply uneasy.

And so, without further protraction, I am leaving Northwood Hills by the same route I took to get here... And I see the two youngsters have discarded their chip bags on the staircase. I am well aware they have returned to a flat paid for at public expense and are pursuing an afternoon of intimacy in which I feel not the slightest interest.

* * *

Happily, the Metropolitan Line is prompt today - and the carriage is warm. As the train pulls out of the station, I begin to detect a new sense of solidity like an arm that regains feeling and blood supply after being heavily slept on.

And now, at last, I am about to re-enter the bustling city. And as I change trains at Baker Street, I know that I am alive again. I have just noticed the date on my watch. And although Father Thames never stands still, the sound of Big Ben at Westminster instantly reminds me that I am real when I grasp the permanence of those consoling booms rising above the din of London traffic.

THE LONG MARCH

Now in his late sixties and with a bald patch to prove it, Paul had been convinced for many years that, among the characteristics of time, there was an elasticity whose cause was very different in nature from those known fluctuations attributed to gravity and the speed of an object's motion. Somehow embedded in the void, he had the odd feeling that consciousness, or even a person's moods and anxieties, could have a certain, albeit indefinable effect on the rate at which individual human beings travel from the past, through the present and on into the future.

An example of how such a perception can arise began simply enough on a bright autumn morning in 2015 when, after breakfast, Paul left home at about twenty to nine and boarded a number 33 bus. Five minutes later, just down the road, given that no single service covered the entire route, he alighted and caught a 271 which, despite its rather roundabout exploration of back streets and council estates, dropped him off, with half an hour to spare, quite close to his destination. He then trudged uphill for a further ten minutes to the Carnegie Eye Unit at the district hospital, arriving comfortably in advance of his appointment. The journey up to that point had taken a total of forty five minutes.

Despite putting in an early appearance, his examination began almost immediately and proved a straightforward, congenial affair comprising a field test, a pressure test, the usual drops of yellow chemical to dilate the pupils and a close look at both retinas - all of which concluded with a clean bill of health pending another six-monthly check-up scheduled for the following June. He then hurried to the nearby station where he waited twenty minutes for a train to New Malden - and it was only when he got there, in the waiting room, that he tackled the ham sandwiches he'd brought with him. He also glanced at a discarded copy of the 'Metro' newspaper and purchased a hot coffee from the station buffet. Finally, he returned to the waiting room where, between that moment and his emergence into the town centre, his mind was occupied by matters having little bearing on the day's other, perhaps equally unremarkable events.

* * *

Apart from a number of far-eastern food shops catering for the local Korean community, it's hard to describe New Malden as anything other than a drab and nondescript suburb of Greater London in which, having scoured all the charity shops with no pleasant surprises to add to his collection of Victorian glass, Paul boarded the third bus of the day, this time to the similarly bleak backwaters of Worcester Park where, before beginning an investigation of the high street, he paused for a moment of quiet reflection on the muddy path overlooking a public recreation ground.

In themselves, he had no interest either in recreation grounds or in sports generally. However, it was in this particular recreation ground, between the thirties and late fifties of the last (the twentieth) century, that his lean, rather spinster-like aunt Ethel had spent most of her Saturday afternoons watching the football or the cricket accompanied by her pleasant, somewhat docile husband, Billy, whose permanently flushed cheeks and amiable grin Paul still remembered. It was a regular form of leisure activity, endlessly repeated, that remained at the very heart of their togetherness until, in the natural course of events, they died, one after the other, leaving behind them no offspring to cherish their memory. And so, as always on his occasional trips to Worcester Park, and now more than fifty years after the two of them were reunited in a better place (or so Paul trusted), he paused to say a prayer for the souls of Ethel and William Clarke.

The sun was generous that morning with its brilliant, late autumn light; the wind had dropped; and he encountered both stillness and melancholy when confronted by the sheer indifference of the passing years as he thought about that unremarkable couple and the fact that he was the only person left alive to remember them. To Paul's way of thinking and prompted by hindsight, the recreation ground, despite the radiance of the autumn sun, assumed the character of a wasteland lingering mournful yet unmindful of that pair of virtual nobodies who, to all intents and purposes, could just as well never have existed.

In due course, he moved on. He left the past behind him; he resumed the present, and he reentered the twenty first century as it saw fit to present itself in the lacklustre guise of Worcester Park's shopping area. As a person with a decidedly sweet tooth and an eye for a bargain, he bought a large Toblerone in the branch of Poundland at the foot of the hill. After which, without the slightest glimpse of anything worthwhile in the charity shops, he made his way to the railway station where, after an extremely tedious fifteen minutes, he was whisked off in a reassuringly spick-and-span carriage to the busier environment of Wimbledon where he braved unexpected rain and a sudden cold wind without encountering anything other than disappointment in Oxfam, Cancer Research and several other charity shops strung out along the lower section of the main road known as The Broadway.

* * *

Back at Wimbledon station, after a very short, sharp and not-all-that-sweet walk up and down the crowded, soaking wet pavements, Paul then leapt on to another train and travelled two stops on to Southfields where, in surroundings even drabber than New

Malden, having unsuccessfully scoured a further two charity shops, he purchased a large wedge of pâté de campagne and a baguette from the excellent French delicatessen which was one of only two plus-points in that neighbourhood. From the other, a British butcher just a few doors away, he then bought two steak and kidney pies whose like he'd sampled previously and judged far more appetising than their supermarket rivals which experience told him were generally more than half crust with predominantly fluid fillings containing one or two dubious nuggets of whatever sort of pie it was supposed to be. Just enough, he considered, to conform with the Trade Descriptions Act!

Paul's next move was to take advantage of the bus service to Wandsworth where the charity shops joined the ranks of the day's similar disappointments elsewhere - after which, this time on an overcrowded double-decker, he set out for Putney where, after two more charity shops and a bottle of Schweppes bitter lemon obtained from Sainsbury's, he discovered that somewhere between there and Wandsworth, he'd lost the righthand lens of his reading glasses which he'd been using on and off for a variety of purposes such as scrutinising price tags or bus-stop timetables.

* * *

This proved something of a pivotal moment; and it was then, more than at any other time during the course of his travels, that Paul's heart sank! At the conclusion of seemingly endless foot-slogging punctuated by a few admittedly comfortable intervals on public transport, it came as a shock to lose something on which he was so heavily dependent. But despite being tired as well as frustrated, he made up his mind to deal with the problem instantly by taking a train back to home ground where he called in at his regular optician. And it was there that good luck soon restored his equanimity when the process of replacing the lost lens was undertaken without a hitch. Cheered up by a promise that the repair would be complete within a few days, he left the premises with a spring in his step accompanied by the words 'mission accomplished' ringing in his ears. It was rather like a wartime air-raid siren sounding the 'all clear' after the enemy has finally returned to base!

Determined to offset the inconvenience of being without reading glasses for a day or two, Paul dodged nimbly in and out of the traffic, reached the other side of the main road and slipped into a conveniently placed supermarket where he grabbed the bottle of gin he'd forgotten at the Putney Sainsbury's. He then boarded his last bus of the day, reached home, and closed the door behind him. It was a relief to find himself once again in such a comfortable, trouble-free environment where, in response to a sudden impulse and within reach of a well filled glass, he sat down on the sofa and cast his mind back over the many ups and downs he'd encountered since he first boarded the number 33 at twenty to nine that morning!

And after a few sips of gin and bitter lemon to soothe his nerves, it all seemed a very long time ago.

* * *

But there was more to be considered in this somewhat parochial set of circumstances than the simple recollection of time spent out and about in southwest London. 'Parochial' is one way of describing it. But at the end of such a protracted series of events, the odd perception he'd so often experienced throughout his life struck Paul once again with renewed force at the precise moment when, still mulling over the day's twists and turns, he happened to notice the time.

He was instantly amazed. And what amazed him was the discovery that it was still only half past three. In the light of his experience, as he looked back at similar busy days with their humdrum character occasionally varied by unexpected surprises, it would have taken until evening to complete the same sum total of activity which, by mid afternoon, he'd managed to accomplish without even noticing it. Indeed, on this exceptionally remarkable occasion, Paul was more impressed than he'd ever been in the past: for it looked as if he'd travelled in double-quick time through a succession of so many disparate worlds that some unaccountable influence must have altered whatever it is that the hands of a clock, *any* clock, are supposed to be measuring!

MAN ABOUT TOWN

Mr Nigel Atkinson, aged seventy six, was keeping abreast of life on planet earth by pausing in the short-term No Alcohol Zone at Piccadilly Circus under the oblivious eye of Eros who was discharging an arrow whilst an improbably obliging wind covered his private parts with a loose strip of clothing.

Looking like a swarm of bees and chattering like budgerigars, groups of tourists were sprawled all over the steps beneath this famously iconic landmark. Adopting the casual postures typical of youth, most of them were blissfully unaware of those older visitors whose dress code was similar to their own but absurdly out of keeping with their greater age and outlines. For all that, profusely vivid colour and informality of appearance added charm to a crowd of holidaymakers some of whom overdid their efforts to look younger than they really were.

Disregarding his years despite some unavoidable evidence of stiff joints, Nigel Atkinson sat down with the loungers on the dirty steps, casually eavesdropped on their conversations and gazed vacantly at an old Chinaman feeding the feral pigeons. And as time wore on, he found himself feeling at an agreeable loss: busy lives were milling all around him; yet although he was conscious of being fundamentally alone, he nevertheless drew energy from the colour, the fascinating range of ethnicities and from the general youthfulness, largely benign, which he was pleased to observe as if it were a technicolour film - and one which happily cost him nothing! Consequently, on a sunny afternoon at a loose end and with nothing better to do, the crowds seemed somehow to be living his life *for* him. In fact, an awareness of this vicarious circumstance flashed briefly through his own unfocussed mind and then dissolved into the summery air all around him.

Gradually, he began to feel almost as if he too were away on holiday like the free spirits on which he cast a casual eye as they slumped at all angles on the hard paving. But he also felt pleasantly relieved at not having to socialise with people whom he thought he might find exhausting at close quarters - but who otherwise enhanced and enlivened an afternoon outing that kept him quietly entertained.

Later on, when the sun resumed its brilliance after about ten minutes simulating a bank holiday Monday, Mr Nigel Atkinson was sufficiently at ease to imagine himself on a weekend break in Paris - minus the attendant anxiety about travel arrangements. Then, as successive groups of cyclists sailed past in disorderly flotillas, he dreamed of sunning himself on the banks of the Seine; and the thought of returning home to his perfectly comfortable flat in West London gave rise to a depressingly accurate reminder of the Monday morning blues in those far-off days before his retirement!

LUCY

Slouching on the seat of a London underground carriage, Miss Lucy Frampton, once a pretty young girl about the quiet lanes of Hurtwood, now looks as crumpled and forlorn as she feels. She has never married and has ended up living alone in a Stockwell bedsit where she feels no hankering for the sunny backwaters of her childhood home where, to this day, only the absence of the cuckoo signals those changes she is too worn out to notice.

WORLDS APART

In the back yard of the unknown, there is a hill too steep for climbers where outcrops of chalk breach the surface like waterfalls frozen in time as they extend vertically downwards through the forest, parting the dense mass of the trees whose wild domain has never been challenged. There, in the impenetrable darkness, I hear the crackle of dry leaves trodden by unseen feet; and I sense a hollowness made light of by the woodpecker's madcap yaffle.

Within the forest's vastness, in its eerie chambers, there are comings and goings no one has ever set eyes on: randomly distributed centres of wordless thought that make little noise and shine no light in the gloom… And yet, there they are, those minute specks of awareness, forever active beneath the billowing cumulus of the treetops.

And now, all of a sudden, there is a deadly silence in that feral province where deciduous variation and seasonal outburst mingle with the changeless foliage of the yews that halt at the foot of the slope where a stream, as clear as glass, quietly transports a fallen leaf whose motion is the only measure of time. But beyond, in that closeted realm, there are no such yardsticks or devices. Safe on the far side of the furthest bank, an ancient presence still lingers, unaffected by the alien, far-off bluster of engines.

For transient man, those primaeval slopes are out of bounds; and yet they offer enduring consolation beneath the ragged outlines of the high canopy whose green bonfires tremble at the sound of voices that no one can hear.

JO VAN BUREN

Like his mother, Jo van Büren was as English as a bank holiday Monday... and of uniquely eccentric character. But although the eccentric Englishman is an acknowledged commonplace, Jo was a far from commonplace eccentric.

He never realised I knew who he was. And although our paths crossed from time to time, no word or look was ever exchanged, since he rigorously shunned all human contact - indeed, the truth is that Jo van Büren lived for at least twenty years alone in a tent on Hampstead Heath where I discreetly observed his comings and goings.

I had long known of the carefully concealed tent in a wooded depression. Quite often, laundry was left hanging from near-by branches... and as the tent-flaps were sometimes left open, I occasionally caught sight of folded-up blankets, stacks of plastic bags and other more personal items such as the tube of toothpaste projecting neatly from a plain white mug. On the other hand, it was a matter of some months before I finally concluded that one recurrent passer-by of repeatedly downcast gaze was the hitherto unidentified 'wild man of the heath'.

Jo van Büren survived all those years of unpredictable weather because, despite his rough and ready lifestyle, he fell just short of penury. Unexpected sightings in the busy high street nearby showed that he worked as a road-sweeper... and amazingly that he submit-ted to occasional human contact late on Fridays at the local branch of Lloyds Bank.

* * *

But change inexorably beset the heath. Jo's tent suddenly disappeared without trace; and a full year passed until, wandering home at dusk, I heard what sounded like a news bulletin coming from somewhere in the gloom of a thicket where curiosity uncovered a softly glowing tent battened down for the night whose sole occupant was listening (as he did for many months thereafter) to a Dutch-speaking radio station. It appeared, then, that Jo van Büren of no fixed abode was still the same citizen of planet earth, and was possessed of hitherto unsuspected qualifications.

Sadly, however, Jo has vanished again. Two years have passed and he has not been seen. No photo has appeared in the Missing Persons charity shops - because no photo exists. And no individual has reported him missing because nobody knew him personally. The Corporation has gone so far as to inform the police, but no body corresponding to that of Jo van Büren has been found on the heath or anywhere else. Jo van Büren is profoundly missing - and strangely, he is profoundly missed.

* * *

The reason Jo has not been found - and never *will* be - is because in a very real sense he *is* nowhere to be found. He does not *wish* to be found - nor *can* he be, for Jo has withdrawn to an impenetrable forest far to the south. There at last he has found a friend; it is the only friend he has ever really wanted - a friend in whose gift lies the ultimate solace of loneliness.

A FRIENDLY ENQUIRY

Mr Phillip Allcock had a very high opinion of himself - an understandable necessity in the light of the very small number of acquaintances who shared it. He also had an exaggerated confidence in his ability to manipulate circumstance such that he often continued to conceal those aspects of his life which everyone knew about already.

Mr Phillip Allcock persistently aspired to high office - a factor often associated with persons of under-average height who by dint of trying sometimes obtain a position of authority over their betters who, being aware of the fact, are prone to snigger or to kick each other's shins under the table after an amusing faux pas in the board room.

But Mr Phillip Allcock, in defence of his own dignity when under fire, was seldom lost for words. Faced with awkward truths, he was a convincing and bare-faced fibber to the point that artful colleagues out for a laugh (or revenge) were sometimes reduced to doubting their own testimonies.

On one particular occasion, in pursuit of an evening's 'alternative' entertainment after widespread rumours, Mr Phillip Allcock was tracked by associates to a dingy backstreet pub where he was secretly observed carrying on an out-of-hours relationship with a somewhat junior female subordinate.

A smiling Mr Allcock, confronted the next day with the evidence of an exhilarated eyewitness, nevertheless flatly denied the allegation in its entirety. And in a curiously backhanded way, this effrontery immediately evolved into a more jovial set of relations.

Initiated by the enterprising gentlemen who had provided the conclusive evidence, a greeting under cover of a friendly enquiry was formulated which soon gained general currency. Mr Phillip Allcock responded warmly, and seemed to feel he had at last gained an appropriate level of recognition when anyone asked him the following million-dollar question.

'O good morning, Phil', they used to say, 'has anything interesting happened recently which you'd like to deny'?

And it was laughter all round as Mr Phillip Allcock sailed serenely into his study, trailing an ambiguous yet smiling 'no' dissolving into a 'maybe' or a 'yes' behind him!

TYPICAL OF HER CLASS

At an exhibition of paintings by Vilhelm Hammershøi, and as part of the written introduction to a particular portrait, the advice of Walter Sickert was quoted to the effect that the only authentic way to treat working class women was not only to depict them dressed in their customary manner but also to present them in their every-day environment. To act otherwise would be a distortion of reality.

The introduction then moved on from Sickert's recommendations and launched into a detailed analysis of the portrait itself. And this naturally reflected the curator's individual attitudes at a point in time very different from that of the sitter and the artist who painted her.

* * *

Dated 1908, the portrait represented an East End coster girl fresh from the London streets where she purveyed fruit and vegetables in all weathers just over a century ago.

Visitors to the exhibition were privileged to glimpse this young woman at home, attired in the flat, black straw hat described in the text as being typical of her class; and the caption, with a certain presumption, also mentioned her blank look of resignation to the run-down domestic circumstances in which she found herself...

More than a hundred years later on, however, I have seen surround-ings far more run-down than pink floral wallpaper by a marble fireplace. And on a daily basis, I observe far sorrier sights than that of this modest-looking young girl.

The same hat referred to above as typical of a social class would have been better described in terms of its elegant proportions, neatly crowning carefully tied-back hair. Her dimly lit face conceivably illustrated poverty - but showed not a trace of disorderliness. Her dress was inclusive of a notably high collar. And her hands drooped unpretentiously over loosely sketched knees.

The house she lived in was inevitably rented. And in it she survived both world wars, scraped a living into her seventies and was buried with the simple anglican rites typical, in those days, not only of *her* class but also of wider society...

Unfortunately, by the time she died, she was completely overwhelmed by the changes affecting *all* classes - changes that were increasingly visible everywhere on the streets of a city she could no longer recognise in an age when nostalgia was deemed naïve as well as politically questionable.

Sadly unnamed, she is already long forgotten; even the whereabouts of her grave is a mystery. But her image survives, as fresh now as on the day it was painted.

UNFAMILIAR GROUND

I could still hear the old priest's voice as I strolled downhill through a wooded section of the park towards an area of open meadowland not far from the river. Father David had died quite recently. He had been greatly revered during his lifetime; and now that he was gone, the inevitable result was that many parishioners still looked back with nostalgia at his whimsical, head-in-the clouds sermons - sermons, and a mindset most evident in the confessional, which gave the impression that he was already half way to the object of his desire where uncertainty is dirty word. And for that reason, if for no other, his death at a respectable old age appeared less of a tragedy: in a weird sort of way, we all knew he was taking his leave many years before he finally bade farewell as the bishop celebrated his requiem in the presence of a packed congregation.

It was recognised that his replacement of only three months' standing, Father Rippon, was a good man and a man destined to be an effective parish priest. But somehow, he had so far failed to arouse the admiration accorded to his predecessor. His sermons were competent and orthodox - but sadly, somewhat on the dry side when compared to what people had got used to. And for the time being at least, many among Father David's surviving flock yearned to hear more, not less about the mystics and visionaries who for so long had illuminated their grasp of christian history - not to mention their traditional picture of the Kingdom of Heaven.

I have to admit that, as I continued my stroll through the woods among the flickering leaf-shadows cast by the sun, I was myself in sympathy with those who felt an undiminished desire for a glimpse of the world that lies beyond the here and now. Fresh from mass, I was perfectly at ease on a sunny day in an environment which, not to beat about the bush, seemed to have more affinity with Father David's visions than with Father Rippon's pleas on behalf of a local charity. From the moral standpoint, I may not have had a leg to stand on. But when I looked around me, it was Father David's words emerging from within that seemed best able to interpret my own experience of reality.

'Today, my dear people', I heard him say, 'the wind is in thought-mode - the enabling device for informed exchange on this pleasant May afternoon. It is already in rapt conversation with the birches and the limes which remain indifferent to mortality whilst still in early leaf and under the influence, strong as alcohol, of the wisteria's comforting scent'.

'Children of God', the voice went on 'the wind thinks deeply but speaks without articulation of words. It is exploring among the boughs two profound mysteries: namely, the incomprehensibility of time which it carries along in procession from the past… and with a sound like running water which for now remains its chief vehicle of expression mediated by the sibilance of the leaves'.

'My friends, I remind you that today, like every other day, is a *particular* day on which the sun that shines so benignly will never shine again. Therefore let your nostrils absorb the scent of flowers and the ligneous odour like walnut husks exhaled by rotting logs'.

I knew, of course, that it was myself rather than anyone else who was thinking these things; but it was still Father David who was giving voice to the words. I looked around me; I carried on with my walk. And I let the sound-patterns reach me from whatever source they might be coming.

'For a brief while', (surely it was Father David speaking to me now), 'notice there is a lull as if the wind has been constrained by a vow of silence. I hear the cracked voices of an ageing couple… seated on a bench…in thrall to recollection. And I draw your attention to the blades of the mower lopping the dandelions' yellow flower-heads that will burst forth again presently like an Easter Proclamation'.

A warning came next - thankfully bereft of anything by way of menace.

'Pause therefore, all of you, on the brink of another age; inscribe your petitions on the headstones by the tower. And attend in detail so that you can hear the toings-and-froings of forgotten lives that the breeze, once more, is quietly celebrating'.

SHADOW PLAY

Being by then shorn of its most wearisome hours, the day posed less of a challenge from which his inner self found cause to shield him. Consequently, his tensions subsided and his drowsiness lessened while seemingly baseless anxieties were absorbed in the sultry, quiet gloom of the redwood shadows.

Quiet... Quiet was for him an ever-recurrent remedy now working its magic among leaning trunks and down-slanting boughs obscured by the needlelike leaves through which he glimpsed occasional solitary figures: the woman with a pram who strayed too close; the old man who ambled past, unaware of the observer seated nearby on a bench; the elderly widow who enquired at what time the park would close; the couple whose bored-looking son wore a blue t-shirt and glasses; and vignettes of picnicking families seen through gaps in the foliage.

* * *

At last, with his head resting in his hands, Norman fell into a reverie: he was struck by the fact that he'd never before cast eyes on those strangers he'd observed buried in their private worlds as they crossed his field of vision; and he acknowledged he was unlikely ever to see again those unidentified day-trippers whose voices floated on the summer air. He watched them drifting slowly away; and noticed how their faces brightened and grew dim again as they passed from light into shade... and then vanished altogether.

WEEKEND BREAK

I

On board the 08:10 from London Charing Cross to Ramsgate it was spring all the way. Trees in the first flush of youth that lined the tracks from right to left glowed resolutely green despite a lingering mist that changed a completely cloudless sky from blue to an almost equally benevolent ivory.

Against this agreeable background, as the train halted half an hour into the journey at Sevenoaks, a youngish gentleman whose dignity was not enhanced by three-quarter-length shorts was thwarted by the guard in his attempt to make it as far as Ramsgate without buying a ticket.

Both parties to the encounter instinctively adopted a breezy approach designed to clothe an indictable offence in the garb of routine fare-collection. This device was intensified as soon as the young man's first suggestion for solving the problem posed by inadequate funds had been shot down.

Eventually, after the devil-may-care handover of a rather tawdry assortment of coins and banknotes, incidental enquiries were made as to the expected arrival time at Canterbury West - to which the answer given was 09:49. The youngish man in unsuitable shorts promptly followed this with a quick call on his mobile and then slumped into the corner of the seat for an interim nap.

Just as the train was approaching Canterbury, the guard, in pursuit of good customer relations, gently tapped the same young man on the shoulder, noting for the second time that he was not quite as youthful as his outfit was intended to suggest. His main concern, however, was to prevent the youngish man in unsuitable shorts from landing up in Ramsgate unable to pay a substantial surcharge.

Not long thereafter, at 11:05, the girlfriend of this resilient not-so-young adventurer took up a pre-arranged position on the Ramsgate platform while she awaited the 10:49 from Canterbury where her accomplice, with his distinguished portfolio of bedroom skills, had been obliged to disembark. And she had with her enough cash to bear out any assurances that might have been given to a guard in the subsequent train when his duties, in any case, were likely to be over and done with, so close to the scheduled arrival time in Ramsgate at 11:11.

2

Fortune at last favoured the ill-clad but confident commuter under a now perfectly blue sky - and no guard was encountered on the final lap of the journey. For good measure, too, it must be added that as both parties to the conspiracy leapt unscathed over the last hurdle, they were confident from experience that, as usual, the Ramsgate ticket barrier would be unmanned - a labour-saving measure based on the knowledge that the necessary checks are invariably carried out on board all trains from London Charing Cross and Victoria!

THE DUELLING GROUND

There are moments in the daily round when the only viable course of action is to do nothing - perhaps when you're tired after a swim; or in the midst of a long walk when you flop down on a convenient log. This is the moment when doing nothing is both a creative act and a needful concession to healthy living.

Take Matthew's leisurely afternoon on the Kenwood Estate, for example. Seated in the shade, surrounded by beech, birch and oak he has abandoned the day's endeavours in favour of recuperation. He is *doing* nothing, but is seeing and hearing much that escapes notice in the crowded streets far from this isolated spot.

Beneath his feet, the otherwise dark surface of the leaf mould is littered with medallions of sunlight; and in one of these, a winged insect of indescribable insignificance is basking in the only world it knows for what is probably the first and last day of its life. A green woodpecker, after an outburst of raucous laughter, has just flown off; and a blackbird, confronted by the glaring eyes of an owl, has shunted its chicks out of the way to the accompaniment of high-pitched, agitated bleeps. But silence is the overall master: there is no wind, and the stillness of the green canopy imposes calm on this hilltop clearing which, as if to shatter illusions, served as a duelling ground in times not long gone.

Matthew is fully aware that the painter, John Constable, was once a regular presence on the surrounding heath where he was memorably persuaded to wield his brush. He is therefore in good company when the outward tranquillity slowly dissolves the uneasiness which, until this moment, was building up inside him. And his mood is further softened when a bee, flying like a bullet in a straight line, ignites and annihilates like a virtual particle as it snags a beam of photons in the sombre woods.

Thus far, not a single soul has passed Matthew on his makeshift seat in this fortress garrisoned by sturdy trunks. No one has spotted the ageing man of nondescript appearance whose thinning hair obstinately refuses to turn grey. And there is no one to take notice as he looks and listens.

Beyond the woods, a dog barks; and closer to home, the fall of a single leaf is surprisingly audible as it strikes a fence. The distant noise of an aircraft drones on in praise of summer; and patches of sunlight creep across the shadowy ground as the planet revolves. Matthew has indeed behaved sensibly; he has finished his contemplations and has shared them with no one. For him, here and for a brief moment of time, beauty has been dispensed unsparingly by the unseen hand of one who alone is of any consequence.

STORM IN A TEACUP

For the various organisms that live there, storms in teacups can be cataclysmic events - a fact clear to me as a general proposition and confirmed by my present vantage point, here, seated at the edge of a wood from which I am gazing lazily at a broad hillside bristling with tall grasses. The field is bounded on its farthest side by a long line of oaks; and above them, peacefully motionless, is a single white cloud in a blue sky that is otherwise quite empty. There is no disturbance to be seen anywhere; and nothing I can think of would add to such perfect harmony.

Relative to the shallow enclave at the forest edge where I am lounging on a bench, the field of corn-coloured grasses seems enormous. It is currently bereft of all human presence and the only sign of life is the occasional, somewhat drunken motion of a cabbage white butterfly - which seems to tell us that, today, all purposeful action belongs elsewhere. Otherwise, the simplicity and quietness of this mid-July morning creates a picture of well-being that embodies, in its entirety, the present time and place. We therefore have a teacup without a storm.

To the right of the shadows that are keeping me cool, the picture is very different among the brambles whose disorderly clumps are drenched in sunlight and covered with blossoms at all stages of development from unopened bud through to full flower and on to the incipient green berries. Here, the teacup is a scene of lively activity carried out by a multitude of pollinators which, although they are mainly varieties of bee, are apparently untainted by the infection that threatens them elsewhere. In this spot at least, not a single floret is left unvisited: and over and above the sound of wind among the trees, there is the constant, cumulative drone of insect wings that vibrate too rapidly to be visible.

I have a suspicion there is dampness hereabouts; and I now recall that just behind me beyond the tree line, there is something whose description as a stream would be an exaggeration. But its presence is enough to explain why a blue damselfly, its body as long and as slender as a darning needle, has settled on a blade of grass close to its life-support system. I also notice the first hints of purple on the tall spikes of willowherb. And amidst the general comings and goings, I rather sympathise with the plight of that butterfly, its wings the colour of powdered rust, which has just been driven from its perch by a wasp.

* * *

All is seemingly at peace in this pleasant, tucked-away little spot which I regard as a microcosm of the planet itself as it travels through the darkness that surrounds it... But perhaps I have spoken too soon, now that an aircraft, with unwelcome suddenness, has cut across the blue canopy overhead like the angel of death.

Not only is there a disturbance in the sky; at ground level, too, trouble is brewing in the thicket behind me where a pair of black-birds is sounding the alarm. I can hear the whirr of their wings as they swoop from branch to branch in a desperate effort to defend their young; and as I peer through the flickering layers of green and black, light and dark, there is a sudden, fast-moving onrush of feet through the dry leaves and the snap of breaking twigs as some sinister, barely visible, unidentifiable prowler darts in and out of sight amidst the tangle of wild vegetation. The timescale is short; and now, my ears are being assaulted by the fluid, choking cries of pain that come to an abrupt end after a minute or two's dreadful suffering that seems like an age; and only later, having passed its climax, does the shrill fortissimo of parental complaint begin gradually to subside into intermittent, disconsolate bleeps as the bereaved pair, hopping from one twig to another, seek comfort through instinctive activity.

* * *

Like nature red in tooth and claw, the storm in all its ruthlessness has come and gone and will soon be forgotten. Things are now seemingly just as they were: the bees are still busily buzzing; and with comparable optimism, the willowherb's early purple tells us that autumn, though only a distant prospect, is nevertheless on its way and should be welcomed when it finally comes.

Some may regard the whole episode as a storm in a teacup. But is this perhaps a teacup that was, and indeed still is, a sign of uncertain significance in an unexceptional yet idyllic backwater on a mysterious globe orbiting around its sun in a galaxy that is nowhere in particular in a universe that is nowhere at all?

Whichever way one looks at it, such reflections imply an almost limitless degree of strangeness; and perhaps this familiar backwater, once again at peace, is as great a mystery as quantum mechanics, wave/particle duality or the invisible dark matter that forms the greater, yet most elusive, portion of the cosmos!

Kenwood Estate, N. London. A more or less factual account of twenty minutes spent on the southern fringe of West Meadow.

Cabbage white butterflies: the large white and/or the small white, pieris brassicae and artogeia rapae.

Damselfly: common blue damselfly, enallagma cyathigerum.

Willowherb: rosebay willowherb, epilobium angustifolium.

Wings the colour of powdered rust: comma butterfly, polygonia c-album.

Nature, red in tooth and claw: Tennyson, In Memoriam A.H.H.

THE SADNESS OF NUALA SINGLETON

Nuala Singleton was pale faced, smooth skinned and had fair hair which was cut short and looked boyish - though there was no hint of masculinity with or without any further implications. She was nervous and shy in manner, obliging in her dealings and eager to be helpful despite the impression of remoteness arising from her quiet way of speaking.

The library in which she worked was poorly lit; and the electrical economies there led to conditions which were environmentally friendly to a high degree and in consequence depressingly stygian. On top of this, the November afternoon was profoundly grey, moody and inclined to drizzle - all of which influences had their effect on Nuala's workspace where she sat checking books in and out or answering the phone. Never a dull moment, you might have said in irony if you'd been there - for when there were no other distractions, the computer screen fully occupied her time as she quietly tapped away at the keyboard.

A young man called Ben who was studying English literature approached the desk. He had a short dark beard, a vague little moustache and deep brown, almond-shaped eyes with a faraway look that gave an almost buddhist impression of tranquillity although, actually, he was a nominal catholic of Spanish descent. This hint of passivity in his character served the moment well because as soon as he reached the counter, the phone rang; and since the other two assistants were chatting in the adjacent office, he had to wait while Nuala obligingly sorted out the caller's request for an extended time limit on a borrowed book.

Being in no hurry and having the easy-going disposition discernible in his features, Ben spent the interval examining Nuala's apparently timid demeanour. He was struck by the overemphatic willingness of her telephone manner and by the way she repeatedly nodded agreement with the invisible caller to whom she spoke so quietly that he wondered whether her voice was audible at the other end of the line. But it was only when he was several minutes into his reflections that he realised that what had primarily aroused his interest was the fact that she was holding the telephone receiver with a Kleenex tissue at a short but significant distance from her ear lobe.

Nuala's behaviour was very little different when it came to signing out Ben's copy of Douglas Dunn's New Selected Poems. She began with the briefest glance of friendly acknowledgement during which their eyes scarcely had time to meet. This was followed by rapt attention to screen and keyboard as she accessed his membership page. A few more taps and a jab with the electronic sensor furthered the requisite process; but the high point in the transaction came when she printed '10.12.14' on the slip facing the inside cover: Ben noticed with astonishment - he could hardly have missed it - that she carefully gripped the date stamp with a Kleenex tissue just as she had done with the telephone… and with the same fastidious misgiving.

Ben thanked her with a warmth of expression that fell short of intimacy and moved off. He then briefly flipped through some of the leaflets in a dispenser near the exit; and finally, as he pushed open the double swing doors, he looked back over his shoulder and noticed the mournful remnants of a smile on Nuala's face as she hurriedly averted her eyes.

MR JAMES SUTCLIFFE
IN MEMORY OF CAPTAIN MAINWARING

Mr James Sutcliffe doesn't like to be on the receiving end of information. It makes him feel demoted and undervalued. He finds it at variance with the standing he not only feels he has earned, but to which he also believes he was born - factors that carry with them an appeal for explicit acknowledgement. Consequently, he is likely to respond brusquely to being informed. And he is not above anticipating what's coming by interrupting his interlocutor with the information he has hurriedly surmised - thus preserving his reputation as the fount of all wisdom. He is also inclined to assert the exact opposite of statements made to him - ignoring the possibility that the bewildered speaker has relied on solid supporting evidence. And under these circumstances, any hint that he's made a fool of himself angers Mr James Sutcliffe more than almost anything else.

Mr James Sutcliffe is a retired bank manager and local Conservative Party activist who defected from Labour following the purchase of his second, grander residence. He is therefore accustomed, in a small way, to being looked up to; and in retirement, he expects more rather than less of the same. Accordingly, he satisfies his craving for admiration each year by inviting a group of friends to dine aboard a Thames pleasure boat. And these dinners are undoubtedly excellent, although the company errs on the drab side. But James is no fool and instinctively understands that his unexceptional speeches in the ears of such flatlanders are bound to evoke respect. And if it suits him on such occasions, he is sometimes emboldened to dish out his remarks in ways calculated to shame or irritate one or other of his guests (seeing this, ironically, as a feather in his cap)... After all, a lifetime of experience has taught him that most men are fools - and that it takes an exceptional dude such as Mr James Sutcliffe to knock some sense into them!

THE NEPALESE PAVILION

A portly gentleman had acquired a rip in the back of his trouser leg. This occurred when a chair-stroke-artwork collapsed under his weight in the absurdly flimsy Nepalese Pavilion designed by a prize-winning Italian architect as a temporary structure and erected in one of Liverpoool's public spaces.

The embarrassed gentleman sustained no injuries, was repositioned on an identical chair by two quick-acting junior assistants, and was then subjected to voluble expressions of regret.

After some protraction, a manager was called who professed further heartfelt concern - and then withdrew in double-quick time from the scene of his manifest insincerity.

* * *

It was at this point that the rip came to light after the gentleman's attention was drawn to it by a thoughtful observer. This occasioned great consternation whereupon, through the medium of a flashy mobile, an assistant secured the manager's immediate return.

The previous conversation was then resumed, although embellished this time round by somewhat livelier gesticulation… whereafter the disgruntled pair withdrew to a private office for further discussion with the top brass.

Almost inevitably, the incident ended in rancour, a banged fist and threats of legal action when, although phrased in the most delicate language, the injured party was asked whether he could prove that the rip had *not* originated prior to the accident with the chair.

PICCADILLY LINE

If, on the one hand, you are acquainted with the ups and downs of the London Underground and, on the other hand, are inclined to philosophical reflection, you would have had a unique opportunity to consider these two disparate areas on one particular afternoon aboard a Piccadilly line train bound for Heathrow Airport. And if you were entertaining ongoing concerns about the durability of truth in relation to the arrow of time, your situation would have been even more fortunate.

The events I refer to occurred in early March 2008 on a westbound train whose stop at Piccadilly Circus was showing unwelcome signs of protraction - a plain fact that soon dawned on the many passengers… not least on those with a plane to catch. You would then have heard an announcement via the platform PA system in the customary, somewhat stilted style of language; furthermore, the train being stationary, you would have had the unusual advantage of being able to hear the words without cupping your ears or giving up altogether. The message was very short - and not all that sweet. I remember it distinctly.

Ladies and gentlemen, we are ahead of schedule, and there will be a brief delay at this station.

* * *

The same announcement was repeated at intervals several times whilst the appropriateness of the word 'brief' became more and more questionable - a fact articulated by the censorious looks on the passengers' faces. The impression was reinforced by snappy glances at watches and a certain amount of fidgeting on the part of travellers who were already anxious about reaching their destinations in accordance with tight schedules. There were also some wordless, eyeball-to-eyeball exchanges in response to the next official bulletin which was straight to the point and clearly at variance with the account given previously.

Ladies and gentlemen, we are now waiting for the train ahead of us to clear the platform at Green Park. We will be moving on in a few minutes, and I will keep you informed.

* * *

A long silence followed, lasting well over five minutes during which there was a perceptible heightening of tension in the carriage where I happened to be sitting. Facial expressions were now blacker than before, inspections of watches were more prolonged; and an exchange of whispers began to take place - productive, in some quarters of the beginnings of group solidarity with a potential for militant action.

On top of the general dismay, among some of the less mature passengers there was also an outpouring of colourful nouns and adjectives which, apart from a couple of disdainful looks, caused much burying of faces in newspapers. The interlude was then interrupted by a further announcement which, although strictly compatible with its predecessor, was as imprecise as it was thoroughly unhelpful - at which point two passengers lost patience and left the compartment.

Ladies and gentlemen, there has been an incident on board the train at Green Park, and the police have taken charge of the situation. We will be moving on as soon as matters are sorted out. Transport for London wishes to apologise for any inconvenience.

* * *

Following this, there was a further five or six minute pause terminating in another very disappointing announcement which led to a great deal of cursing and agitation accompanied by a mass exodus from the train and several minutes of confused gazing up and down the platform. Given the content of the message, this was not at all surprising.

Ladies and gentlemen, I regret we have no further information while the police are pursuing their enquiries. You are therefore advised to continue your journey by alternative means. Passengers en route to Heathrow Airport should travel to Paddington from platform 1 via the Bakerloo line. Your tickets will be accepted on the Heathrow Express.

* * *

Whilst the exodus continued, leaving those who remained behind focussed on various forms of literature, a young man rose to his feet with an expression on his face which told me that those without a pressing engagement might be in for a treat. Contrary to any obvious stereotype and notwithstanding the bottle in his hand, he was well dressed, owned a briefcase and wore a smart grey suit enhanced by an exceedingly belligerent tie. His cheeks were unnaturally red, it has to be admitted; his smile was provokingly mischievous - and in a move to hide embarrassment, his companion was leaning forward with his head buried in his hands whilst the following creditable and confidently voiced imitation of an official announcement roused the remaining passengers from the pages of Pride and Prejudice, The Road to Wigan Pier and a broad range of newspapers!

Ladies and gentlemen, passengers proceeding to Heathrow Airport on the Heathrow Express will reach their destination in good time to discover by what margin they have missed their flights!

This story pre-dates the now established alcohol ban on the London underground.

SECOND CLASS CITIZEN

Miss Laura Tremayne, long-term resident of Camden Town, was on an old folks' coach trip to Kew Gardens where, amidst the exotica of a conservatory, her desire to read an information plaque about the history and benefits of the cocoa plant was being frustrated by a considerably taller and better dressed female visitor standing in front who was reading it at a dreadfully slow pace.

Miss Laura Tremayne, from her much lower vantage point some-what to the rear of her rival, was casting upward glances which, being unnoticed, completely failed to communicate her feelings to the object of irritation; and a feeble lunge forward was equally ineffective in dislodging the offender who carried on regardless. It is therefore unsurprising that by this time Miss Laura Tremayne was extremely agitated - a fact reflected in a red face with glinting blue eyes reminiscent of the parrots that share their Mexican home with the cocoa plant.

After a further frustratingly long interval, the root cause of annoyance made a leisurely exit without even noticing Miss Laura Tremayne who, thus deprived of the satisfaction of landing a censorious look and despite a now uninterrupted view of the plaque, was so furious that she walked off in a huff, having exhausted both the energy and the interest necessary in order to read it!

Cocoa (Theobroma Cacao): name taken from a Spanish/Nahuatl word originating in Southern Mexico.

A POINT OF NO RETURN

It is a fundamental error to identify
the latest with the best - and even worse
to confuse it with the truest.

M. H

On the afternoon of the fourteenth of October 2012 in Kensington Gardens, there was a large gathering of young people involved in an 'Art Marathon'. At the time under review, they had ceased progressing towards their destination, having come to a brief halt outside the Serpentine Gallery; and happening to be there, it suddenly struck me how the frenetic, antlike spectacle of their comings-and-goings among themselves betrayed an enthusiasm which was decisively out of tune with my own lukewarm curiosity. Neither was I in any way awed by the messianic zeal of a bunch of juveniles spearheading an attempt at social reform as though the arts were a recently discovered panacea.

Haranguing this eager crowd was a pleasant, hail-fellow-well-met, plumpish sort of chap fronting a getting-to-know-you, hi-ya-guys, we're-all-in-it-together bonding session. This took the form of a rather awkward, iffy sequence of verbal improvisations based on the name of each person as he or she yelled it out in response to a smile and a pointed finger. 'Brian', for example, evoked references to the film 'The Life of Brian'; and 'Robin' generated allusions to 'Robin Hood' and the 'Sheriff of Nottingham'. But given the number of clichés and weak jokes, forgivable perhaps in the light of the need for an instant response, I was embarrassed not only for the speaker but also for myself!

It wasn't long before I concluded that many of the placards draped around dedicated necks lacked both originality, deducible message -

or even straightforward English. I was particularly flummoxed by the following example, marker-penned by a bedraggled-looking youth with these words: 'I blow *my* nose. You blow *your* nose. So who's got it right?' For me at least, things had reached a point of no return, of ultimate inconsequence - and being not only embarrassed but bored, I decided it was time to move on.

Although continuing to feel somewhat nonplussed by slogans of this sort, I eventually broke free from the stultifying mood of pointlessness that pursued me and observed that the afternoon was exceptionally brilliant despite a wind with a very sharp edge to it. Something greater than local events seemed to inflate the atmosphere; and although the sunset was still a long way away, I nevertheless sailed off eagerly, if metaphorically, towards it - passing beneath the overhanging immensity of the London planes and then onwards until I came abreast of the Albert Memorial whose familiar embellishments met me with the reflected glint of gold and its reassuring complement of secondhand sunshine.

ALDERMAN BROWN'S RECEPTION

'It is amazing', said some long forgotten soul on his deathbed, 'that in so small a space so great a tragedy can occur'… words quoted by a friend who has now followed the deceased into the emptiness beyond the burning-ghats where I imagine him fighting shy of the further, personal tragedy of being born again… as somebody else.

Incoherently, this same voice from the past has suddenly resurfaced in my mind at Alderman Brown's reception where I stand alone with my own unimportance in the company of a broad cross-section of persons busily engaged in spurious self-congratulation or insinuating small talk.

* * *

But now that the town-hall worthies and unworthies alike are back at their desks earning their bread, here am I seated unaccompanied beside the sunlit surface of a pond where the dragonflies are as blue as heaven and the tawny skippers scavenge on the ragwort's swaying heads. All of these are my subordinates, and yet they are my lifelong companions as well. By heart I know their speeches; and that is why I feel no call to exercise superfluous influence whilst they jog along nicely and leave me peacefully at home in their quiet, enduring and ever-renewable presence.

URSULA MACFARLANE
SPINSTER OF THIS PARISH

Miss Ursula MacFarlane, though of slightly under-average height, is always exceedingly well dressed; and she always presents herself in explicitly female garments to the total exclusion of trousers. It is plainly important to her always to be of excellent appearance - and this she has regularly accomplished through her choice of the material, weave, pattern and cut of her clothes. In a personal world where haute couture plays such an important part, Miss Ursula MacFarlane chooses her connections carefully - and dress code is therefore an important factor among her criteria.

In the light of these pressing concerns, she has so far turned her back several times on a neighbour - the first instance being due to the fact that his attire reflected a busy morning at the allotment. On another occasion, she precipitately about-turned to face her front door as if she'd forgotten something just as the same gentleman was ducking behind a hedge in order to thwart the satisfaction it gave her to snub him!

* * *

Only a week after again falling into Miss Ursula MacFarlane on the steps of a charity shop in Leatherhead where greetings proved unavoidable, there was a further close encounter between the two parties at a 'thé dansant' attended by the local mayor and dignitaries in whose presence, being affronted by the formalities and the top-down pressures of status, Miss Ursula MacFarlane was minded to diminish her unimportance by handing round a smörgåsbord of snacks at the same time as munching a succession of smoked salmon and cucumber sandwiches with disturbing vulgarity and noise. Unsightly crumbs were also seen around her mouth, their presence underlined by a generous helping of lipstick.

Her conversation continued somewhat too volubly, with a nervous tremor underlying her voice. Clearly, Miss Ursula MacFarlane was not at ease when it came to socialising with well-placed persons above the rank of a John Lewis shop assistant or the frail pensioner-in-charge at a branch of Oxfam!

THE TALL STORIES OF GERHARD ROHM

I am sitting comfortably on a bench in Kew's Princess of Wales Conservatory during the annual Orchid Festival which, by any standard, is a joy. Despite this fact, however, and up to the point when my attention was forcibly transferred to the immediate environment, the exotic blooms all around me were merely incidental to the following circumstance in which I was absorbed.

Moments ago, although only briefly, I was attempting to read some equally brief pieces of creative prose translated by Deborah Jupp from the German of Gerhard Rohm. As the book's introduction collectively describes them, these 'fictions' trade heavily on the absurd in such a way that the stories turn back on themselves and self-destruct as they develop; and consequently, one tends to end up more or less where one started - namely, nowhere.

Unlike the author's acclaimed collection of fifty two tales, I favour a more straightforward and meaningful way of looking at things as my interest shifts - a process already begun in that I have abandoned Gerhard Rohm's pages in favour of the orchids to which I have just alluded in such glowing terms. Consequently, like a teenager in love, I am admiring the colourful flower-heads present on every side amongst the tropical foliage - a scene greatly enhanced by the brilliant February sun. February it certainly *is*, and so it *feels*, beyond the panes; but beneath the resilient membrane of glass above me, I am warm and increasingly at ease.

The result of my redirected interest is one of immediate liberation from a sense of disenchantment and pointlessness - and I am breath-ing more freely. Instead, my eyes are now focussed on a tiny child who is struggling to clamber up some steps in order to gaze into a fish pond. I also notice something else that I've frequently observed at other tourist hot spots: namely, the number of people taking photographs of various objects (today it's the orchids) at whose material reality they seldom look *directly*. Here too, in that omission, one can see an underlying current of pointlessness - at least until the images are viewed on a home computer. Today, of course, in a more forgiving vein, perhaps we should soft-pedal on the charge of pointlessness because I notice that, after all, some people *are* attending to what they see, albeit superficially and in passing, because they openly demonstrate the fact by means of finger-pointing and verbal exclamation.

The muse is therefore leading me to a positive conclusion rather than to the backward-facing reversals of Gerhard Rohm which I consider much less witty than the blurb on the book jacket would have me believe. Bathed in light, I feel growing optimism: I know that it's February; but the sun is shining. The orchids are gaudy (though some are exquisitely muted); and given that it's half term, there is heartening evidence of happy family lives all around me. In consequence, the picture is various and complex, but comforting. I shall not be returning to the fictions of Gerhard Rohm. Instead, I shall abandon myself to the marvels of nature - and to the contemplation of a nearby titan arum which evolved in the Sumatran jungle and whose flower, the biggest in the world, is taller than a man.

Gerhard Rohm: I have disguised the names of this book and its author because my object is to illustrate a psychological transition rather than to criticise another's work.

Titan arum, amorphophallus titanum. See 'A Year at Kew' by Rupert Smith with a foreword by Alan Titchmarsh, page 100. Published by BBC Books.

DARLING OF THE GODS

The darling of the gods was displaying his virility behind the bike sheds to an enthusiastic (if tremulous) onlooker. But an eagle-eyed gym mistress had spotted the proceedings and was herself observed taking down detailed particulars before reporting the matter to the headmaster.

'In future', said the headmaster, 'you have my full permission to put a stop to anything similar before things get so hopelessly out of hand again'!

A LESSON LEARNED

Before alighting from the train at Acton Town, one young man asked another young man for the time; but the second young man couldn't oblige because he had no watch and was too lazy to check on his mobile. The first young man then approached a third young man and said 'excuse me, mate, have you got the time?' He was in luck, was answered politely; and having at last achieved his objective, he disembarked without any further acknowledgement.

Now although this record of an observed event cannot be taken as an indictment of all young men (or young women, for that matter), it signals a lesson worth remembering in relation to discernible cultural change. When he was really up against it, this particular young man said 'excuse me, mate'; but as soon as he got what he wanted, he just made off without so much as a thankyou, a smile or even a glance in response. In other words, for him, the third young man was closer to a robot than he was to a real-life a person.

THE WILES OF WILLIAM CRAWLEY

Mr William Crawley, works manager at Barlowe & Higgins Seedsmen, had two nicknames - one that he knew about and one that he didn't. The one he knew about was Willy - and he rather liked it despite the obviously lewd undertone. This was because the mild humour running alongside the covert abuse made him feel, in a back-handed sort of way, that he was popular with his team - somewhat *more* popular, in fact, than was actually the case.

For William, the question of popularity was bound up with a fear of being undervalued; and this was an issue at the heart of his social relationships. The root cause was as simple as it was commonplace: namely, that being someone of under-average height, he was forever in need of reassurance - a need which at times resulted in behaviour that diminished rather than advanced his cause. He also had a struggle on his hands fighting off the effect on others of his premature bald patch - not to mention the comic aspects of dark and droopy eyebags which were taken as evidence of late nights and, rather unfairly as it happened, of loose living.

The overt symptoms of these underlying problems were many. In the first place, William had a tenacity in pursuit of his various goals which irritated those he came up against along the way. In his eagerness to excel, he was also a stickler for exactitude which he viewed, somewhat too openly, as a source of pride. And incidentally, this latter tendency also provided him with a very useful tool when the question was one of money! For example, in the works canteen when touched for the loan of a few pence by colleagues in the lunch queue, he was known to impose a deadline for restitution on the grounds of some spurious private circumstance. And the unfortunate borrower, if he or she strayed more than a few hours beyond the agreed time, was subtly reminded of Nelson's famous remark about an Englishman's duty!

A much more telling incident, however, consisted of a one-off, niggardly gesture in the not-too-distant past which proved a massive giveaway as well as a fertile source of ridicule on the part of everyone acquainted with William Crawley. The story which became a legend and was passed on to all newcomers, was this: that having once agreed to transport some friends on a day trip to Norfolk, he had not only accepted the price of the petrol (which was reasonable) but had also requested an additional sum to cover wear-and-tear on the car!

All of these foibles, and many more like them, had given rise to the second nickname of which Willy was *not* aware - even though he guessed he was under fire when a huddle of sniggering workmates, well out of earshot, were referring to him not as *Willy* but as *Creepy Crawley*. This, of course, was a borrowed allusion which had come to signify a host of known shortcomings but which arose originally from the pernickety, fussy precision with which Willy filled out his worksheets - a daily routine that involved using a shiny metal ruler not only to secure straight lines but also to achieve an unnecessarily exact level of neatness and typographical finesse.

* * *

The outcome of all these universally known factors was that staff relations were a fluctuating amalgam of amusement and irritation in not-quite-equal proportions - with a perceptible leaning towards the negative side. The latter imbalance was strengthened by a very ironical inconsistency on Willy's part which, like other matters, was associated with the canteen lunch queue. It was here that Works Manager Crawley, at his most creepy, mysteriously ran out of small change with improbable frequency; and this landed him in need of stop-gap assistance from his friends. To make matters worse, like many familiars of sharp practice, William misjudged his personal credit balance and was unrealistically confident about his ability to smooth things over. He therefore convinced himself that his colleagues never remembered he owed them money unless they asked for it and accompanied their requests with a sing-song parody of William's own stock response of 'Oh, I forgot'. As time passed, this way of dealing with the matter had become a standard comedy act; and the essence of the game was to utter the well-worn catch-phrase *before* the astute Mr Crawley got a chance to come out with it himself for the umpteenth time!

At the end of the day, though, this charade and several others meant that all parties could convert their varying degrees of irritation into laughter... thus enabling the world to keep on turning in the shared conviction that everybody was *one up* on everybody else - at the same time as leaving the moderately creepy Mr Crawley stubbornly convinced that he was well ahead in a struggle that everyone else regarded as a joke!

SWEET SIXTEEN

There is a strong suspicion that the young gentleman ambling along the banks of the Serpentine is sixteen years old. His whole life is before him, you might say. And from the outset, even *I* am prepared to compliment him on *not* wearing a hood. Clearly, he wishes to stand out in the public eye: he is fair-haired and handsome and is keen to arouse female admiration. For this purpose, he seeks to add individuality to his natural endowments which he believes he has achieved by wearing his jeans so extravagantly low that the belt divides his backside in two - the scantily clad upper half being carefully exposed by a shirt unaccustomed to being tucked in (a deliberate practice based on the idea that nonconformity is original). Young women who are so minded can therefore relish the sight of freshly laundered white underpants with assertively large blue polka dots. Moreover, pernicious sections of bare skin glimpsed through the assiduously contrived holes in his trouser legs are calculated to whet appetites even further.

The parading peacock thus surreptitiously documented is by no means iniquitous. But neither has he much to show in the way of originality, given that his costume is worn by numberless lookalikes from John o'Groats to Land's End. His good looks are neither better nor worse than many thousands of his peers - for which reason he is plainly ordinary. And sadly, there is no evidence as to whether he is more (or less) ordinary than the others.

THE UNDERSTOREY

Sheen Common, situated in the Royal Borough of Richmond Upon Thames, Surrey, does indeed have a small area of what can genuinely be called 'common' to its credit. This comprises a piece of open land just about big enough to accommodate a cricket pitch and the smallish equivalent of a pavilion. The vast bulk that forms the rest of the so-called *common*, however, is not actually a common at all but woodland - ancient woodland too - which, moreover, is distinctively English in being made up, almost entirely, of closely packed oaks with a dense holly understorey which, a few years ago, was partially cleared.

Here and there, yew saplings - none of them mature trees - fight a losing battle beside the paths that weave in and out of the hollies. And bordering the main, often muddy walk leading from the main road to Bog Gate, there are more saplings, beeches this time, which are at their most attractive when autumn transforms the regular colour of their foliage into cheerful yellows, rich mahogany and a medley of citrus greens.

* * *

There is a solemnity about these woods - derived in part from the blackness of the hollies and from the great height of the oaks contending among themselves for the light. In fact, before the recent clearance, this was really a *forest* rather than a wood in that the summer canopy so obscured the sun that virtually nothing could grow at ground level except the hollies. Nowadays, of course, one may reasonably expect to find an increasing number of grasses, weeds and wild flowers. Indeed, of late, there are sporadic picture-postcard areas where bluebells manage to flourish before the oaks, in full leaf, cast their encroaching shadows.

Some people might argue that this forest is only at its best when visited by the spectral presence of mist and hoar frost or by a light covering of snow when the only sounds are the plaintive tweets of a robin or the whispers of a wind that rattles the dry and seemingly lifeless twigs. Others, by contrast, as the land tilts away from the sun, will take heart from the damp Septembers and Octobers when earth balls and funnel caps inch their way upwards as if by magic through the carpet of decaying leaves.

In winter, despite their vast number, the Sheen Common hollies are consistently sparing with their traditional, blood-red berries - though perhaps, just once in a decade, there is an abundance so great that the woodpigeons can make no impression on the glut. On the other hand, as if to compensate for their usual inadequacy, these hollies do have one rather surprising secret to their credit: in just three out-of-the-way spots, well hidden from view, there are lone relatives of the standard variety whose berries are not red at all, but pure yellow.

There is one last evocative presence in this forest which appears while the barrenness of winter still dominates February and not a single green leaf breaks the monotony of mist or drizzle. This is the white blossom of the cherry plum which, like a snow shower frozen in time, brightens the seasonal gloom like a ray of hope while the sun, if visible at all, is still as pale and as vague as a ghost behind a wafer-thin layer of cloud.

Bog Gate: a pleasantly obscure way into Richmond Park from the Sheen Common woods.

Fungus species: common earth ball, scleroderma citrinum; and funnel cap, clitocybe geotropa.

Yellow berried holly: ilex aquifolium bacciflava.

OPEN TO DEBATE

A bright May morning at a London bus stop and the hottest day so far that year. Awaiting the 493 to St Mary's Hospital was a gentleman called Sam who would have looked just as unwell without the black scar that disfigured his bald head. Sam was deeply immersed in personal concerns - so much so that he forgot he was standing at a request stop. And for that reason, his relief at an exceptionally short wait came unstuck as he raised his arm only when it was clear that the bus driver, whom no one had hailed, was driving straight past on the assumption that those standing in the queue were waiting for one of the other buses that stopped there. Roused abruptly from the obscurity of his daydreams, Sam had barely enough time to note the driver's ethnicity. However, once the penny dropped, he immediately embarked on a lengthy outpouring of abuse. The words 'effing foreigner' were repeated over and over again amidst a broader motley of curses: 'no manners... no bloody consideration... they just don't give a damn... not like the old days... Effing foreigners'... And so it went on.

There was another elderly man present with long white hair and genial features rather like Father Christmas whose quiet remonstrations advised against stereotyping. But Sam stuck to his guns. However, there was a third pensioner standing beside him who also butted in, maintaining that neither prejudice nor political correctness could reasonably compete with the merits of simple observation when it came to judging the conduct of London bus drivers.

But there's an inconsistency at the heart of this entirely true story which the third, more observant gentleman was acutely aware of: namely that Sam's international accent placed him in a vulnerable position that left the current of his remarks *conspicuously* open to debate!

SWEET HOSANNAS

Although summer is dead and buried, beneath this vast riverside plane it is summer for the second time...The nerve ends of the tree, those limp tentacles furthest from the trunk, dangle like creepers casting dark shadows on to the footpath. Straight ahead between the spiked leaf-clusters, the surface of the river is a twitching membrane - dull pewter and black except for the trail of silver coins seething in the wake of a pleasure boat.

A jogger thumps past, earnestly challenging the ravages of time. Family groups amble along at a leisurely pace, chatting in German and Lithuanian. A grey squirrel streaks across the grass, vaulting in a series of loops like the wave motion of a rope repeating the movements of the hand holding it.

Other disparate events continue simultaneously. A dead leaf rattles in the breeze as its crumpled points scrape the gravel. An angler is having no luck. A canoeist paddles upstream against the ebb-tide into a cauldron of light that consumes him. The ring-necked parakeets squawk and heckle in the high canopy. The rough sleeper's bedding is packed in boxes beneath the arches. A woman in blue and mauve flashes on and off like a lamp as she glides in and out of the shadows.

But who would have guessed that alongside this peaceful gallery of concord and unbloody-mindedness lies a melting pot of inner city turmoil at loggerheads with the angler's sudden good fortune? And how tragic it seems that on the dark side of the moon, even the lips of children buzz like a hornets' nest, oblivious to the anthems of paradise.

THE SHADOWS FADE AWAY

It was early May, a bank holiday and a drowsy afternoon. This was a welcome change that persisted despite the invisible currents of cool air forcing their way, with vague hints of malevolence, beneath the blanket of early spring warmth. Water trickled consolingly and just audibly from the small pond that served as a watering hole for the deer. And beside it, a white hawthorn at its finest scattered a thick, bewitchingly ambivalent scent over the bracken's fiddleheads emerging through the débris of the previous year's growth. The intermittent whine of aircraft en route to Heathrow barely disturbed the peace of this gently sloping, miniature valley between the hillsides that fed the pond where, in the absence of the deer, a succession of dogs of all shapes and sizes leapt recklessly into the water and stirred up the mud.

To the east, along the ridge where the two hills enclosing the valley coalesced into a single escarpment, juvenile oaks spread their greening fans against the sky's blue background; here also, a pair of white spots, little more than pinpricks, moved almost imperceptibly to the right in tandem with a smaller, much more mobile pink shape reminiscent of a blip flashing its way across a computer screen; and it was these indistinct signs, diminished by distance and taken together, that provided the sole evidence from which an observer, lounging by the pond, might deduce the progress of a family out for an afternoon stroll. Nearer to hand, there were larger, brighter patches of colour beneath the trailing willows and the paler greens of the poplars where the first picnics of the season were being concelebrated on showy chain-store rugs. That the grass blades, not far beneath their fresh green tips, were still damp was something no one seemed to notice; nor, in the first flush of spring, did anyone seem to care.

Thus, among crumpled shorts and flimsy dresses rescued in haste from packed wardrobes, yet another year had begun its endlessly repeated cycle of coming and going - although inevitably, for some of those enjoying their first real glimpse of the sun, the 'going' might well prove both premature and final. How could anyone tell? But nature, at least for the moment, provided a built-in censor that constrained all thoughts at variance with the newness and brightness of the day. Consequently, given an unforeseeable future, the tranquillity of those few hours beneath an insistently cheerful sky remained uninterrupted, unspoilt and seemingly immune from the darkside. After all, there was the clear promise of more fine weather to come; there was another bank holiday at the end of the month - and despite the fears of environmentalists, the skylarks were still warbling in the vastness overhead.

TRANSITIONAL VALUES

The Thames was gliding at snail's pace downstream towards Rich-mond Bridge - and then onwards, via the city, to the sea. The water was grey like scoured pewter but with a green undertone from the reflections of the trees along its banks. Further highlights were bestowed at random by white clouds playfully vying with an intermittent sun. And each of these contributing factors was trans-formed by the river itself into vertical columns of colour which seemed to plunge straight down beneath its surface.

Such was the scene as viewed from Buccleuch Gardens about a third of a mile upstream from the bridge. Straight ahead, an eyot situated at the sharp right-hand bend was suddenly ignited, rather theatri-cally, by a brief outburst of sunshine. And it was then that Mildred, who at seventy seven had hobbled all the way from the town centre, took advantage of a shady bench. In fact, acknowledging her years, she decided it was unwise to go any further despite the allure of Petersham Meadows just ahead and the river's numberless and nameless enticements which she knew lay out of sight and beyond her reach.

Mildred's neatly trim blue skirt with white blouse and a modest brooch perpetuated a lifelong aversion to wearing trousers. And despite the degree to which age now curtailed her activities, her habitually prim appearance, orderly grey hair and the faint perfume she was wearing all betokened a willingness to soldier on with-out caving in either to the advancing years or to newly established customs.

Nevertheless, as she contemplated the ceaseless jostling of the waves and felt the sultry benevolence of the summer air, she took the risk of telling herself that if she closed her eyes for the last time then and there and carried away the prospect laid out before her, heaven itself would be hard put to it to rival the earthly paradise she was leaving behind.

Soon, after a brief interruption, the sun emerged again with renewed brilliance; and a rising breeze stirred the water. These combined circumstances erased the former reflections in an instant and transformed the river's surface into a glittering mass of white dots floating on a restless, ever-shifting membrane. It was as if it were a painting by Seurat, set in motion by the wind and glimpsed out of focus through bewildered eyes.

SEEN FROM ABOVE

As I gaze out of this inaccessible region from among deep shadows where dry leaves underfoot are sprinkled with the gold coins of my eternal light, I am watching you and I notice how you scuttle like cockroaches along the highways… like worms abandoning one dark hole for another as if mimicking the artful fox who seeks in vain to escape attention. And you… you whom I released from the puppetry of my imagination into a state of independent self-governance…you are *not* a pretty sight!

Even I who dwell out of reach might ask myself a question… even though I knew the answer before I gave rise to the source of my own doubts when I *thought* your ancestors into existence and imposed free will on them so that they became autonomous beings rather than heavenly robots.

Because I am the Lord neither of legend nor hindsight but of overarching foreknowledge, I was well aware of the misuse to which your liberation would be put. And I intervened; I entered your space-time and I made careful arrangements at my own considerable cost to secure your well-being.

And now, finally, I advise you to look again at my holy face, albeit hidden behind the veil, and to take advantage of yet another opportunity. I who have no beginning desire that you, like me, should have no end - and the choice, now as it has been from the outset, lies in the exercise of your own right-minded obedience to the rule of law inscribed on history's pages with the red ink from my veins.

AN ODD SORT OF CHAP

Martin was thought by some to be very well informed. And especially in the eyes of those with whom his connection was superficial, this impression was strengthened by his class accent of which he was unaware until a market stallholder spoke to him in so affected a way that he realised he was being made a fool of and guessed the reason. Martin was also the sort of person whom strangers approached, thinking from some indefinable aspect of his bearing that he was sure to know the whereabouts of the Old Vic, the Serpentine or one of the capital's lesser-known museums. As an elderly, lifelong Londoner, of course, he certainly did know the answer to such questions; and yet, strangely, as soon as he was asked, he tended to become muddled.

In reality, none of these favourable impressions was entirely false; but such as they were, they also conveyed a very incomplete picture. For example, no one would have guessed from his outward demeanour that when he was a boy Martin frequently concealed himself in the dark upper reaches of a holm oak where, with a cheap bakelite flute, he perfectly reproduced the call of a cuckoo. Nor could anyone have imagined that in old age he still remembered the results with glee, often bursting into laughter as he pictured the swift dispersal of the many pedestrians, hitherto completely fooled, as they abandoned the pavement beneath his hiding-place when the cuckoo's song assumed an unmistakable resemblance to the National Anthem!

Compounding these eccentricities, but at the very opposite end of the spectrum, Martin was something of a recluse: he was attached to and dependent on a smallish circle of friends; but he was also a lover of the Surrey and Sussex wilds where he spent many hours alone by the Mole or the Ouse, gazing at the play of light among the ripples, looking out for rare butterflies - or just picking blackberries in due season. By contrast, closer to his London home and as a lover of the arts, he repeatedly attended all the major galleries and exhibitions where, alongside taking pleasure in the work, he was also occasionally embarrassed when a visitor who had obstructed his view turned and stared back at him - having overheard the unmistakable abuse that Martin had whispered, insufficiently quietly, under his breath.

Taken all in all, the foregoing brief outline justifies an interim conclusion; and on this basis, as readers will surely appreciate, Martin can only be summed up as an unusually complex and contradictory sort of person who combined insight with absurdity, impishness with regular church attendance and sobriety with foibles such as a delight in listening to other people's rows.

Honest reportage must also be open about the fact that the memory of cuckoo calls in a holm oak was supplemented by the recollection of a second incident at which Martin continued to snigger for years after it occurred, although his rôle at the time was merely that of an onlooker. This had also been much later in life in his mid-sixties; and it began on a 465 bus passing through Tolworth, an undistinguished Surrey suburb near Surbiton, when a sprightly young man in his mid-twenties leapt on board clad in an obviously new and slightly-too-glossy black suit. He carried with him an equally brand-new-looking briefcase, almost certainly purchased a few days earlier from the John Lewis store at Kingston; and, in Martin's eyes, he looked suspiciously like a trainee estate agent, full of enthusiasm on the first rung of the ladder to fame and fortune as a branch manager.

Unfortunately, however, having gained access, the athletic newcomer immediately tripped up and fell to his knees with conspicuous indignity; and as he did so, he added to his own embarrassment by letting drop a very inappropriate turn of phrase. But whilst this caused an exchange of disapproving looks among the other passengers, Martin who was making his way home after a day on the Surrey downs, was obliged to conceal his own predicament behind the pages of a discarded newspaper where his laughter remained unnoticed until he arrived at the Kingston terminus where, with a lingering smile on his face, he finally escaped and transferred to another bus. This carried him on the very last leg of his journey home - and he was still smiling when he got there!

After reading 'Essays in Idleness' written by the Japanese monk Yoshida Kenko, 1283 to 1352 AD.

MARCUS BARRACLOUGH'S BIRTHDAY

I have just been reading some short stories by Lydia Davis. The book's title 'Can't and Won't' is an allusion to the publisher's alleged dislike of her frequent use of contractions such as - yes, you've guessed it - *can't* and *won't*; and this pedantic attitude has reminded me of a friend, a certain Marcus Barraclough, who conceals his lack of imagination by criticising the use of commonplace idiom or even street language which, in English at least, I consider a uniquely fertile source of inventiveness.

This friend of mine can be extremely pompous in laying claim to ideas whose ordinariness is by no means disguised by his output of polysyllables among which he sometimes loses track and stumbles - after which, as a last resort, he appeals to popular consensus. His aim, in most of these cases, is simply to establish as fact what is no more than a personal preference that just *happens* to underpin his unconventional lifestyle and acquired class affiliation. He is, in fact, true to a very recognisable type in the sense that his advancing years combine with a pot belly and a bald head to lend weight to his volubly expressed convictions.

His inferiors may be fooled by his strategies; but keep your eyes open if you happen to be dining at the Reform Club on the evening of Marcus Barraclough's birthday where you may be lucky enough to glimpse a few of those privy to his ways whispering behind the shelter of a menu - or sharing ungrateful asides behind the backs of their hands as they tuck into an excellent dinner at their host's considerable expense.

THE TOP FLOOR BALCONY

After a busy morning gadding about between Richmond where I live and Camden Town where a friend lives, I returned to Richmond, got the shopping hurriedly out of the way in Tesco's, and after a frustrating interlude consigning it to the fridge-freezer at home, I took advantage of the warmest day so far that year and settled down in the comfort of my top floor balcony.

After all the hustle and bustle, I began to relax almost at once under the soothing influence of the red geraniums - a process enhanced by the 'tree of heaven' (ailanthus altissima) which far exceeded the height of the roof above my head. Bursting into early blossom, it swallowed me up in its welcome shade as I paused for a few minutes and allowed myself to adjust fully to the mood-change. After this, with all former tensions expunged, I embarked on the short stories of Hermione Finch whose work, as described in the book's introductory text, was judged worthy of lavish praise.

* * *

There is nothing about the short stories of Hermione Finch that would justify me in being rude about them. But they do tend to dwell on the ordinariness of everyday life which, for me at least, they failed to illuminate quite as profoundly as the blurb suggested. In consequence, they did little to offset my other competing inclination that afternoon: namely, they failed to prevent me from dozing. Indeed, in just over twenty minutes I was forced to fight off drowsiness at least three times.

At this point, there may well be some who feel that I too am wasting time on very ordinary information. After all, there I was, a London flat-dweller, hidden away on a smallish balcony on the afternoon of what was at last a genuine and seemingly propitious spring day. Millions of others, I have to admit, must have been absorbing the same long-awaited change in the weather. But, for a number of considered reasons, I make no apology. I noticed that the woodpigeons were making a meal of the florets dangling like upside-down lupins from the tree of heaven; and I twice had to flick a honey bee off the front cover of the book. It also struck me that the pilots heading for Heathrow in the sky above me were as unaware of my presence as I was indifferent to the noise of their aircraft; and I remember thinking that the intermittent swish of the traffic in the street below me was reminiscent of the waves pounding a sandy shore.

In the light of all this, there is just one thing I might perhaps draw to the attention of Hermione Finch if she hasn't thought of it already - and it's this. Unremarkable as that sunny day may have been, there is a particular sense in which it was unlike any other day insofar as the 'now' of those moments, as well as those of the short stories, can never be duplicated… regardless of how similar another thousand days might genuinely be in countless parallel universes!

Viewed in this way, ordinary things can be (and are) as mysterious as a nebula or the big bang because, when you boil it down, *everything* is mysterious by definition. And that is because no one knows what anything really is nor where it ultimately came from. And to those minded to conclude that it came from nowhere, I make this suggestive reply: namely, that coming from nowhere would make things even *more* mysterious, inexplicable and extraordinary than they already are.

What matters, therefore, is being aware of the mystery implicit in ordinary things - and making it felt.

Hermione Finch: To avoid irrelevant discussion, I have withheld the true name of the author to whom the text refers.

PROMENADE

Lucinda closed the front door behind her, having tossed aside the dishcloth, the duster and the familiar brand of detergent. She was anxious to take advantage of one of the few fine afternoons of April 2012 - a month also notable for the wettest drought* on record. And so, with relaxation primarily in mind, she made straight for the Thames Path at Richmond where, with the Georgian bridge behind her back, she ambled south-west towards Petersham Meadows, pausing for contemplation on a wooden bench in front of which the grass verge was partially flooded due to the high tide.

Soothed by the silver shimmer of the waves, Lucinda's fraught consciousness revived as she took in the billowing green silhouettes of the trees that lined both shores and totally engulfed a small eyot at the bend just upstream from where she was sitting. And her spirits rose still further at the sight of a flotilla of small craft moored midway between the two banks. Her interest was also aroused by the swift, arrowlike movement of some small canoes - although she counted herself lucky at not being on board such fragile-looking craft that seemed to sit perilously low in the water.

As a crowded pleasure boat chugged upstream towards Teddington, and as the voice of the tour guide grew dimmer, Lucinda was struck by the numberlessness of the ripples and by their ceaseless motion. And then, increasingly in thrall to benevolent nature, she also noticed the cattle in the meadows ahead of her, lazily flopped on their bellies and chewing the cud as if the universe had been drained of purpose. Influenced by this novel thought, Lucinda herself slowly abandoned her plans for further exploration, rested content with the idyll spread out in front of her and, after a few more minutes' thought, drifted off into a state of pleasantly unfocussed reverie.

*In 2012, there was a period of official drought accompanied by a great deal of unforeseen rain.

CONTRAFLOW

*Time travel may seem the sole province of fiction writers and fantasists -
but the past (if not the future) gathers around us like a mist in all those
special places that have never altered and where time's arrow, instead of
moving in a straight line, goes round and round in circles. It is in odd
corners like these that the genius loci, if acknowledged, will venture into
the open.*

Here on the banks of a shallow river, a meadow full of tall grasses is
dreaming. And on the far side at the bend, a mature forest plunges
precipitately downhill, halting abruptly at the water's edge whilst
from east to west the intractable downs fix us benignly in their gaze.
This surely is the time and the place to sit quietly and breathe deeply
- the better to keep a close watch and catch whispers.

Notice how the heron poised to strike at short notice scrutinises
the same ripples as in a former life. A damselfly settles on reeds
unchanged for a hundred years. The gentle air rustles in the aspens,
repeating the same hollow whispers heard by children who are now
grown men. And discern the dim ancestral figures, those insubstantial
wraiths, gathering close at hand on the river-bank. They have
assembled here once again, bearing witness to a shared and changeless past viewed from differing standpoints on opposite sides of a
delicate, transparent membrane.

The sound of white water in spate beneath the weir is smoother than
tinnitus and speaks the same familiar dialect as it returns from exile
in atlantic skies to repeat its sleepy drone within range of welcoming
ears. This is the stream that gives sustenance to the life along its
banks where the kingfisher's dart, like subtle poison, flashes round
the bend where dead eyes are watching.

Crimson, the five-spot burnet moth zigzags through the tall grasses
- a conscious, querying vehicle of shadowy indecision parked at

the crossroads. Time now to halt and inhale that ageless smell of mudflats and reed beds that is our overwhelming consolation - whilst on the far bank stands an army of yews whose bark, like armour, shields the growth rings that are the vestiges of former carefree days.

* * *

The stream flows backwards from the present to the past. Looking down from a higher prominence, it is broad epochs that we see. A dark cloud-shadow glides across the moor. The wind cools and drops to a steady breeze whose conflict with the oaks sounds like a waterfall washing over us.

And now, surely you can hear those ancestral voices... voices that whirr and gossip like the wings of dragonflies?

WRITER'S BLOCK

There is no benefit in writing about ordinary things and people if your writing is just as ordinary as the people and things you're writing about.

On the other hand, people who seem to be ordinary may still have merit; and there may also be things about them that are genuinely interesting. But unless you can probe deeper and transcend the everyday profile of your subject matter without short-changing the truth by subverting it, no amount of media coverage acquired through useful contacts will override the fact that you too are on the ordinary side - even though a proportion of fools, influenced by your name and reputation, will believe the exact opposite.

It is, of course, clear that being ordinary is no grave sin. But being boring, if that is the consequence, is a drag for any writer; and the most obvious answer is to be vigilant. I will put my cards on the table: I have just given up on a much-acclaimed author whose short stories, contained in a very nicely produced hardback, I finally abandoned a few moments ago because I found the themes flat and the treatment no better. Instead, I have diverted my attention to what is a pleasant, sunny afternoon, here, where the brambles are flowering among thorns beneath the flight path to Heathrow Airport…and where the aggressive roar of aircraft engines, by dint of familiarity, has failed to subdue the skylarks. In other words, it is a perfect summer afternoon whose ordinariness nevertheless has abundant character and interest.

The bracken, I notice, provides shelter for the deer; and already, I have more or less forgotten about the stories, having found two butterflies spiralling in aerial combat far more entertaining. There is a muddy little pond in front of me where I have often watched wildlife drinking and where, just seconds ago, two dogs out for a walk seemed to find the idea of resisting a plunge as impossible as I did to attempt yet another short story.

Given such circumstances, therefore, I have happily pursued inclination and have disregarded the paid experts' exhortations on the back cover of a rather dull book. As to their polysyllables and reliance on fashion, you can forget about it! It is summertime that is my far greater love, here, where darters and dragonflies flit like arrows an inch above the ripples. With simple pleasure, I watch them navigating nimbly in and out of the commonest, you might even say the most *ordinary*, of waterside rushes that benefit, as do I, from the mud and silt washed down over time from that insignificant little spring I discovered not far away, further up the hill among the poplars.

PINPOINTS OF CONSCIOUSNESS

The broad river that moments ago was a dull pewter flares up suddenly at the bend as if shattered ice and glass were advancing in alien splendour from some outpouring further upstream. Lacking the bird's-eye view from my vantage point halfway up the hill, a pleasure boat has rounded the corner and has disappeared again behind the foreground trees. The passengers on board and the matchstick men on the muddy towpath have no inkling of my existence; yet here I am, gazing at the willows on an island now transformed in a flash by the sun - rather like the scene on a Tiffany lampshade when a child inadvertently switches the light on.

Areas of brightness and shadow chase each other in ragged disorder, advancing uphill towards me. Like a hot shower, warmth pours over me; yet to the west, overrun as if by some nameless menace, the woods darken and then reignite at the whim of the intermittent sun.

Beside the park bench I am sitting on, ants navigate the highways between the concrete slabs, halting at junctions to plot their onward course. Like those strollers at the water's edge, they too are unaware of my presence. And yet I perceive that within their own unknowable world, they represent mysterious pinpoints of consciousness in a multi-storeyed biosphere of inaccessible awarenesses.

* * *

Even so, when it comes to ants, I think ill of them; and on them I plant my foot. I act to their detriment; I deplore their numberless cohorts and their relentless orderliness. I abominate their swarms and seething nests; and I loathe those winged vagrants that infect high summer, crawling like locusts over footpaths and in through open windows!

EINE KLEINE NACHTMUSIK

When you look at another human being, you are contemplating a great mystery: not only are you glimpsing a familiar, observable material form - although today's counter-intuitive understanding of matter is far from familiar; but you are also witnessing an indiscernible, non-dimensional conscious self. And this is no 'ghost in a machine', but rather an undivided combination of physical and mental worlds for which no ultimate description is yet available.

Patrick, who was sitting up in bed, yawned and withdrew his pen from the page. It was late; the line of reasoning was exacting; and the intrinsic profundity made provisos and subordinate clauses into obstacles obscuring a barely accessible theme. Even the noise of the bedside clock was a distraction: it wasn't the usual, relaxing 'tick tick' seamlessly measuring out the passage of time; instead, it was a cluttered, battery-generated, muddled sound - much at variance with the silence of the night sky and the cold smell of autumn air which had first initiated Patrick's reflections.

And so, the creative impulse died and he switched off the light. Then, as his eyes grew accustomed to the darkness, the stars appeared through the window and breached the boundary between the cosy bedroom and an untamed universe. Thereafter, a welcome emptiness took the place of cumbersome thought as awareness of the void became a dim presence embracing Patrick as he sank, finally at ease, into the soft oblivion of the pillows.

THE BYSTANDER

I

He felt increasingly like a fish out of water among the building works and scaffolding that obscured the sky near the vast edifice that had once been a power station but was now an art gallery. And moment by moment, as inward reflection imposed itself on external reality, he began to imagine he was in the middle of some un-familiar, almost intangible no-man's-land which was sullen in all its details and as grey as the March afternoon that overshadowed it.

To make matters worse, the gloom that confronted him was accent-uated by the turbulent gusts that tradition rightly associates with the third month of the year. Loose cables clanked against exposed metal joists; and plastic sheeting, flapping wildly in the wind, sounded like the clash of pigeon wings after shotgun fire. Taken all in all, it was a depressing picture that strongly and negatively affected Neville's state of mind as the influence of the exhibition that he'd just enjoyed began to dwindle.

The grim mood of the moment stood in contrast to the nearby riverside flower beds where daffodils, prompted by the northern hemisphere as it leaned towards the sun, proclaimed the arrival of spring… though with no supporting evidence other than the urgent fluttering of their petals. It was cold, unseasonably so, and as hostile as any windswept moorland. On top of this, almost inevitably, it began to rain, leaving Neville feeling exposed and diminished - rather like a lone survivor washed ashore on an island where there was nothing but rock and stunted vegetation.

For Neville, in his mid-sixties, balding, and a childless widower with no taste for further entanglements, there was an alarming affinity between his immediate environment and the negative aspects of his existence as it then was. He kept moving. After all, there was nothing to detain him. But at the same time, caught in a blast of icy wind, he became conscious of a misgiving that grew stronger as a powerful sense of isolation bore down on him.

2

Whilst he continued in that sombre mood, a boy and a girl in their late teens, oblivious to his presence, sauntered past en route to the former power station which had long ago gained worldwide renown as the Tate Modern Gallery. Arm-in-arm, brightly if scattily dressed, and indifferent to the rain, they were pursuing an imprecise plan of action. Starting first with the in-house bookshop, they were hoping to flip through the catalogue of the special exhibition (whose entry charge they couldn't afford) before dawdling aimlessly in and out of the other permanent display areas to which access was free. Thus occupied, and alone together, they would most probably glance right and left at paintings or sculptures which, by reason of their mutual self-absorption, they wouldn't actually *see* at all - although they would almost certainly be unaware of their indifference.

Of course, these were indications of what was to come that Neville could never have guessed at; but what hit home most was the violent contrast of the gloom that surrounded him seen alongside the young couple's vitality and technicolour dress sense. It was a perception that greatly reinforced his feeling that something odd was afoot - perhaps some inexplicable twist in the substructure of reality which led him to think, in a rare moment of inspiration, that he was at a crossroads: namely, at the intersection of two distinct worlds in at least *one* of which he was little more than a bystander.

It was a fleeting moment - perhaps an even briefer insight. Neville knew he would never again encounter that inward-looking pair whose detachment and animation made him feel they were part of another reality that had left him behind. But then, in a split second of discernment, he experienced a volte-face and took heart: was he not privy to an experience of the future where that boy and girl, wholly absorbed in their present, were unaware of their participation in his (Neville's) past at a moment when his time-line coincided with theirs as they approached the Tate Modern? And was this not the most plausible explanation for the indifference of those youngsters to the rain and March winds of the early twenty first century in which he himself, for an unspecified number of years, was inexplicably embedded?

A TURN-UP FOR THE BOOKS

Members of the Bexford Grammar School Old Boys' Association surviving from the nineteen fifties may possibly recollect a fellow pupil called Twaddle for whose unusual name I can personally vouch. From the same period, they may also remember Charles Channon, a prefect who, by the time of this narrative had moved on to Jesus College Cambridge where he was an undergraduate. He'd been a close friend of mine for many years; and it was from him that I heard the following remarkable anecdote.

During a formal college reception, ablaze with the stars of academia, Charles caught sight of the once familiar figure of Twaddle being introduced to a young woman in terms that amused him so much that he withdrew at speed to the terrace. Luckily, although he'd been standing perilously close, he hadn't been spotted.

There is no record as to whether his reaction was widely shared. However, I still recall his vivid account of how desperate he'd been to escape notice lest he be caught off-guard after hearing his professor of Anglo-Saxon Studies making the straight-*laced* and straight-*faced* introduction which he (Charles) had found so hilarious.

The incident itself, as he described it, formed only the briefest of interludes during that gathering of dignitaries, dons and freshers when the two undergraduates were introduced to each other. But the unexceptional words used were nevertheless sufficient to propel Charles from the scene for fear of embarrassment.

'It's kids' stuff, really', he explained. 'What drove me to the exit was the conciseness of Professor Tomkins' introduction. It was the sheer economy of *Mr Twaddle, meet Miss Twiddle* that did it'.

And we both burst out laughing like a pair of idiots.

NO GOLDS TODAY!

Early on the morning of the eighth of August 2012, responding to unconfirmed reports, James battled his way from South London to Stratford much further east where he discovered that tickets for the Olympic Park were definitely *not* available on site. He felt hard done by: on both rail and tube, it had been 'standing room only' from the start; and now it seemed as if a door had been slammed in his face with pointed indifference - although the capable, somewhat scrawny steward who gave him the news did her best to soften the impact.

In Stratford City's brand new shopping precinct built alongside the park as an 'Olympic legacy', James half imagined that the acres of steel and glass surrounding him were part of an alien planet where mesmerised humanoids were cruising around like cleverly programmed machines. He was ill at ease, out on a limb and his former disappointment was by no means diminished by panoramic views of the Olympic site itself as seen from an elevated observation deck. The much vaunted architectural masterpieces (judged from the outside and from above) looked strikingly akin a twenty-first century junk yard - and this was an impression strongly reinforced by one particular contribution, crookedly reminiscent of the Eiffel Tower and made, or so it seemed, from lengths of scaffolding and a random selection of spare parts.

No prizes for guessing that within forty five minutes of his arrival, James was back on the tube; and in ninety minutes more he was home again where he lost no time in dumping his baggage… after which, armed with a book, he wandered off to a bench in the leafy quiet of a churchyard nearby.

The refreshingly natural sound greeting him almost at once was a noisy exchange between two squirrels in the throes of territorial conflict. And his peace of mind was further enhanced when he noticed that, despite the virus currently threatening them, honey bees were busily at work among flowering weeds on an otherwise neglected grave. As to the rumbustious magpies: he made the decision, just this once, to turn a deaf ear to their prattle which harmonised surprisingly well with the far-off laughter of school-children.

DIGBY BUTTERWORTH'S UNDOING

Digby was in many ways a master of English usage, allowing that, in the present context, the focus is more on strategic application than on the elegance of his style. He was able, very convincingly, to navigate any tricky situation; without apparent deceit, he could worm his way out of innumerable tight corners. And he frequently volunteered lucid advice for friends to follow which drew not only on skilful invention but also on snippets of genuine personal experience. He was a person in whom sincerity and insincerity were perfectly combined - as was his concern for others with a subtly concealed brand of indifference.

The consequence of all this was that many people played along without really knowing where they were when it came to Digby Butterworth, a departmental manager aged forty at a well-known West End chain store. On the other hand, there were also those individuals, the rare exceptions, with whom he entirely failed to carry conviction; and these included his immediate boss and one of his wife's sisters - both of whom had independently spotted a particularly glaring fact: namely, that Digby's advice, lines of argument and his circumnavigation of awkward truths, taken collectively, were so consistent, so smoothly expressed and so bereft of provisos that they lacked the credibility they were designed to establish.

As his wife's sister, Emma, told an intimate friend 'I wouldn't trust a word that so-and-so says'! To her mind and that of his boss, the fluency that exposed the flaw in his character made his perform-ances a matter of mere spectacle. In Emma's case, she rather enjoyed despising him; and she also enjoyed the enthusiastic support of her intimate friend who rubber-stamped each and every acid criticism. In the eyes of his boss, however, Digby's verbal skills possessed clear value on the shop floor and made a measurable contribution to sales.

But coming from a social background quite unlike Digby's, this had no effect on his judgement of character - which boiled down to an unequivocally disdainful, top-down rejection.

The general outcome was predictable, even if a little sad for someone like Digby whose appearance at forty bore an uncanny resemblance to a Van Gogh self-portrait *minus* all the colour and energy of the brush strokes; and this effect was even more marked when, thinking he was unobserved, his face was at rest. Unsurprisingly, therefore, he featured very low down on the Christmas card lists of his wife's sister and that of his boss - judiciously tempered in the latter case, of course, by the twists, turns and contrivances of office politics!

DECLINE AND FALL

The winter, like a state funeral, has established its presence on the public highway. It is cold; a strong wind is wailing like a banshee and the sleet, still partially liquid, is driving against the window panes. From the safe refuge of a warm interior, I hear the hard droplets striking the glass like grit whilst I listen to the reckless turmoil of the air from the security of my comfort zone.

Slumped in the velvet softness of an armchair, reconciled to having to stay indoors, I could seize the moment (if so minded) to reflect on the meaning of life. But meaning implies purpose; and as a religious believer, I have a ready-made formula in that department. But on another level, as someone subject to the moods and the mortality of my fellow men, today's outlook is grim.

Given the negative assumption that cosmic and biological evolution are governed neither by reason nor destiny, the meaning of life boils down to the fact that there *is* no meaning other than the simple truth that any imagined meaning is illusory. And so the rain goes on falling with cold indifference and the north wind drums on the casement. The sky darkens to a wilderness of grey; and the birds, now silent, are shuddering. Even the hungry foxes, confined to their quarters by the icy blast, have shut up shop; and the weightless owl, deprived of star-shine, clings to the rafters of a creaking barn.

From my comfortably lit drawing room, I hear an alien universe hammering on the resilient layers of glass. Weird faces peer in at me, barely visible. Ghosts moan and rivers burst their banks. Bungalows in the West Country are swilling with muddy water that resembles chocolate and tastes of dirt; and the emergency services are stretched beyond breaking point. Seemingly, the sun has quit the galaxy. Without anchorage or tangible defence, but not without hope, I feel in danger of being swept away.

MAX

Richard was struck by the scene in front of him. Not for the first time, he was made aware that certain individuals are liable to display indifference to those around them by more or less disregarding their existence. People of that ilk are often prepared to make themselves at home by extending their territory rather like recently hatched cuckoos whose nature it is to oust the other innocent fledglings from their rightful inheritance. Lounging about on a shopping mall bench like a pile of luggage or sprawling on the grass in unsightly, loose-limbed, often suggestive postures, they seem blind to the negative reaction they arouse in others and to the inconvenience that sometimes goes with it. Richard's long-term observations had also convinced him that the offenders, on the whole, tend to be men rather than women. That, at any rate, was his firmly established opinion.

Some might say it was a rather peculiar, perhaps unduly selective view of the world; but it was one which, having matured over time, was borne out on this occasion by a young man sitting opposite him on the District Line of the London underground. As the carriage rattled along, Richard also observed that, according to the letters printed on his t-shirt, the name of this somewhat bedraggled-looking individual was Max. Aged in the region of twenty six, he was gazing fixedly downwards at his mobile phone with the consequence that a few strands of oily-looking black hair dangled from his forehead which, by contrast, seemed unhealthily pale. In addition to this, strongly supporting the general impression, his blue jeans had faded almost to grey - having clearly absorbed a great deal of dirt.

* * *

Oblivious to the picturesque panorama that opened up as the west-bound train crossed the Thames from Gunnersbury to Kew, what was most noteworthy about this young man was the way he was sitting with each leg from thigh to knee sloping upwards at an angle from its starting-point on the seat - added to which his knees were about as far apart as was anatomically possible and further apart than was decent. This ill-considered stance prevented other passengers from sitting beside him - on top of which, in his self-absorption, it was not only to the river that he was oblivious; he was also unaware of the woman who, with a look of contempt in her eyes, was seated on the far side of the unoccupied space to his immediate left. Focussed on his mobile as he was, he had no inkling that she was watching him out of the corner of her eye as he casually picked his nose after which he twiddled the result between thumb and forefinger before flicking it casually into the gangway without even looking up.

Middle-aged and neatly but informally dressed as befitted the bright September day, Richard was amused rather than otherwise by the unspoken censure he observed in progress on the opposite side of the carriage. And this was explained by the fact that, due to his particular vantage point, the affront to public hygiene was a minor peccadillo compared with the unpleasantly intimate view between Max's legs. Consequently, with considerations like these prominent in his mind, he rose to his feet and made ready to leave the train at the next stop. It was not a moment too soon; and it came as something of a relief after the noise, the close atmosphere and the squalid scene that he'd witnessed. Nevertheless, when all was said and done, what remained with him longer than anything else was the look on that woman's face - the shock-horror of superior disdain visible through the heavy layers of make-up. It was a picture that kept him smiling as he disembarked at Kew and made his way along the short, tree-lined avenue towards the Botanic Gardens where he found that the air was clear, the light green and the silence a welcome bonus.

R S V P

Mr Francis Barrington has just telephoned me to enquire after my health - given the fact that I failed to attend his seventy first birthday party or to answer his RSVP.

I politely explained that after the small difference of opinion during our last encounter, he hadn't actually *invited* me and was only ringing me now in order to cover his tracks. I also pointed out that if a long-standing annual tradition needed to be cancelled for credible reasons, he would certainly have rung me in advance to explain...

Mr Francis Barrington's quietly managed reaction to this riposte (which, if false, would have been explosively irritating), served only to accentuate the farce of that gentleman's efforts to have it both ways - especially when set alongside my recent observations from a parked car as the guests arrived for festivities held on exactly the same date - that of his birthday - every year.

STILL EARLY MAY

The rain fell heavily aslant, driven from west to east out of a dark grey sky in which were present no features whatsoever that suggested the likelihood of improvement. The monotony, with so little character that it barely warrants description, was bereft of distinct cloud-forms; and the effect was so consistently bleak that it added weight to an overall sense of foreboding, given the plain fact that spring was already a month old.

These conditions, however, did not unduly affect Deirdre who was preoccupied by her own inner world and by the mood swings that went with it. On the contrary, aboard the number 33 bus, as she gazed out of the window, she was mildly encouraged by the prospect of morning coffee in her friend's nice little period semi on the borders of Twickenham. And yet she knew, from past experience, that by the time she left that cosy dwelling with its scents of wax polish and home cooking, there would be renewed cause for misgivings despite the total absence of concrete evidence. In other words, she was at the mercy of a persistent hunch, to her friend's disadvantage, which something in the air told her was not entirely imaginary!

* * *

It was still early May - leaving more than a month of lengthening days for her worries to build up, whereafter (or so she thought) they would very likely fester on as the hours of light began to shorten. Sadly, it seemed, there was more than enough time (with no predictable limit to it) for her anxieties to gain an even firmer foothold.

Her misgivings were numerous and came in a selection of shapes and sizes; but her principal concern centred on Fenella, her friend of over fifty years' standing. Fenella was also nine summers short of Deirdre's age of seventy eight, a fact of life which had by no means dimmed her wits. Consequently, for a decade or more, she had gradually become conscious of a cooling down, of something having altered: something almost imperceptible that affected their relationship. And the conclusion she drew boiled down to a suspicion: namely, that Fenella had an interest in her (Deirdre's) demise and in the benefits to be gained under the terms which she had reason to hope were enshrined in her older friend's Will. But although these suspicions contained an element of truth, Fenella believed she had by no means let the cat out of the bag, leaving a supposedly innocent Deirdre, under a halo of wispy grey hair, in a state of blissful ignorance.

As for Deirdre herself, although in two minds as to whether she was right, it was the thought of being taken for a fool that was as painful as the betrayal implicit in Fenella's presumed expectations - although she recognised that such expectations were not necessarily incompatible with sincere friendship. Time, of course, was on the side of neither of them; but the idea that all their familiar get-to-gethers over chocolate cake and coffee might have a connection with the dark side of the moon deeply depressed Deirdre who therefore resented her long-standing trust which increasingly presented itself as a weakness. But although consumed by unwanted suspicions and by the uncertainty, and although uncomfortably alert to risk, Deirdre continued to hope against hope that she'd got it all wrong whilst ambiguously convinced that she hadn't! She felt like a veteran oak besieged by devouring larvae: an oak whose centuries-old wood was at risk from the determined assault of malevolent burrowers acting according to their nature!

Nevertheless, following these resumed rumblings and soon after arriving at Fenella's comfortable little home, things developed pleasantly enough... and Deirdre's mood brightened. The *gas* fire, convincingly burning like a *coal* fire in the grate, was a source of good cheer; the chocolate cake which on this occasion turned out to be lemon meringue pie was delicious… on top of which Fenella was unusually attentive, refreshingly willing to listen; and she also seemed to have taken extra care with her appearance. Deirdre was aware of these subtle configurations. She reflected on them and, as on many previous occasions, she vacillated. 'Perhaps I've been imagining things,' she thought.

* * *

And yet… and yet, when late morning gave place to mid afternoon, she began to think about moving on as the conversation wore thin. She found herself repeating her praise for the lemon meringue pie more than once; enquiries about where Fenella had obtained such nice coffee sounded hollow; and allusions to the weather among friends who had known each other for fifty years were an even surer sign that it was time to heave herself up from the comfortable chintzy sofa.

And so, after farewells that were slightly on the gushing side, Deirdre was glad when she found herself once more on the bus, looking forward to getting back to her comfort zone, to her own armchair, to the Channel 4 News and to something a little stronger than Fenella's undoubtedly excellent cups of freshly ground coffee! And as she alighted from the bus, she was confronted by something even stranger, something even flimsier than a line of thought, when she reflected that it was a very odd thing indeed that she felt so much more relaxed now that the event which had cheered her up had come to an end.

PLANTATION

After an uphill slog and a bumpy ride in the hot sun, I have taken refuge from the heat in the shade of an oak and I am waiting for the woods to hose me down with their cooling silence.

And now, as my heart slackens pace, I can tell that true silence is not a featureless continuum but an active plurality in a state of rest. Today there is no wind and nothing stirs, but still the quietness has unspecified substance and elusive dimensions yet to be discerned: the trickling of a stream is also like air flowing through aspens or the tinnitus in my ear that it cancels out. Here too silence is splintered by a blackbird's protest; it vibrates to the beat of pigeons' wings; it is dry leaves rustling beneath the feet of mice. Silence is golden, they say… and its influence is as tangible as the scent of nard on the feet of Christ.

* * *

But now, I can no longer hear it. It has been shattered by a strimmer at the margins. It has taken fright and fled from the eco-friendly chain-saw preparing logs for the larvae of stag beetles.

The woodsmen are assiduous but rowdy. Once more I am a refugee on the open road in pursuit of sanctuary.

ON HOLMWOOD COMMON

I am standing at the edge of a wood. It is a dreary day and I am unaccompanied. The branches of the oaks are bare; and the dead leaves under foot betray no vestige of the summer they have left behind. Above them, the sky that was blue in August has faded. The mornings now are hostile, and as grey as the fur of a rabbit. This is only to be expected; it is the middle of winter.

All the same and despite appearances, today is not an ordinary day. Remember that apart from history's knack of repeating itself, nothing is truly ordinary - not even the simple rasping of twigs jostled by the wind to my left, the quiet pit-a-pat like the footsteps of a mouse over there in the undergrowth, or the forlorn chirp of a wren in the blackthorn thicket on the other side of the footpath.

Experiences such as these, of course, are familiar to everyone; they are happenings like countless others of similar ilk from time immemorial. But they are not the *same* as those former events. Instead, they are unique by association with a moment: with the very moment that has just come and gone, in an instant, leaving no trace.

Consider once again the proposition that *nothing* is ordinary and that *everything* is strange if confronted head-on. Yet to engage with this strangeness, there is no need to seek confirmation in the uncertainties of quantum weirdness. As to the question of what we mean by 'strange' or 'weird' and by what measure we distinguish any given example, there is no clear answer. Even the everyday realities of the macrocosm, although seemingly commonplace, nevertheless remain impenetrable if we take a second look.

Today, there is a body of opinion which, finding its world view threatened by allusions to mystery, is quick to dismiss all consideration of the void - at the same time turning a blind eye to the dissolution of all that is solid as each successive layer of subatomic reality is peeled away. Yet these are the very people, the physicists and the chemists, who are best placed to supply answers where as yet none exists. Even if the final solution is forever beyond reach, which for the moment we cannot know, a dead end is inevitable without some acknowledgement and understanding of the counter-intuitive implications of the questions being raised.

* * *

And so, I rejoice as I stand at the edge of the wood. It is a dreary day and I am unaccompanied. The branches of the oaks are bare; and the dead leaves under foot betray no vestige of the summer they have left behind. Above them, the sky that was blue in August has faded. The mornings now are hostile, and as grey as the fur of a rabbit. And yet the spring is coming. Long before its leaves open, far whiter than a blizzard, the blackthorn will burst into flower. And snowdrops can be seen already where the ivy protects them from the wind.

There is something else, too: it is only faint, but I still hear that sound like footfall in the undergrowth which tells me there is more than meets the eye, here on the common beneath the leafless and deceptively lifeless boughs. It is an invisible, insistent presence; yet although I cannot see it, and even if it proves all-too-familiar, I feel sure it shares an origin that is very far from *ordinary*.

But it defies definition, like the universe itself. And I welcome it, although I cannot give it a name.

THE CHURCH AT SOUTH CREAKE

Memory takes me back to those youthful, high-anglican days when I was on one of several pilgrimages to the shrine of Our Lady of Walsingham in rural Norfolk. Whilst there, an afternoon trip was arranged to the nearby parish of South Creake which was a tiny, remote village with a lovely mediaeval church whose vicar was a certain Father de La Haye Maltby.

To the accompaniment of suggestive smiles, I was confidentially informed that Father de La Haye Maltby was also known to fellow clergymen as Twinkletoes. This was because he habitually wore shiny black shoes with silver buckles. It was also said that he shared the vicarage with a somewhat odd housekeeper of indeterminate gender who, broadly speaking, was thought to be a woman.

One thing I *didn't* need telling, however, was that over the years this allegedly eccentric parish priest had so beautified and restored the South Creake church that any mediaeval peasants returning from the grave would have felt just as much at home there today as they would have done before almost every original embellishment was either looted or reduced to dust by the unbounded zeal of the king's agents.

SALVE, FESTA DIES

There are particular days, mostly in summer, when the sun seems as unsparing with its light as was Christ with the outpouring of his blood. These are days when nature has never before appeared so marvellously green; when insects flit without effort through the bright, transparent air; when, almost imperceptibly, something invisible stirs in the bracken and revives an unstated, barely remembered fancy.

On days like these, perhaps for just a few moments, there is a brief transition from one state of being to another when, knowingly but willingly, one can fool oneself into thinking that all is well with the world and his wife. And thus affected, it's all too easy to believe that wherever the sun dispenses such benevolence, perfect peace, although fragile, is the likely outcome.

And so, with all sharp sound blunted by the heat, the mood of the wanderer softens into complacency; and if at such times he or she were to fall into a quiet drowse, it might be - just *might* be - more advantageous never to reawaken.

Salve, Festa Dies: Hail, Festival Day. The English Hymnal, Easter Sunday.

LIKE I SAY

Mr Jim Pethybridge, just turned twenty, is a confirmed member of the 'Like-I-Say Society' and a keen supporter of the 'You-Woz Brigade'. He is the eldest son of a family that has lived in East Ham since time immemorial whose habitual language is the street talk proper to that area and to the many generations of factory workers and barrow boys who have lived there.

In that context, 'like I say' represents a perfectly acceptable local brand of English which is entirely out of place on the lips of supposedly well educated broadcasters and journalists - not to mention a sprinkling of unqualified teaching assistants occasionally to be found leading children up the garden path in a mismanaged infants' school whose principal is organising a campaign against private h'eddication!

YOUNG FELLA M'LAD

The golden May sunshine trickled down through the overhead canopy of leaves which had only recently emerged from their buds. Bernard, alone and in his teens, noticed a faint shudder high up where the foliage engaged with the pure blue of the sky.

It caused him to wonder. What precisely was it, he asked himself, that brought about that gentle motion? Was it perhaps the vestige of a gravitational wave from the first billionth of a second in the life of the universe? Was it caused by the wings of a tiny bird that he'd failed to notice? Or was it just the action of an invisible, wholly unremarkable breeze?

Such was the gist of Bernard's reverie that morning, in the early years of a life that would encounter much beauty… along with the repressed sniggers and incomprehension of the friends with whom he tried to share his ideas and perceptions.

OCTOBER REVOLUTION

Today is the sixth of October. Already, the nights are getting cold; and in a few rural areas, the first frosts have been reported. Nevertheless, it is mid-afternoon; and for a short while the sun is shining brilliantly. At the same time, there is an undercurrent of autumnal stillness; and although it is warm enough to sit comfortably on a bench here at the edge of the wood, a cutting chill lurks like a ghost among the shadows.

In the meantime, and for the moment, it is sufficiently hot to have lured a butterfly out of retirement. I am watching it struggle like a drunk, fitfully clearing a laurel bush whose smooth leaves glisten under the sun's relentless glare. Sadly, it is very much on its own, this small insect... frail, plain white and of the commonest breed. But against all the odds, it seems hell-bent on celebrating the demise of summer in sure and certain ignorance of the fact that, although a far-off, equally dogged ice-cream van is chiming unseasonal songs, this is more than likely to be the very last day of its life.

In sure and certain ignorance: a play on the words 'in sure and certain hope of the resurrection' from The Book of Common Prayer's Burial of the Dead.

THE SKINFLINT

Mr Nikolai Karamzin, having been granted political asylum during the communist era and, in due course, a British passport to go with it, persistently overlaid his excellent command of English, despite the passage of many years, with a strong Russian accent; and this, when he was reading passages out loud from his translations of obscure Central Asian epics, added a sonorous, regional quality to the basic raw material - thereby expressing that magical something which the text merely hinted at.

Mr Karamzin, now in his seventies, had a lively yet dignified, rather private personality, and had made his way in the West as an academic, ending up at the University of London where he specialised in the literature of his native land and its associated territories. As his career prospered, he had attracted an entourage of admiring friends, both literary scholars and creative writers, many of whom, accompanied by winks and nods, had learned (amongst themselves) to dilute their admiration with an extraneous element of banter falling just short of ridicule - although the strength of their positive feelings saved them from accusations of anything other than the mildest form of ambivalence. Nevertheless, it was an ambivalence of sorts; and at the heart of it lay one particularly pivotal circumstance among a host of others.

* * *

Sooner rather than later, given the many disparate factors involved, readers will be looking for an explanation of the winks and nods so readily exchanged by the friends of Nikolai Andreyevich Karamzin. And to satisfy this need is an easy enough task: for the plain fact was that Nikolai, with all his accomplishments, was regarded as a perfect example of the most commonplace expression used to describe individuals with a reputation for penny-pinching. And as a result, many of his acquaintances (out of earshot, of course) were often heard with the name 'Scrooge' on their lips when referring to the grey eminence of Nikolai Karamzin and his diminishing mop of wispy, professorial hair.

This, then, was the equivocal light in which Nikolai was seen by those whose admiration for his well-earned status was not wholly undermined by their observation of his human failings. It sprang from a blemish of which almost all of them were aware and by which most of them (except for one) were amused. And it centred most famously on a particular incident which, amongst many lesser examples, was cited whenever his friends were alone together. And more wordlessly, of course, the same event was at the heart of the surreptitious winks and nods whenever they and Nikolai were gathered over a few drinks which they (but not Nikolai) had paid for!

The time has now come to set out precisely what this incident amounted to. It was occasioned by the fact that one of Nikolai's group of friends had moved to a rather grand house in Brighton, the remaining friends (including Nikolai himself) being steadfastly committed Londoners. A visit to Brighton was therefore proposed; and to everyone's astonishment, Nikolai offered to drive - even before the unanimous undertaking to share the cost of the fuel was agreed.

It was a beautiful summer's day when the gang of five set out from Little Venice in rather cramped conditions. Spirits were high, jokes were light-heartedly bandied about and on the feeble side, academia was forgotten - and no one noticed the frown that darkened Nikolai's face when a deviation through the North Downs via Abinger Common was suggested and submitted to - the object being the particularly splendid scenery in that part of Surrey. The consequent delay was minimal; the sun bore down unremittingly on field and hedgerow, scattering for good measure its jumble of gold coins among the woodland shadows. And despite the détour, the ageing companions, still cracking jokes, arrived in good time at their destination where they were welcomed by their host with an excellent, well lubricated lunch enhanced by much laughter, a fair dose of reminiscence and the surprising absence of winks and nods!

Nikolai, with a strength of mind consonant with the possibility of being the driver of a band of drunks, had restrained his own drinking - with the result that his wish to begin the homeward journey forestalled that of his friends by a wide margin. Departure for London at 4:00pm, whilst agreed to by those dependent on it, naturally depressed spirits; there were exchanges of looks; and one red-faced novelist privately raised two fingers whilst the others chuckled on having it pointed out that Nikolai was the only guest who had failed to bring a gift - a fact which the betrayer of this dark secret had gleaned from their host's wife!

* * *

There were no hitches on the journey back to Little Venice where each of the friends, dumped just outside Nikolai's flat, prepared for his or her dreary bus ride home. It remained only to hand over the cash for the fuel after hearing Nikolai's amazingly precise estimate of costs. But in the midst of all the fumbling in pockets, the rustling of banknotes and the clink of coins, Nikolai had another, remarkably telling surprise in store when he explained that the sum suggested was a little higher than it would have been, were it not for the increased mileage of the route via Abinger Common.

And like an embarrassingly exposed boil, it was *this* niggardly manifestation, reluctantly agreed to amidst sidelong glances, that underpinned all future winks and nods when the name of Nikolai Andreyevich Karamzin was mentioned!

THE WRONG END OF THE STICK

Mrs Margaret Delaunay is firmly convinced that the Ark of the Covenant is hidden away somewhere in Ethiopia - although she is by no means clear that Ethiopia is the home of an ancient branch of Orthodoxy, namely the Ethiopian Orthodox Church, which tends to specialise in arks and covenants.

Mrs Margaret Delaunay has no idea whether the original stone tablets are still *inside* the Ark about which she is otherwise so certain. Indeed, there is little likelihood that she knows what the Tablets of the Law really are. And she would certainly be unable to quote many of the commandments inscribed on them other than the stark-staringly obvious one 'thou shalt not kill'. As to 'thou shalt not commit adultery', Mrs Delaunay (married several times) might well wish to dismiss it as tribal primitivism when set alongside her own brand of twenty-first century liberal enlightenment which her rather wild mop of grey hair very subtly hints at!

Notwithstanding all of this, Mrs Delaunay remains fully convinced that the Ark of the Covenant is in Ethiopia - even though such conviction must surely imply solid back-up that would have led long ago to overwhelming demands for restitution by the Jews!

* * *

Sadly, Mrs Margaret Delaunay has no interest whatsoever in religion; but she has certainly been stimulated by the sort of numinous aura, as in the present case, which carries no penalties such as the need to sing boring hymns or to espouse principles which are even more boring due to their claim to be binding.

Although she would hotly deny it, Mrs Delaunay's convictions are solely attributable to the film 'Indiana Jones and the Raiders of the Lost Ark' and to a TV documentary on Ethiopia's mysterious rock churches which fanned the flames of a susceptibility supported by faint recollections of sunday-school bible stories that somehow, during her teens, got muddled up with the first thrilling report that flying saucers had landed.

In short, Mrs Margaret Delaunay is a sucker for ripping yarns ennobled (as in the present case) by the sort of inconclusive mystery which, ironically, fills the gap left by the sheer nonsense she considers religion to be!

CITY ASSIGNMENT

September the first 2013, Piccadilly Circus. And once again I'm here at the foot of Eros. Immediately, as I sit down on the hard stone steps, my interest is aroused by an outbreak of hand-clapping directed, it would seem, at a couple in their mid twenties. By all appearances, they've just got married despite the fact that it's Sunday; and they are posing for a photograph in this carefully chosen spot.

The male party is dressed conventionally in a black suit enlivened by a bright red tie - whereas his wife or partner (we don't know in what form the knot has been tied) is celebrating in a traditional white wedding dress which is conventional enough viewed from the front but which, having no back at all between the shoulders and the waist, leaves much skin exposed to the late summer sun. This may hasten the certainty, later on this evening, that the marriage will be consummated - though on second thoughts, it's probably been consummated already.

* * *

The sun today is warm and pleasant. And yet, given the close proximity of autumn, the shadows are lengthening and in the shade the temperature is dropping - none of which has so far been noticed by the world, his wife and their abundance of rowdy offspring.

There is a welter of swirling activity, hectic perambulation and eager chatter - indeed, there is so much high-spirited babble that I can only just hear the voice-recording on which I am preserving this account. On the other hand, I see no events that suggest an incipient narrative - although the celebration of a fine summer weekend is rampant and tumultuous.

The feral pigeons are scrawny, persistently hopeful but largely unsuccessful in their hunt for scraps. A teenager wearing shorts is squatting high above me on the Eros monument with his feet dangling a little too freely, given his precarious position. Meanwhile and as usual, cameras by the dozen are being focussed on things that the photographers themselves do not actually look at until they get home - although the newly-weds are now gathered in a semicircle with their friends, gazing at the digital images of their big day.

Close to my left elbow, a rather ghastly-looking, oily salad is being consumed by a teenage girl. The rice is glistening at the end of her fork in the bright sunshine; and her conversation, which betrays an indeterminate regional accent, is voluble between mouthfuls, irritatingly fruity, and far too loud.

A mother and daughter from somewhere like Brixton or Trinidad have just passed me dressed in two rather beautiful shades of shocking pink - in contrast to a woman from Saudi Arabia, almost entirely veiled in black, who is plainly gob-smacked by the hustle and bustle all around her and is standing stock-still in wonderment.

Displayed on the wall of a well-known sports retailer, a rather brashly designed poster declares that the Lillywhites sale is offering 'massive discounts'. At the same time, I remain surrounded, as I have been since I arrived, by a tsunami of apparent purposelessness that may or may not be trivial and which I cannot make head or tail of. And to cap it all, plunging me suddenly into shadow, there now stands in front of me a pair of young men who are obviously at loggerheads - although, given the general hubbub, it's hard to catch the gist. One of them, with a mediterranean appearance, has raised his hand and is shaking a pointed forefinger at the other fairer, possibly American youth aged about twenty whose face, turned momentarily towards me, bears a wan smile that somehow betrays incomprehension. And now as I watch his attempt to let matters rest and wander off, his southern-sun-kissed adversary has grabbed him by the shoulder - and escalation seems imminent.

In these circumstances, I'm afraid I'll have to consider my position. I have never been a boy scout, but 'be prepared' has always been my motto, and it still is - so I think I ought to move on.

Best to be on the safe side, I always say!

HILDA

Hilda has thwarted a stranger's child attempting to kick a feral pigeon. She rose swiftly from the park bench where she was feeding the birds, took him gently by the arm and, in sober language, ticked him off. Angered, the boy's mother made reference to human rights. But Hilda maintained that it was not among the rights of man to kick pigeons. Her precise language and tone of voice made it clear that the child should have known this.

Red-faced and abusive, the mother pulled a scant white blouse down over her midriff and retreated from the scene of her castigation. Sadly, the child she trailed behind her did not know why he was crying.

THE NUMBER 65 TO KEW GARDENS

Vic Penny, a retired postman of amiable if forthright disposition, was comfortably seated on the number 65 bus as it halted opposite the Richmond upon Thames branch of Tesco. He was minding his own business and thinking about nothing in particular when a married couple, evidently from somewhere out of town, climbed on board. They were in their early fifties and looking forward to a pleasant afternoon in Kew Gardens. The husband, however, got into an immediate muddle with the driver who was obliged to point out that London buses no longer took cash. 'I'm afraid we're not from around these parts', explained the confused visitor apologetically.

His wife, whose flushed features betrayed irritation, was clearly more abreast of the practicalities than her other half. All the same, as she whipped two prepaid passes from her handbag, she glared angrily at the driver and was clearly about to say something which took no account of the fact that had her spouse not leapt ahead in conformity with what he saw as a husband's traditional duty, the question of cash payment would never have arisen in the first place.

From a whisper later on as the pair alighted at Kew, it turned out that the woman's name was Ruby. And, in a voice loud enough to be heard by everyone as she slapped the passes down on the reader, she went on to take a swipe at the country's capital in terms which, at a push, could have been taken as a smear with a politically incorrect slant to go with it.

'Coming to London is like being in a foreign country', she exclaimed with an expression on her face that matched the sentiment!

On hearing this, Vic woke up from his daydreams, leant forward and caught Ruby's eye just as the doors closed and the bus continued on its way to Kew. At the age of sixty eight, and as a senior citizen, he considered himself entitled to take liberties.

'Excuse me, madam', he said; 'the reason why coming to London is like being in a foreign country is because that's just what it is!'

And although some passengers buried their faces behind news-papers, there was much discreet laughter on the lower deck of the number 65 as it picked up speed.

RUNNING COMMENTARY

There are moments which are the same as any other; and there are *particular* moments like the present moment when a pause or a deep breath is the wisest move. And so, for today at least, I have made a decision: I am taking measures to deal with the drudgery of repetitious action; and I am placing myself out of reach of enemy fire.

Summer, after a multitude of false starts, has at last firmly established itself. In response, I have taken a stand: I have turned my back on the wearisome tasks forever bearing down on me; I have sought a remedy in wilful neglect and I rejoice in the consequent lack of purpose.

Even glancing at the news headlines, or harbouring recollections of things that were irksome... even an unfriendly-looking envelope on the hall floor - all of them mount up and create a sense of hard labour, of foreboding - and they tire me out. And so, I am resolving matters in my own familiar way. In perfect harmony with long-established, self-imposed habit, I am sounding the retreat. I am turning tail, I have lifted two fingers - I am on the run!

Like an anchorite, I have set out in search of tranquillity: I have withdrawn to the wilderness - to the manicured wilderness of a public garden. Surrounded by well-clipped, well-watered shrubs, I am lounging beneath a pear tree where few passers-by have even noticed my presence. What, after all, is *'presence'*? And what is *'place'* in a universe where a particle can occupy more than one location in apparent defiance of common knowledge?

In a clear and almost cloudless sky, with their undercarriages dangling from a thread like beads, transcontinental aircraft are poised to land at Gatwick. Out of sight, a baby is innocently howling; and a butterfly, dark as the shadow of a falling leaf, has been absorbed as if into a black hole by the penumbra of an apple tree.

Consequently, the sharp edge of consciousness is blunter; and soaring summer heat has diminished the speed of time; it has muffled sound and softened the air to the consistency of cotton wool. As an extra defence, I have switched off my phone: I am insulated from unwanted interference; and for a while I feel secure from the violence of world events.

This then, here and now, in the wake of today's simple remedy, is all that lies within sight of the ordinary park bench where I am comfortably seated: the sun is shining down on a green, unshaded lawn; and above me, forming a shelter, the leaves of the pear tree are as smooth as candlewax.

A WELSHMAN BORN AND BRED

Meredith slid like a ghost between the grim bulk of the hollies lining either side of the path. In harmony with their colourless gloom, he presented almost as dismal a picture himself: tall, slender as a reed and dressed in a nondescript plastic mackintosh, he looked friendless and forlorn - on top of which there was something slightly absurd about his gangly, unwaveringly upright silhouette.

His middle-aged features, more furrowed than he liked to admit, were surmounted by a battered flat-cap which, in its pristine state at the London Scotch Shop, had shown a more obviously explicit affinity with the glens. Its latterday decline, of course, was easy to explain: after the first flush of youth, the cap's now faded tartan had been the victim of many winters. Thus demoted, its only current function was to provide cover for a balding scalp that was nevertheless fighting back in stubborn opposition to grey hair. Quality, it seemed, was holding its own against quantity - but only by a very narrow margin!

It was the second day of an unnaturally warm November. The sky looked as heavy as lead, resolutely miserable and was broken only occasionally by capricious outbursts of pale wet sunlight that emerged between gaps in the clouds. These brief interludes ignited into wildfire the autumnal yellows of the beeches, the flaming reds of the maples and, like wind-fanned embers, the glimmering extravagance of a smoke tree. Even the green blades of the grass, sprinkled with colourless drops of rain, had their moments of emerald splendour.

It took no more than the briefest glance to work out that Meredith was not only alone but lonely… *lonely*, that is *as a cloud*… and likewise detached yet without the encumbrance of melancholy. And the reason, although it was simple enough, was also strangely ironical.

In the presence of nature, he preferred to be unburdened by the distractions and obtuseness of other people: people who never even *noticed* the glint in the eye of an angry swan; people who considered it ridiculous that the upside-down reflections in a puddle might be seen as glimpses of another world - who were indifferent to autumn colour unless it was exuberant and primary... whose perceptions, in other words, were dull, short-lived and easily subverted.

With these attitudes dominant, and being influenced by the solemnity of the low light, Meredith was undismayed when the sun surrendered decisively to gloom and it began raining again. Notwithstanding a Scottish flat-cap, was he not after all a son of Brynamman, born and bred in the Black Mountains where wet Atlantic weather was part of his heritage? Accordingly, he turned left immediately into one of Kew's grandest woodland areas; and as his outline dissolved like a spectre into the darkness of the understorey, he listened with enchantment to the raindrops as they pitter-pattered among the leaves.

It was a transitional moment experienced in routinely familiar isolation. Only just visible in the sombre confines of the wood and dead to the rowdier world beyond it, Meredith was aware of a handful of watchful eyes, those of the birds looking down with indifference from above and twittering faintly. For a short while, he was conscious of something close to detachment - and slowly, yet with the same inevitable brevity, he was released from his daily concerns.

Meredith: a Welsh forename, typically masculine, but very occasionally applied to women.

I wandered lonely as a cloud: Poem by William Wordsworth.

MYSTERIES OF THE TAO

I

When an entire army has blundered past, the soil is scarred and good only for weeds, blackthorn and nettles. No crops can be sown in these conditions. Consequently, there can be no harvest and the people will suffer.

Where battle is unavoidable, there are lessons to be learned: never act with undue violence; never abuse the power you have gained; nor, if you are the victor, should you ever triumph by rubbing salt into the wounds of the enemy.

In the final analysis, those who use excessive force will be the losers: their cruel indifference is at variance with the True Way; and in the eyes of history they will be marked men. The praise they hoped for will never be voiced, and they will be turned back at the gates of Heaven.

2

People with inner understanding do not make a great din; it is the empty vessels that make the most noise. Therefore act wisely: guard your tongue and keep tabs on unnecessary bragging. At the end of the day, it is far better to be at one with the Earth - not to mention its Maker who, although infinitely powerful, is also serenely silent.

3

The source and architect of all things is to be found everywhere: above, below and around you. It fills the entire emptiness of space.

It is inherent in everything that breathes, yet it demands no recognition. It nourishes all creation, yet it makes no fuss about it.

Without stressing its power, it sustains the whole universe. And with consummate humility, it thrives among the meek and lowly.

It never loses its grip on what it has made - yet it refrains from using force to impose its will.

It is for all these reasons that we call it omnipotent: like a gentle breeze at the entrance of a cave, it is more powerful than fire and more disturbing than an earthquake.

4

When the Right Way is acknowledged, the horses remain yoked to the plough. But when the Way is disregarded, they are taken to the training ground and prepared for battle. There is no greater curse than the desire for conquest or the envy of another man's goods. And the lesson is clear: those who discover that enough is enough and stick to the straight and narrow will find the greatest contentment.

Very loosely based on numbers 30, 56, 34 & 46 of the Tao Te Ching by Lao Tsu. 6th century BC.

Designed and typeset by David Bloomfield
Cover illustration by Michael Hill